T0144774

Mademoiselle of Monte Carlo

Mademoiselle of Monte Carlo

William Le Queux

MINT EDITIONS

Mademoiselle of Monte Carlo was first published in 1921.

This edition published by Mint Editions 2021.

ISBN 9781513280929 | E-ISBN 9781513285948

Published by Mint Editions®

 MINT
EDITIONS

minteditionbooks.com

Publishing Director: Jennifer Newens
Design & Production: Rachel Lopez Metzger
Project Manager: Micaela Clark
Typesetting: Westchester Publishing Services

Contents

I

The Suicide's Chair

Yes! I'm not mistaken at all! *It's the same woman!*" whispered the tall, good-looking young Englishman in a well-cut navy suit as he stood with his friend, a man some ten years older than himself, at one of the roulette tables at Monte Carlo, the first on the right on entering the room—that one known to habitual gamblers as "The Suicide's Table."

"Are you quite certain?" asked his friend.

"Positive. I should know her again anywhere."

"She's very handsome. And look, too, by Jove!—how she is winning!"

"Yes. But let's get away. She might recognize me," exclaimed the younger man anxiously. "Ah! If I could only induce her to disclose what she knows about my poor father's mysterious end then we might clear up the mystery."

"I'm afraid, if all we hear is true about her, Mademoiselle of Monte Carlo will never do that," was the other's reply as they moved away together down the long saloon towards the trente-et-quarante room.

"*Messieurs! Faites vos jeux*," the croupiers were crying in their strident, monotonous voices, inviting players to stake their counters of cent-sous, their louis, or their hundred or five hundred franc notes upon the spin of the red and black wheel. It was the month of March, the height of the Riviera season, the fetes of Mi-Careme were in full swing. That afternoon the rooms were overcrowded, and the tense atmosphere of gambling was laden with the combined odours of perspiration and perfume.

Around each table were crowds four or five deep behind those fortunate enough to obtain seats, all eager and anxious to try their fortune upon the rouge or noir, or upon one of the thirty-six numbers, the columns, or the transversales. There was but little chatter. The hundreds of well-dressed idlers escaping the winter were too intent upon the game. But above the click of the plaques, blue and red of different sizes, as they were raked into the bank by the croupiers, and the clatter of counters as the lucky players were paid with deft hands, there rose ever and anon:

"*Messieurs! Faites vos jeux!*"

Here English duchesses rubbed shoulders with the most notorious women in Europe, and men who at home in England were good churchmen and exemplary fathers of families, laughed merrily with the most gorgeously attired cocottes from Paris, or the stars of the film world or the variety stage. Upon that wide polished floor of the splendidly decorated Rooms, with their beautiful mural paintings and heavy gilt ornamentation, the world and the half-world were upon equal footing.

Into that stifling atmosphere—for the Administration of the Bains de Mer of Monaco seem as afraid of fresh air as of purity propaganda—the glorious afternoon sunlight struggled through the curtained windows, while over each table, in addition to the electric light, oil-lamps shaded green with a billiard-table effect cast a dull, ghastly illumination upon the eager countenances of the players. Most of those who go to Monte Carlo wonder at the antiquated mode of illumination. It is, however, in consequence of an attempted raid upon the tables one night, when some adventurers cut the electric-light main, and in the darkness grabbed all they could get from the bank.

The two English visitors, both men of refinement and culture, who had watched the tall, very handsome woman in black, to whom the older man had referred as Mademoiselle of Monte Carlo, wandered through the trente-et-quarante rooms where all was silence, and counters, representing gold, were being staked with a twelve-thousand franc maximum.

Those rooms beyond are the haunt of the professional gambler, the man or woman who has been seized by the demon of speculation, just as others have been seized by that of drugs or drink. Curiously enough women are more prone to gamble than men, and the Administration of the Etablissement will tell you that when a woman of any nationality starts to gamble she will become reckless until her last throw with the devil.

Those who know Monte Carlo, those who have been habitues for twenty years—as the present writer has been—know too well, and have seen too often, the deadly influence of the tables upon the lighter side of woman's nature. The smart woman from Paris, Vienna, or Rome never loses her head. She gambles always discreetly. The fashionable cocottes seldom lose much. They gamble at the tables discreetly and make eyes at men if they win, or if they lose. If the latter they generally obtain a "loan" from somebody. What matter? When one is at "Monty" one is not in a Wesleyan chapel. English men and women when they go to the Riviera leave their morals at home with their silk hats and Sunday gowns. And it is strange to see the perfectly respectable Englishwoman admiring the same daring costumes of the French pseudo-"countesses" at which they have held up their hands in horror when they have seen them pictured in the papers wearing those latest "creations" of the Place Vendome.

Yes. It is a hypocritical world, and nowhere is canting hypocrisy more apparent than inside the Casino at Monte Carlo.

While the two Englishmen were strolling over the polished parquet of the elegant world-famous *salles-de-jeu* "Mademoiselle of Monte Carlo" was experiencing quite an extraordinary run of luck.

But "Mademoiselle," as the croupiers always called her, was usually lucky. She was an experienced, and therefore a careful player. When she staked a maximum it was not without very careful calculation upon the chances. Mademoiselle was well known to the Administration. Often her winnings were sensational, hence she served as an advertisement to the Casino, for her success always induced the uninitiated and unwary to stake heavily, and usually with disastrous results.

The green-covered gaming table, at which she was sitting next to the end croupier on the left-hand side, was crowded. She sat in what is known at Monte as "the Suicide's Chair," for during the past eight years ten men and women had sat in that fatal chair and had afterwards ended their lives abruptly, and been buried in secret in the Suicide's Cemetery.

The croupiers at that table are ever watchful of the visitor who, all unawares, occupies that fatal chair. But Mademoiselle, who knew of it, always laughed the superstition to scorn. She habitually sat in that chair—and won.

Indeed, that afternoon she was winning—and very considerably too. She had won four maximums *en plein* within the last half-hour, and the crowd around the table noting her good fortune were now following her.

It was easy for any novice in the Rooms to see that the handsome, dark-eyed woman was a practised player. Time after time she let the coups pass. The croupiers' invitation to play did not interest her. She simply toyed with her big gold-chain purse, or fingered her dozen piles or so of plaques in a manner quite disinterested.

She heard the croupier announce the winning number and saw the rakes at work dragging in the stakes to swell the bank. But she only smiled, and now and then shrugged her shoulders.

Whether she won or lost, or whether she did not risk a stake, she simply smiled and elevated her shoulders, muttering something to herself.

Mademoiselle of Monte Carlo was, truth to tell, a sphinx to the staff of the Casino. She looked about thirty, but probably she was older. For five years she had been there each season and gambled heavily with unvarying success. Always well but quietly dressed, her nationality was as obscure as her past. To the staff she was always polite, and she pressed hundred-franc notes into many a palm in the Rooms. But who she was or what were her antecedents nobody in the Principality of Monaco could ever tell.

The whole Cote d'Azur from Hyeres to Ventimiglia knew of her. She was one of the famous characters of Monte Carlo, just as famous, indeed, as old Mr. Drewett, the Englishman who lost his big fortune at the tables, and who was pensioned off by the Administration on condition that he never gamble at the Casino again. For fifteen years he lived in Nice upon the meagre pittance until suddenly another fortune was left him, whereupon he promptly paid up the whole of his pension and started at the tables again. In a month, however, he had lost his second fortune. Such is gambling in the little country ruled over by Prince Rouge-et-Noir.

As the two Englishmen slipped past the end table unseen on their way out into the big atrium with its many columns—the hall in which players go out to cool themselves, or collect their determination for a final flutter—Mademoiselle had just won the maximum upon the number four, as well as the column, and the croupier was in the act of pushing towards her a big pile of counters each representing a thousand francs.

The eager excited throng around the table looked across at her with envy. But her handsome countenance was quite expressionless. She simply thrust the counters into the big gold-chain purse at her side, glanced at the white-gloved fingers which were soiled by handling the counters, and then counting out twenty-five, each representing a louis, gave them to the croupier, exclaiming:

"*Zero-trois!*"

Next moment a dozen persons followed her play, staking their cent-sous and louis upon the spot where she had asked the croupier at the end of the table to place her stake.

"*Messieurs! Faites vos jeux!*" came the strident cry again.

Then a few seconds later the croupier cried:

"Rien ne vas plus!"

The red and black wheel was already spinning, and the little ivory ball sent by the croupier's hand in the opposite direction was clicking quickly over the numbered spaces.

Six hundred or more eyes of men and women, fevered by the gambling mania, watched the result. Slowly it lost its impetus, and after spinning about unevenly it made a final jump and fell with a loud click.

"Zer-r-o!" cried the croupier.

And a moment later Mademoiselle had pushed before her at the end of the croupier's rake another pile of counters, while all those who had followed the remarkable woman's play were also paid.

"Mademoiselle is in good form to-day," remarked one ugly old Frenchwoman who had been a well-known figure at the tables for the past ten years, and who played carefully and lived by gambling. She was one of those queer, mysterious old creatures who enter the Rooms each morning as soon as they are open, secure the best seats, occupy them all the luncheon hour pretending to play, and then sell them to wealthy gamblers for a consideration—two or three louis—perhaps—and then at once go to their ease in their own obscure abode.

The public who go to Monte know little of its strange mysteries, or of the odd people who pick up livings there in all sorts of queer ways.

"Ah!" exclaimed a man who overheard her. "Mademoiselle has wonderful luck! She won seventy-five thousand francs at the *Cercle Prive* last night. She won *en plein* five times running. *Dieu!* Such luck! And it never causes her the slightest excitement."

"The lady must be very rich!" remarked an American woman sitting next to the old Frenchwoman, and who knew French well.

"Rich! Of course! She must have won several million francs from the Administration. They don't like to see her here. But I suppose her success attracts others to play. The gambling fever is as infectious as the influenza," declared the old Frenchwoman. "Everyone tries to discover who she is, and where she came from five years ago. But nobody has yet found out. Even Monsieur Bernard, the chief of the Surveillance, does not know," she went on in a whisper. "He is a friend of mine, and I asked him one day. She came from Paris, he told me. She may be American, she may be Belgian, or she may be English. She speaks English and French so well that nobody can tell her true nationality."

"And she makes money at the tables," said the American woman in the well-cut coat and skirt and small hat. She came from Chelsea,

Mass., and it was her first visit to what her pious father had always referred to as the plague spot of Europe.

"Money!" exclaimed the old woman. "Money! *Dieu!* She has losses, it is true, but oh!—what she wins! I only wish I had ten per cent of it. I should then be rich. Mine is a poor game, madame—waiting for someone to buy my seat instead of standing the whole afternoon. You see, there is only one row of chairs all around. So if a smart woman wants to play, some man always buys her a chair—and that is how I live. Ah! madame, life is a great game here in the Principality."

Meanwhile young Hugh Henfrey, who had travelled from London to the Riviera and identified the mysterious mademoiselle, had passed with his friend, Walter Brock, through the atrium and out into the afternoon sunshine.

As they turned upon the broad gravelled terrace in front of the great white facade of the Casino amid the palms, the giant geraniums and mimosa, the sapphire Mediterranean stretched before them. Below, beyond the railway line which is the one blemish to the picturesque scene, out upon the point in the sea the constant pop-pop showed that the tir-aux-pigeons was in progress; while up and down the terrace, enjoying the quiet silence of the warm winter sunshine with the blue hills of the Italian coast to the left, strolled a gay, irresponsible crowd— the cosmopolitans of the world: politicians, financiers, merchants, princes, authors, and artists—the crowd which puts off its morals as easily as it discards its fur coats and its silk hats, and which lives only for gaiety and without thought of the morrow.

"Let's sit down," suggested Hugh wearily. "I'm sure that she's the same woman—absolutely certain!"

"You are quite confident you have made no mistake—eh?"

"Quite, my dear Walter. I'd know that woman among ten thousand. I only know that her surname is Ferad. Her Christian name I do not know."

"And you suspect that she knows the secret of your father's death?"

"I'm confident that she does," replied the good-looking young Englishman. "But it is a secret she will, I fear, never reveal, unless— unless I compel her."

"And how can you compel her?" asked the elder of the two men, whose dark hair was slightly tinged with grey. "It is difficult to compel a woman to do anything," he added.

"I mean to know the truth!" cried Hugh Henfrey fiercely, a look of determination in his eyes. "That woman knows the true story of my father's death, and I'll make her reveal it. By gad—I will! I mean it!"

"Don't be rash, Hugh," urged the other.

"Rash!" he cried. "It's true that when my father died so suddenly I had an amazing surprise. My father was a very curious man. I always thought him to be on the verge of bankruptcy and that the Manor and the land might be sold up any day. When old Charman, the solicitor, read the will, I found that my father had a quarter of a million lying at the bank, and that he had left it all to me—provided I married Louise!"

"Well, why not marry her?" queried Brock lazily. "You're always so mysterious, my dear Hugh."

"Why!—because I love Dorise Ranscomb. But Louise interests me, and I'm worried on her account because of that infernal fellow Charles Benton. Louise poses as his adopted daughter. Benton is a bachelor of forty-five, and, according to his story, he adopted Louise when she was a child and put her to school. Her parentage is a mystery. After leaving school she at first went to live with a Mrs. Sheldon, a young widow, in an expensive suite in Queen Anne's Mansions, Westminster. After that she has travelled about with friends and has, I believe, been abroad quite a lot. I've nothing against Louise, except—well, except for the strange uncanny influence which that man Benton has over her. I hate the fellow!"

"I see! And as you cannot yet reach Woodthorpe and your father's fortune, except by marrying Louise—which you don't intend to do—what are you going to do now?"

"First, I intend that this woman they call 'Mademoiselle of Monte Carlo,' the lucky woman who is a decoy of the Administration of the Bains de Mer, shall tell me the true circumstance of my father's death. If I know them—then my hand will be strengthened."

"Meanwhile you love Lady Ranscomb's daughter, you say?"

"Yes. I love Dorise with all my heart. She, of course, knows nothing of the conditions of the will."

There was a silence of some moments, interrupted only by the pop-pop of the pigeon-shots below.

Away across the white balustrade of the broad magnificent terrace the calm sapphire sea was deepening as the winter afternoon drew in. An engine whistled—that of the flower train which daily travels express from Cannes to Boulogne faster than the passenger train-deluxe, and bearing mimosa, carnations, and violets from the Cote d'Azur to Covent Garden, and to the florists' shops in England.

"You've never told me the exact circumstances of your father's death, Hugh," remarked Brock at last.

"Exact circumstances? Ah! That's what I want to know. Only that woman knows the secret," answered the young man. "All I know is that the poor old guv'nor was called up to London by an urgent letter. We had a shooting party at Woodthorpe and he left me in charge, saying that he had some business in London and might return on the following night—or he might be away a week. Days passed and he did not return. Several letters came for him which I kept in the library. I was surprised that he neither wrote nor returned, when, suddenly, ten days later, we had a telegram from the London police informing me that my father was lying in St. George's Hospital. I dashed up to town, but when I arrived I found him dead. At the inquest, evidence was given to show that at half-past two in the morning a constable going along Albemarle Street found him in evening dress lying huddled up in a doorway. Thinking him intoxicated, he tried to rouse him, but could not. A doctor who was called pronounced that he was suffering from some sort of poisoning. He was taken to St. George's Hospital in an ambulance, but he never recovered. The post-mortem investigation showed a small scratch on the palm of the hand. That scratch had been produced by a pin or a needle which had been infected by one of the newly discovered poisons which, administered secretly, give a post-mortem appearance of death from heart disease."

"Then your father was murdered—eh?" exclaimed the elder man.

"Most certainly he was. And that woman is aware of the whole circumstances and of the identity of the assassin."

"How do you know that?"

"By a letter I afterwards opened—one that had been addressed to him at Woodthorpe in his absence. It was anonymous, written in bad English, in an illiterate hand, warning him to 'beware of that woman you know—Mademoiselle of Monte Carlo.' It bore the French stamp and the postmark of Tours."

"I never knew all this," Brock said. "You are quite right, Hugh! The whole affair is a tangled mystery. But the first point we must establish before we commence to investigate is—who is Mademoiselle of Monte Carlo?"

II

Concerns a Guilty Secret

Just after seven o'clock that same evening young Henfrey and his friend Brock met in the small lounge of the Hotel des Palmiers, a rather obscure little establishment in the Avenue de la Costa, behind the Gardens, much frequented by the habitues of the Rooms who know Monte Carlo and prefer the little place to life at the Paris, the Hermitage, and the Riviera Palace, or the Gallia, up at Beausoleil.

The Palmiers was a place where one met a merry cosmopolitan crowd, but where the cocotte in her bright plumage was absent—an advantage which only the male habitue of Monte Carlo can fully realize. The eternal feminine is always so very much in evidence around the Casino, and the most smartly dressed woman whom one might easily take for the wife of an eminent politician or financier will deplore her bad luck and beg for "a little loan."

"Well," said Hugh as his friend came down from his room to the lounge, "I suppose we ought to be going—eh? Dorise said half-past seven, and we'll just get across to the Metropole in time. Lady Ranscomb is always awfully punctual at home, and I expect she carries out her time-table here."

The two men put on light overcoats over their dinner-jackets and strolled in the warm dusk across the Gardens and up the Galerie, with its expensive little shops, past the original Ciro's to the Metropole.

In the big hall they were greeted by a well-preserved, grey-haired Englishwoman, Lady Ranscomb, the widow of old Sir Richard Ranscomb, who had been one of the greatest engineers and contractors of modern times. He had begun life as a small jerry-builder at Golder's Green, and had ended it a millionaire and a knight. Lady Ranscomb was seated at a little wicker table with her daughter Dorise, a dainty, fair-haired girl with intense blue eyes, who was wearing a rather daring jazzing gown of pale-blue, the scantiness of which a year or two before would have been voted quite beyond the pale for a lady, and yet in our broad-minded to-day, the day of undressing on the stage and in the home, it was nothing more than "smart."

Mother and daughter greeted the two men enthusiastically, and at Lady Ranscomb's orders the waiter brought them small glasses of an aperitif.

"We've been all day motoring up to the Col di Tenda. Sospel is lovely!" declared Dorise's mother. "Have you ever been there?" she asked of Brock, who was an habitue of the Riviera.

"Once and only once. I motored from Nice across to Turin," was his reply. "Yes. It is truly a lovely run there. The Alps are gorgeous. I like San Dalmazzo and the chestnut groves there," he added. "But the frontiers are annoying. All those restrictions. Nevertheless, the run to Turin is one of the finest I know."

Presently they rose, and all four walked into the crowded *salle-a-manger*, where the chatter was in every European language, and the gay crowd were gossiping mostly of their luck or their bad fortune at the *tapis vert*. At Monte Carlo the talk is always of the run of sequences, the many times the zero-trois has turned up, and of how little one ever wins *en plein* on thirty-six.

To those who visit "Charley's Mount" for the first time all this is as Yiddish, but soon he or she, when initiated into the games of roulette and trente-et-quarante, quickly gets bitten by the fever and enters into the spirit of the discussions. They produce their "records"—printed cards in red and black numbers with which they have carefully pricked off the winning numbers with a pin as they have turned up.

The quartette enjoyed a costly but exquisite dinner, chatting and laughing the while.

Both men were friends of Lady Ranscomb and frequent visitors to her fine house in Mount Street. Hugh's father, a country landowner, had known Sir Richard for many years, while Walter Brock had made the acquaintance of Lady Ranscomb a couple of years ago in connexion with some charity in which she had been interested.

Both were also good friends of Dorise. Both were excellent dancers, and Lady Ranscomb often allowed them to take her daughter to the Grafton, Ciro's, or the Embassy. Lady Ranscomb was Hugh's old friend, and he and Dorise having been thrown together a good deal ever since the girl returned from Versailles after finishing her education, it was hardly surprising that the pair should have fallen in love with each other.

As they sat opposite each other that night, the young fellow gazed into her wonderful blue eyes, yet, alas! with a sinking heart. How could they ever marry?

He had about six hundred a year—only just sufficient to live upon in these days. His father had never put him to anything since he left Brasenose, and now on his death he had found that, in order to recover the estate, it was necessary for him to marry Louise Lambert, a girl for whom he had never had a spark of affection. Louise was good-looking, it was true, but could he sacrifice his happiness; could he ever cut himself adrift from Dorise for mercenary motives—in order to get back what was surely by right his inheritance?

Yet, after all, as he again met Dorise's calm, wide-open eyes, the grim truth arose in his mind, as it ever did, that Lady Ranscomb, even though she had been so kind to him, would never allow her only daughter to marry a man who was not rich. Had not Dorise told him of the sly hints her mother had recently given her regarding a certain very wealthy man named George Sherrard, an eligible bachelor who lived in one of the most expensive flats in Park Lane, and who was being generally sought after by mothers with marriageable daughters. In many cases mothers—and especially young, good-looking widows with daughters "on their hands"—are too prone to try and get rid of them "because my daughter makes me look so old," as they whisper to their intimates of their own age.

After dinner all four strolled across to the Casino, presenting their yellow cards of admission—the monthly cards granted to those who are approved by the smug-looking, black-coated committee of inspection, who judge by one's appearance whether one had money to lose.

Dorise soon detached herself from her mother and strolled up the Rooms with Hugh, Lady Ranscomb and Brock following.

None of them intended to play, but they were strolling prior to going to the opera which was beneath the same roof, and for which Lady Ranscomb had tickets.

Suddenly Dorise exclaimed:

"Look over there—at that table in the corner. There's that remarkable woman they call 'Mademoiselle of Monte Carlo'!"

Hugh started, and glancing in the direction she indicated saw the handsome woman seated at the table staking her counters quite unconcernedly and entirely absorbed in the game. She was wearing a dead black dress cut slightly low in the neck, but half-bare shoulders, with a string of magnificent Chinese jade beads of that pale apple green so prized by connoisseurs.

Her eyes were fixed upon the revolving wheel, for upon the number sixteen she had just thrown a couple of thousand franc counters. The ball dropped with a sudden click, the croupier announced that number five had won, and at once raked in the two thousand francs among others.

Mademoiselle shrugged her shoulders and smiled faintly. Yvonne Ferad was a born gambler. To her losses came as easily as gains. The Administration knew that—and they also knew how at the little pigeonhole where counters were exchanged for cheques she came often and handed over big sums in exchange for drafts upon certain banks, both in Paris and in London.

Yet they never worried. Her lucky play attracted others who usually lost. Once, a year before, a Frenchman who occupied a seat next to her daily for a month lost over a quarter of a million sterling, and one night threw himself under the Paris *rapide* at the long bridge over the Var. But on hearing of it the next day from a croupier Mademoiselle merely shrugged her shoulders, and said:

"I warned him to return to Paris. The fool! It is only what I expected."

Hugh looked only once across at the mysterious woman whom Dorise had indicated, and then drew her away. As a matter of fact he had no intention that mademoiselle should notice him.

"What do you know of her?" he asked in a casual way when they were on the other side of the great saloon.

"Well, a Frenchman I met in the hotel the day before yesterday told me all sorts of queer stories about her," replied the girl. "She's apparently a most weird person, and she has uncanny good luck at the tables. He said that she had won a large fortune during the last couple of years or so."

Hugh made no remark as to the reason of his visit to the Riviera, for, indeed, he had arrived only the day previously, and she had welcomed him joyously. Little did she dream that her lover had come out from London to see that woman who was declared to be so notorious.

"I noticed her playing this afternoon," Hugh said a moment later in a quiet reflective tone. "What do the gossips really say about her, Dorise? All this is interesting. But there are so many interesting people here."

"Well, the man who told me about her was sitting with me outside the Cafe de Paris when she passed across the Place to the Casino. That caused him to make the remarks. He said that her past was obscure. Some people say that she was a Danish opera singer, others declare that she was the daughter of a humble tobacconist in Marseilles, and others assert that she is English. But all agree that she is a clever and very dangerous woman."

"Why dangerous?" inquired Hugh in surprise.

"Ah! That I don't know. The man who told me merely hinted at her past career, and added that she was quite a respectable person nowadays in her affluence. But—well—" added the girl with a laugh, "I suppose people gossip about everyone in this place."

"Who was your informant?" asked her lover, much interested.

"His name is Courtin. I believe he is an official of one of the departments of the Ministry of Justice in Paris. At least somebody said so yesterday."

"Ah! Then he probably knew more about her than he told you, I expect."

"No doubt, for he warned my mother and myself against making her acquaintance," said the girl. "He said she was a most undesirable person."

At that moment Lady Ranscomb and Walter Brock joined them, whereupon the former exclaimed to her daughter:

"Did you see that woman over there?—still playing—the woman in black and the jade beads, against whom Monsieur Courtin warned us?"

"Yes, mother, I noticed her. I've just been telling Hugh about her."

"A mysterious person—eh?" laughed Hugh with well-affected indifference. "But one never knows who's who in Monte Carlo."

"Well, Mademoiselle is apparently something of a mystery," remarked Brock. "I've seen her here before several times. Once, about two years ago, I heard that she was mixed up in a very celebrated criminal case, but exactly what it was the man who told me could not recollect. She is, however, one of the handsomest women in the Rooms."

"And one of the wealthiest—if report be true," said Lady Ranscomb.

"She fascinates me," Dorise declared. "If Monsieur Courtin had not warned us I should most probably have spoken to her."

"Oh, my dear, you must do no such thing!" cried her mother, horrified. "It was extremely kind of monsieur to give us the hint. He has probably seen how unconventional you are, Dorise."

And then, as they strolled on into the farther room, the conversation dropped.

"So they've heard about Mademoiselle, it seems!" remarked Brock to his friend as they walked back to the Palmiers together in the moonlight after having seen Lady Ranscomb and her daughter to their hotel.

"Yes," growled the other. "I wish we could get hold of that Monsieur Courtin. He might tell us a bit about her."

"I doubt if he would. These French officials are always close as oysters."

"At any rate, I will try and make his acquaintance at the Metropole to-morrow," Hugh said. "There's no harm in trying."

Next morning he called again at the Metropole before the ladies were about, but to his chagrin, he learnt from the blue-and-gold concierge that Monsieur Courtin, of the Ministry of Justice, had left at ten-fifteen o'clock on the previous night by the *rapide* for Paris. He had been recalled urgently, and a special *coupe-lit* had been reserved for him from Ventimiglia.

That day Hugh Henfrey wandered about the well-kept palm-lined gardens with their great beds of geraniums, carnations and roses. Brock had accepted the invitation of a bald-headed London stock-broker he knew to motor over to lunch and tennis at the Beau Site, at Cannes, while Dorise and her mother had gone with some people to lunch at the Reserve at Beaulieu, one of the best and yet least pretentious restaurants in all Europe, only equalled perhaps by Capsa's, in Bucharest.

"Ah! If she would only tell!" Hugh muttered fiercely to himself as he walked alone and self-absorbed. His footsteps led him out of Monte Carlo and up the winding road which runs to La Turbie, above the beautiful bay. Ever and anon powerful cars climbing the hill smothered him in white dust, yet he heeded them not. He was too full of thought.

"Ah!" he kept on repeating to himself. "If she would only tell the truth—if she would only tell!"

Hugh Henfrey had not travelled to Monte Carlo without much careful reflection and many hours of wakefulness. He intended to clear up the mystery of his father's death—and more, the reason of that strange incomprehensible will which was intended to wed him to Louise.

At four o'clock that afternoon he entered the Rooms to gain another surreptitious look at Mademoiselle. Yes! She was there, still playing on as imperturbably as ever, with that half-suppressed sinister smile always upon her full red lips.

Sight of her aroused his fury. Was that smile really intended for himself? People said she was a sphinx, but he drew his breath, and when outside the Casino again in the warm sunshine he halted upon the broad red-carpeted steps and beneath his breath said in a hard, determined tone:

"Gad! She shall tell me! She shall! I'll compel her to speak—to tell me the truth—or—or—!"

That evening he wrote a note to Dorise explaining to her that he was not feeling very well and excusing himself from going round to the hotel. This he sent by hand to the Metropole.

Brock did not turn up at dinner. Indeed, he did not expect his friend back till late. So he ate his meal alone, and then went out to the Cafe de Paris, where for an hour he sat upon the *terrasse* smoking and listening to the weird music of the red-coated orchestra of Roumanian gipsies.

All the evening, indeed, he idled, chatting with men and women he knew. *Carmen* was being given at the Opera opposite, but though he loved music he had no heart to go. The one thought obsessing him was of the handsome and fascinating woman who was such a mystery to all.

At eleven o'clock he returned to the cafe and took a seat on the *terrasse* in a dark corner, in such a position that he could see anyone who entered or left the Casino. For half an hour he watched the people passing to and fro. At last, in a long jade-green coat, Mademoiselle emerged alone, and, crossing the gardens, made her way leisurely home on foot, as was her habit. Monte Carlo is not a large place, therefore there is little use for taxis.

When she was out of sight, he called the waiter to bring him a liqueur of old cognac, which he sipped, and then lit another cigarette. When he had finished it he drained the little glass, and rising, strolled in the direction the woman of mystery had taken.

A walk of ten minutes brought him to the iron gates of a great white villa, over the high walls of which climbing roses and geraniums and jasmine ran riot. The night air was heavy with their perfume. He opened the side gate and walked up the gravelled drive to the terrace whereon stood the house, commanding a wonderful view of the moon-lit Mediterranean and the far-off mountains of Italy.

His ring at the door was answered by a staid elderly Italian manservant.

"I believe Mademoiselle is at home," Hugh said in French. "I desire to see her, and also to apologize for the lateness of the hour. My visit is one of urgency."

"Mademoiselle sees nobody except by appointment," was the man's polite but firm reply.

"I think she will see me if you give her this card," answered Hugh in a strained, unusual voice.

The man took it hesitatingly, glanced at it, placed it upon a silver salver, and, leaving the visitor standing on the mat, passed through the glass swing-doors into the house.

For some moments the servant did not reappear.

Hugh, standing there, entertained just a faint suspicion that he heard a woman's shrill exclamation of surprise. And that sound emboldened him.

At last, after an age it seemed, the man returned, saying:

"Mademoiselle will see you, Monsieur. Please come this way."

He left his hat and stick and followed the man along a corridor richly carpeted in red to a door on the opposite side of the house, which the servant threw open and announced the visitor.

Mademoiselle had risen to receive him. Her countenance was, Hugh saw, blanched almost to the lips. Her black dress caused her pallor to be more apparent.

"Well, sir? Pray what do you mean by resorting to this ruse in order to see me? Who are you?" she demanded.

Hugh was silent for a moment. Then in a hard voice he said:

"I am the son of the dead man whose card is in your hands, Mademoiselle! And I am here to ask you a few questions!"

The handsome woman smiled sarcastically and shrugged her half-bare shoulders, her fingers trembling with her jade beads.

"Oh! Your father is dead—is he?" she asked with an air of indifference.

"Yes. *He is dead*," Hugh said meaningly, as he glanced around the luxurious little room with its soft rose-shaded lights and pale-blue and gold decorations. On her right as she stood were long French windows which opened on to a balcony. One of the windows stood ajar, and it was apparent that when he had called she had been seated in the long wicker chair outside enjoying the balmy moonlight after the stifling atmosphere of the Rooms.

"And, Mademoiselle," he went on, "I happen to be aware that you knew my father, and—that you are cognizant of certain facts concerning his mysterious end."

"I!" she cried, raising her voice in sudden indignation. "What on earth do you mean?" She spoke in perfect English, though he had hitherto spoken in French.

"I mean, Mademoiselle, that I intend to know the truth," said Hugh, fixing his eyes determinedly upon hers. "I am here to learn it from your lips."

"You must be mad!" cried the woman. "I know nothing of the affair. You are mistaken!"

"Do you, then, deny that you have ever met a man named Charles Benton?" demanded the young fellow, raising his voice. "Perhaps, however, that is a bitter memory, Mademoiselle—eh?"

The strikingly handsome woman pursed her lips. There was a strange look in her eyes. For several moments she did not speak. It was clear that the sudden appearance of the dead man's son had utterly unnerved her. What could he know concerning Charles Benton? How much of the affair did he suspect?

"I have met many people, Mr.—er—Mr. Henfrey," she replied quietly at last. "I may have met somebody named Benton."

"Ah! I see," the young man said. "It is a memory that you do not wish to recall any more than that of my dead father."

"Your father was a good man. Benton was not."

"Ah! Then you admit knowing both of them, Mademoiselle," cried Hugh quickly.

"Yes. I—well—I may as well admit it! Why, indeed, should I seek to hide the truth—*from you*," she said in a changed voice. "Pardon me. I was very upset at receiving the card. Pardon me—will you not?"

"I will not, unless you tell me the truth concerning my father's death and his iniquitous will left concerning myself. I am here to ascertain that, Mademoiselle," he said in a hard voice.

"And if I tell you—what then?" she asked with knit brows.

"If you tell me, then I am prepared to promise you on oath secrecy concerning yourself—provided you allow me to punish those who are responsible. Remember, my father died by foul means. *And you know it!*"

The woman faced him boldly, but she was very pale.

"So that is a promise?" she asked. "You will protect me—you will be silent regarding me—you swear to be so—if—if I tell you something. I repeat that your father was a good man. I held him in the highest esteem, and—and—after all—it is but right that you, his son, should know the truth."

"Thank you Mademoiselle. I will protect you if you will only reveal to me the devilish plot which resulted in his untimely end," Hugh assured her.

Again she knit her brows and reflected for a few moments. Then in a low, intense, unnatural voice she said:

"Listen, Mr. Henfrey. I feel that, after all, my conscience would be relieved if I revealed to you the truth. First—well, it is no use denying the fact that your father was not exactly the man you and his friends believed him to be. He led a strange dual existence, and I will disclose to you one or two facts concerning his untimely end which will show you how cleverly devised and how cunning was the plot—how—"

At that instant Hugh was startled by a bright flash outside the half-open window, a loud report, followed by a woman's shrill shriek of pain.

Then, next moment, ere he could rush forward to save her, Mademoiselle, with the truth upon her lips unuttered, staggered and fell back heavily upon the carpet!

III

In the Night

Hugh Henfrey, startled by the sudden shot, shouted for assistance, and then threw himself upon his knees beside the prostrate woman.

From a bullet wound over the right ear blood was slowly oozing and trickling over her white cheek.

"Help! Help!" he shouted loudly. "Mademoiselle has been shot from outside! *Help!*"

In a few seconds the elderly manservant burst into the room in a state of intense excitement.

"Quick!" cried Hugh. "Telephone for a doctor at once. I fear your mistress is dying!"

Henfrey had placed his hand upon Mademoiselle's heart, but could detect no movement. While the servant dashed to the telephone, he listened for her breathing, but could hear nothing. From the wall he tore down a small circular mirror and held it against her mouth. There was no clouding.

There was every apparent sign that the small blue wound had proved fatal.

"Inform the police also!" Hugh shouted to the elderly Italian who was at the telephone in the adjoining room. "The murderer must be found!"

By this time four female servants had entered the room where their mistress was lying huddled and motionless. All of them were in *deshabille*. Then all became excitement and confusion. Hugh left them to unloosen her clothing and hastened out upon the veranda whereon the assassin must have stood when firing the shot.

Outside in the brilliant Riviera moonlight the scent of a wealth of flowers greeted his nostrils. It was almost bright as day. From the veranda spread a wide, fairy-like view of the many lights of Monte Carlo and La Condamine, with the sea beyond shimmering in the moonlight.

The veranda, he saw, led by several steps down into the beautiful garden, while beyond, a distance of a hundred yards, was the main gate leading to the roadway. The assassin, after taking careful aim and firing, had, no doubt, slipped along, and out of the gate.

But why had Mademoiselle been shot just at the moment when she was about to reveal the secret of his lamented father's death?

He descended to the garden, where he examined the bushes which cast their dark shadows. But all was silence. The assassin had escaped!

Then he hurried out into the road, but again all was silence. The only hope of discovering the identity of the criminal was by means of the police vigilance. Truth to tell, however, the police of Monte Carlo are never over anxious to arrest a criminal, because Monte Carlo attracts the higher criminal class of both sexes from all over Europe. If the police of the Principality were constantly making arrests it would be bad advertisement for the Rooms. Hence, though the Monte Carlo police are extremely vigilant and an expert body of officers, they prefer to watch and to give information to the bureaux of police of other countries, so that arrests invariably take place beyond the frontiers of the Principality of Monaco.

It was not long before Doctor Leneveu, a short, stout, bald-headed little man, well known to habitues of the Rooms, among whom he had a large practice, entered the house of Mademoiselle and was greeted by Hugh. The latter briefly explained the tragic circumstances, whereupon the little doctor at once became fussy and excited.

Having ordered everyone out of the room except Henfrey, he bent and made an examination of the prostrate woman.

"Ah! m'sieur," he said, "the unfortunate lady has certainly been shot at close quarters. The wound is, I tell you at once, extremely dangerous," he added, after a searching investigation. "But she is still alive," he declared. "Yes—she is still breathing."

"Still alive!" gasped Henfrey. "That's excellent! I—I feared that she was dead!"

"No. She still breathes," the doctor replied. "But, tell me exactly what has occurred. First, however, we will get them to remove her upstairs. I will telephone to my colleague Duponteil, and we will endeavour to extract the bullet."

"But will she recover, doctor?" asked Hugh eagerly in French. "What do you think?"

The little man became serious and shook his head gravely.

"Ah! m'sieur, that I cannot say," was his reply. "She is in a very grave state—very! And the brain may be affected."

Hugh held his breath. *Surely Yvonne Ferad was not to die with the secret upon her lips!*

At the doctor's orders the servants were about to remove their mistress to her room when two well-dressed men of official aspect entered. They were officers of the Bureau of Police.

"Stop!" cried the elder, who was the one in authority, a tall, lantern-jawed man with a dark brown beard and yellow teeth. "Do not touch that lady! What has happened here?"

Hugh came forward, and in his best French explained the circumstances of the tragedy—how Mademoiselle had been shot in his presence by an unknown hand.

"The assassin, whoever he was, stood out yonder—upon the veranda—but I never saw him," he added. "It was all over in a second—and he has escaped!"

"And pray who are you?" demanded the police officer bluntly. "Please explain."

Hugh was rather nonplussed. The question required explanation, no doubt. It would, he saw, appear very curious that he should visit Mademoiselle of Monte Carlo at that late hour.

"I—well, I called upon Mademoiselle because I wished to obtain some important information from her."

"What information? Rather late for a call, surely?"

The young Englishman hesitated. Then, with true British grit, he assumed an attitude of boldness, and asked:

"Am I compelled to answer that question?"

"I am Charles Ogier, chief inspector of the Surete of Monaco, and I press for a reply," answered the other firmly.

"And I, Hugh Henfrey, a British subject, at present decline to satisfy you," was the young man's bold response.

"Is the lady still alive?" inquired the inspector of Doctor Leneveu.

"Yes. I have ordered her to be taken up to her room—of course, when m'sieur the inspector gives permission."

Ogier looked at the deathly countenance with the closed eyes, and noted that the wound in the skull had been bound up with a cotton handkerchief belonging to one of the maids. Mademoiselle's dark well-dressed hair had become unbound and was straying across her face, while her handsome gown had been torn in the attempt to unloosen her corsets.

"Yes," said the police officer; "they had better take her upstairs. We will remain here and make inquiries. This is a very queer affair—to say the least," he added, glancing suspiciously at Henfrey.

While the servants carried their unconscious mistress tenderly upstairs, the fussy little doctor went to the telephone to call Doctor Duponteil, the principal surgeon of Monaco. He had hesitated whether to take the victim to the hospital, but had decided that the operation could be done just as effectively upstairs. So, after speaking to Duponteil, he also spoke to the sister at the hospital, asking her to send up two nurses immediately to the Villa Amette.

In the meantime Inspector Ogier was closely questioning the young Englishman.

Like everyone in Monte Carlo he knew the mysterious Mademoiselle by sight. More than once the suspicions of the police had been aroused against her. Indeed, in the archives of the Prefecture there reposed a bulky dossier containing reports of her doings and those of her friends. Yet there had never been anything which would warrant the authorities to forbid her from remaining in the Principality.

This tragedy, therefore, greatly interested Ogier and his colleague. Both of them had spent many years in the service of the Paris Surete under the great Goron before being appointed to the responsible positions in the detective service of Monaco.

"Then you knew the lady?" Ogier asked of the young man who was naturally much upset over the startling affair, and the more so because the secret of his father's mysterious death had been filched from him by the hand of some unknown assassin.

"No, I did not know her personally," Henfrey replied somewhat lamely. "I came to call upon her, and she received me."

"Why did you call at this hour? Could you not have called in the daytime?"

"Mademoiselle was in the Rooms until late," he said.

"Ah! Then you followed her home—eh?"

"Yes," he admitted.

The police officer pursed his lips and raised his eyes significantly at his colleague.

"And what was actually happening when the shot was fired? Describe it to me, please," he demanded.

"I was standing just here"—and he crossed the room and stood upon the spot where he had been—"Mademoiselle was over there beside the window. I had my back to the window. She was about to tell me something—to answer a question I had put to her—when someone from outside shot her through the open glass door."

"And you did not see her assailant?"

"I saw nothing. The shot startled me, and, seeing her staggering, I rushed to her. In the meantime the assailant—whoever he was—disappeared!"

The brown-bearded man smiled dubiously. As he stood beneath the electric light Hugh saw doubt written largely upon his countenance. He instantly realized that Ogier disbelieved his story.

After all it was a very lame one. He would not fully admit the reason of his visit.

"But tell me, m'sieur," exclaimed the police officer. "It seems extraordinary that any person should creep along this veranda." And he walked out and looked about in the moonlight. "If the culprit wished to shoot Mademoiselle in secret, then he would surely not have done so in your presence. He might easily have shot her as she was on her way home. The road is lonely up here."

"I agree, monsieur," replied the Englishman. "The whole affair is, to me, a complete mystery. I saw nobody. But it was plain to me that when I called Mademoiselle was seated out upon the veranda. Look at her chair—and the cushions! It was very hot and close in the Rooms to-night, and probably she was enjoying the moonlight before retiring to bed."

"Quite possibly," he agreed. "But that does not alter the fact that the assassin ran considerable risk in coming along the veranda in the full moonlight and firing through the open door. Are you quite certain that Mademoiselle's assailant was outside—and not inside?" he asked, with a queer expression upon his aquiline face.

Hugh saw that he was hinting at his suspicion that he himself had shot her!

"Quite certain," he assured him. "Why do you ask?"

"I have my own reasons," replied the police officer with a hard laugh. "Now, tell me what do you know about Mademoiselle Ferad?"

"Practically nothing."

"Then why did you call upon her?"

"I have told you. I desired some information, and she was about to give it to me when the weapon was fired by an unknown hand."

"Unknown—eh?"

"Yes. Unknown to me. It might be known to Mademoiselle."

"And what was this information you so urgently desired?"

"Some important information. I travelled from London to Monte Carlo in order to obtain it."

"Ah! Then you had a motive in coming here—some strong motive, I take it?"

"Yes. A very strong motive. I wanted her to clear up certain mysterious happenings in England."

Ogier was instantly alert.

"What happenings?" he asked, for he recollected the big dossier and the suspicions extending over four or five years concerning the real identity and mode of life of the handsome, sphinx-like woman Yvonne Ferad.

Hugh Henfrey was silent for a few moments. Then he said:

"Happenings in London that—well, that I do not wish to recall."

Ogier again looked him straight in the face.

"I suggest, M'sieur Henfrey"—for Hugh had given him his name—"I suggest that you have been attracted by Mademoiselle as so many other men have been. She seems to exercise a fatal influence upon some people."

"I know," Hugh said. "I have heard lots of things about her. Her success at the tables is constant and uncanny. Even the Administration are interested in her winnings, and are often filled with wonder."

"True, m'sieur. She keeps herself apart. She is a mysterious person—the most remarkable in all the Principality. We, at the Bureau, have heard all sorts of curious stories concerning her—once it was rumoured that she was the daughter of a reigning European sovereign. Then we take all the reports with the proverbial grain of salt. That Mademoiselle is a woman of outstanding intellect and courage, as well as of great beauty, cannot be denied. Therefore I tell you that I am intensely interested in this attempt upon her life."

"And so am I," Hugh said. "I have a strong reason to be."

"Cannot you tell me that reason?" inquired the officer of the Surete, still looking at him very shrewdly. "Why fence with me?"

Henfrey hesitated. Then he replied:

"It is a purely personal matter."

"And yet, you have said that you were not acquainted with Mademoiselle!" remarked Ogier suspiciously.

"That is quite true. The first time I have spoken to her was this evening, a few minutes before the attempt was made upon her life."

"Then your theory is that while you stood in conversation with her somebody crept along the veranda and shot her—eh?"

"Yes."

Ogier smiled sarcastically, and turning to his colleague, ordered him to search the room. The inspector evidently suspected the young Englishman of having shot Mademoiselle, and the search was in order to try and discover the weapon.

Meanwhile the brown-bearded officer called the Italian manservant, who gave his name as Giulio Cataldi, and who stated that he had been in Mademoiselle Ferad's service a little over five years.

"Have you ever seen this Englishman before?" Ogier asked, indicating Hugh.

"Never, until to-night, m'sieur," was the reply. "He called about twenty minutes after Mademoiselle's return from the Rooms."

"Has Mademoiselle quarrelled with anybody of late?"

"Not to my knowledge, m'sieur. She is of a very quiet and even disposition."

"Is there anyone you know who might possess a motive to shoot her?" asked Ogier. "The crime has not been committed with a motive of robbery, but either out of jealousy or revenge."

"I know of nobody," declared the highly respectable Italian, whose moustache was tinged with grey. He shrugged his shoulders and showed his palms as he spoke.

"Mademoiselle arrived here two months ago, I believe?" queried the police official.

"Yes, m'sieur. She spent the autumn in Paris, and during the summer she was at Deauville. She also went to London for a brief time, I believe."

"Did she ever live in London?" asked Hugh eagerly, interrupting Ogier's interrogation.

"Yes—once. She had a furnished house on the Cromwell Road for about six months."

"How long ago?" asked Henfrey.

"Please allow me to make my inquiries, monsieur!" exclaimed the detective angrily.

"But the question I ask is of greatest importance to me in my own inquiries," Hugh persisted.

"I am here to discover the identity of Mademoiselle's assailant," Ogier asserted. "And I will not brook your interference."

"Mademoiselle has been shot, and it is for you to discover who fired at her," snapped the young Englishman. "I consider that I have just as much right to put a question to this man as you have, that is"—he added with sarcasm—"that is, of course, if you don't suspect him of shooting his mistress."

"Well, I certainly do not suspect that," the Frenchman said. "But, to tell you candidly, your story of the affair strikes me as a very improbable one."

"Ah!" laughed Hugh, "I thought so! You suspect me—eh? Very well. Where is the weapon?"

"Perhaps you have hidden it," suggested the other meaningly. "We shall, no doubt, find it somewhere."

"I hope you will, and that will lead to the arrest of the guilty person," Hugh laughed. Then he was about to put further questions to the man Cataldi when Doctor Leneveu entered the room.

"How is she?" demanded Hugh breathlessly.

The countenance of the fussy little doctor fell.

"Monsieur," he said in a low earnest voice, "I much fear that Mademoiselle will not recover. My colleague Duponteil concurs with that view. We have done our best, but neither of us entertain any hope that she will live!" Then turning to Ogier, the doctor exclaimed: "This is an amazing affair—especially in face of what is whispered concerning the unfortunate lady. What do you make of it?"

The officer of the Surete knit his brows, and with frankness replied:

"At present I am entirely mystified—entirely mystified!"

IV

What the Dossier Contained

Walter Brock was awakened at four o'clock that morning by Hugh touching him upon the shoulder.

He started up in bed and staring at his friend's pale, haggard face exclaimed:

"Good Heavens!—why, what's the matter?"

"Mademoiselle of Monte Carlo has been shot!" the other replied in a hard voice.

"Shot!" gasped Brock, startled. "What do you mean?"

Briefly Hugh who had only just entered the hotel, explained the curious circumstances—how, just at the moment she had been about to reveal the secret of his father's death she was shot.

"Most extraordinary!" declared his friend. "Surely, we have not been followed here by someone who is determined to prevent you from knowing the truth!"

"It seems much like it, Walter," replied the younger man very seriously. "There must be some strong motive or no person would dare to shoot her right before my eyes."

"Agreed. Somebody who is concerned in your father's death has adopted this desperate measure in order to prevent Mademoiselle from telling you the truth."

"That's exactly my opinion, my dear Walter. If it was a crime for gain, or through motives of either jealousy or revenge, Mademoiselle would certainly have been attacked on her way home. The road is quite deserted towards the crest of the hill."

"What do the police say?"

"They do not appear to trouble to track Mademoiselle's assailant. They say they will wait until daylight before searching for footprints on the gravel outside."

"Ah! They are not very fond of making arrests within the Principality. It's such a bad advertisement for the Rooms. The Administration like to show a clean sheet as regards serious crime. Our friends here leave it to the French or Italian police to deal with the criminals so that the Principality shall prove itself the most honest State in Europe," Brock said.

"The police, I believe, suspect me of shooting her," said Hugh bluntly.

"That's very awkward. Why?"

"Well—they don't know the true reason I went to see her, or they would never believe me to be guilty of a crime so much against my own interests."

Brock, who was still sitting up in bed in his pale blue silk pyjamas, reflected a few moments.

"Well, Hugh," he said at last, "after all it is only natural that they should believe that you had a hand in the matter. Even though she told you the truth, it is quite within reason that you should have suddenly become incensed against her for the part she must have played in your father's mysterious death, and in a frenzy of anger you shot her."

Hugh drew a long breath, and his eyebrows narrowed.

"By Jove! I had never regarded it in that light before!" he gasped. "But what about the weapon?"

"You might easily have hidden it before the arrival of the police. You admit that you went out on the veranda. Therefore if they do chance to find the weapon in the garden then their suspicions will, no doubt, be considerably increased. It's a pity, old man, that you didn't make a clean breast of the motive of your visit."

"I now see my horrible mistake," Henfrey admitted. "I thought myself wise to preserve silence, to know nothing, and now I see quite plainly that I have only brought suspicion unduly upon myself. The police, however, know Yvonne Ferad to be a somewhat mysterious person."

"Which renders the situation only worse," Brock said. Then, after a pause, he added: "Now that you have declined to tell the police why you visited the Villa Amette and have, in a way, defied them, it will be best to maintain that attitude. Tell them nothing, no matter what happens."

"I intend to pursue that course. But the worst of it is, Walter, that the doctors hold out no hope of Mademoiselle's recovery. I saw Duponteil half an hour ago, and he told me that he could give me no encouraging information. The bullet has been extracted, but she is hovering between life and death. I suppose it will be in the papers to-morrow, and Dorise and her mother will know of my nocturnal visit to the house of a notorious woman."

"Don't let that worry you, my dear chap. Here, they keep the news of all tragedies out of the papers, because shooting affairs may be thought by the public to be due to losses at the Rooms. Recollect that of all the suicides here—the dozens upon dozens of poor ruined gamesters who are yearly laid to rest in the Suicides' Cemetery—not a single report has appeared in any newspaper. So I think you may remain assured that Lady Ranscomb and her daughter will not learn anything."

"I sincerely hope they won't, otherwise it will go very hard with me," Hugh said in a low, intense voice. "Ah! What a night it has been for me!"

"And if Mademoiselle dies the assailant, whoever he was, will be guilty of wilful murder; while you, on your part, will never know the truth concerning your father's death," remarked the elder man, running his fingers through his hair.

"Yes. That is the position of this moment. But further, I am suspected of the crime!"

Brock dressed while his friend sat upon the edge of the bed, pale-faced and agitated. Suppose that the assailant had flung his pistol into the bushes, and the police eventually discovered it? Then, no doubt, he would be put across the frontier to be arrested by the police of the Department of the Alpes Maritimes.

Truly, the situation was most serious.

Together the two men strolled out into the early morning air and sat upon a seat on the terrace of the Casino watching the sun as it rose over the tideless sea.

For nearly an hour they sat discussing the affair; then they ascended the white, dusty road to the beautiful Villa Amette, the home of the mysterious Mademoiselle.

Old Giulio Cataldi opened the door.

"Alas! m'sieur, Mademoiselle is just the same," he replied in response to Hugh's eager inquiry. "The police have gone, but Doctor Leneveu is still upstairs."

"Have the police searched the garden?" inquired Hugh eagerly.

"Yes, m'sieur. They made a thorough examination, but have discovered no marks of footprints except those of yourself, myself, and a tradesman's lad who brought up a parcel late last night."

"Then they found no weapon?" asked the young Englishman.

"No, m'sieur. There is no clue whatever to the assailant."

"Curious that there should be no footmarks," remarked Brock. "Yet they found yours, Hugh."

"Yes. The man must surely have left some trace outside!"

"One would certainly have thought so," Brock said. "I wonder if we may go into the room where the tragedy happened?" he asked of the servant.

"Certainly, m'sieur," was the courteous reply, and he conducted them both into the apartment wherein Mademoiselle of Monte Carlo had been shot down.

"Did you accompany Mademoiselle when she went to London, Giulio?" asked young Henfrey of the old Italian, after he had described to Brock exactly what had occurred.

"Yes, m'sieur," he replied. "I was at Cromwell Road for a short time. But I do not care for London, so Mademoiselle sent me back here to look after the Villa because old Jean, the concierge, had been taken to the hospital."

"When in London you knew some of Mademoiselle's friends, I suppose?"

"A few—only a few," was the Italian's reply.

"Did you ever know a certain Mr. Benton?"

The old fellow shook his head blankly.

"Not to my knowledge, m'sieur," he replied. "Mademoiselle had really very few friends in London. There was a Mrs. Matthews and her husband, Americans whom she met here in Monte Carlo, and Sir George Cave-Knight, who died a few weeks ago."

"Do you remember an elderly gentleman named Henfrey calling?" asked Hugh.

Old Cataldi reflected for a moment, and then answered:

"The name sounds familiar to me, m'sieur, but in what connexion I cannot recollect. That is your name, is it not?" he asked, remembering the card he had taken to his mistress.

"Yes," Hugh replied. "I have reason to believe that my late father was acquainted with your mistress, and that he called upon her in London."

"I believe that a gentleman named Henfrey did call, because when I glanced at the card you gave me last night the name struck me as familiar," the servant said. "But whether he actually called, or whether someone at table mentioned his name I really cannot recollect."

"Ah! That's a pity," exclaimed Hugh with a sigh. "As a matter of fact it was in order to make certain inquiries regarding my late father that I called upon Mademoiselle last night."

Giulio Cataldi turned in pretence of rearranging a chair, but in reality to avert his face from the young man's gaze—a fact which Hugh did not fail to notice.

Had he really told the truth when he declared that he could not recollect his father calling?

"How long were you in London with Mademoiselle?" asked Henfrey.

"About six weeks—not longer."

Was it because of some untoward occurrence that the old Italian did not like London, Hugh wondered.

"And you are quite sure that you do not recollect my father calling upon your mistress?"

"As I have said, m'sieur, I do not remember. Yet I recall the name, as it is a rather unusual one."

"And you have never heard of Mr. Benton?"

Cataldi shook his head.

"Well," Hugh went on, "tell me whether you entertain any suspicions of anyone who might be tempted to kill your mistress. Mademoiselle has enemies, has she not?"

"Who knows?" exclaimed the man with the grey moustache and small, black furtive eyes.

"Everyone has enemies of one sort or another," Walter remarked. "And no doubt Mademoiselle has. It is for us to discover the enemy who shot her."

"Ah! yes, it is, m'sieur," exclaimed the servant. "The poor Signorina! I do hope that the police will discover who tried to kill her."

"For aught we know the attempt upon the lady's life may prove successful after all," said Hugh despairingly. "The doctors hold out no hope of her recovery."

"None. A third doctor has been in consultation—Doctor Bazin, from Beaulieu. He only left a quarter of an hour ago. He told me that the poor Signorina cannot possibly live! Ah! messieurs, how terrible all this is—*povera Signorina*! She was always so kind and considerate to us all." And the old man's voice trembled with emotion.

Walter Brock gazed around the luxurious room and at the long open window through which streamed the bright morning sun, with the perfume of the flowers outside. What was the mystery concerning Mademoiselle Yvonne? What foundation had the gossips for those constant whisperings which had rendered the handsome woman so notorious?

True, the story of the death of Hugh's father was an unusually strange one, curious in every particular—and stranger still that the secret was held by this beautiful, but mysterious, woman who lived in such luxury, and who gambled so recklessly and with invariable good fortune.

As they walked back to the town Hugh's heart sank within him.

"She will die," he muttered bitterly to himself. "She'll die, and I shall never learn the truth of the poor guv'nor's sad end, or the reason why I am being forced to marry Louise Lambert."

"It's an iniquitous will, Hugh!" declared his friend. "And it's infernally hard on you that just at the very moment when you could have learnt the truth that shot was fired."

"Do you think the woman had any hand in my father's death?" Hugh asked. "Do you think that she had repented, and was about to try and atone for what she had done by confessing the whole affair?"

"Yes. That is just the view I take," answered Brock. "Of course, we have no idea what part she played in the business. But my idea is that she alone knows the reason why this marriage with Louise is being forced upon you."

"In that case, then, it seems more than likely that I've been followed here to Monte Carlo, and my movements watched. But why has she been shot? Why did not her enemies shoot me? They could have done so twenty times during the past few days. Perhaps the shot which hit her was really intended for me?"

"I don't think so. There is a monetary motive behind your marriage with Louise. If you died, your enemy would gain nothing. That seems clear."

"But who can be my secret enemy?" asked the young man in dismay.

"Mademoiselle alone knows that, and it was undoubtedly her intention to warn you."

"Yes. But if she dies I shall remain in ignorance," he declared in a hard voice. "The whole affair is so tangled that I can see nothing clearly—only that my refusal to marry Louise will mean ruin to me—and I shall lose Dorise in the bargain!"

Walter Brock, older and more experienced, was equally mystified. The pessimistic attitude of the three doctors who had attended the injured woman was, indeed, far from reassuring. The injury to the head caused by the assailant's bullet was, they declared, most dangerous. Indeed, the three medical men marvelled that she still lived.

The two men walked through the palm-lined garden, bright with flowers, back to their hotel, wondering whether news of the tragedy had yet got abroad. But they heard nothing of it, and it seemed true, as Walter Brock had declared, that the police make haste to suppress any tragic happenings in the Principality.

Though they were unconscious of it, a middle-aged, well-dressed

Frenchman had, during their absence from the hotel, been making diligent inquiries regarding them of the night concierge and some of the staff.

The concierge had recognized the visitor as Armand Buisson, of the police bureau at Nice. It seemed as though the French police were unduly inquisitive concerning the well-conducted young Englishman and his companion.

Now, as a matter of fact, half an hour after Hugh had left the Villa Amette, Ogier had telegraphed to Buisson in Nice, and the latter had come along the Corniche road in a fast car to make his own inquiries and observations upon the pair of Englishmen. Ogier strongly suspected Henfrey of firing the shot, but was, nevertheless, determined to remain inactive and leave the matter to the Prefecture of the Department of Alpes Maritimes. Hence the reason that the well-dressed Frenchman lounged in the hall of the hotel pretending to read the "Phare du Littoral."

Just before noon Hugh went to the telephone in the hotel and inquired of Cataldi the progress of his mistress.

"She is just the same, m'sieur," came the voice in broken English. "*Santa Madonna!* How terrible it all is! Doctor Leneveu has left, and Doctor Duponteil is now here."

"Have the police been again?"

"No, m'sieur. Nobody has been," was the reply.

So Hugh rang off and crossed the hall, little dreaming that the well-dressed Frenchman had been highly interested in his questions.

Half an hour later he went along to the Metropole, where he had an engagement to lunch with Dorise and her mother.

When they met, however, Lady Ranscomb exclaimed:

"Why, Hugh, you look very pale. What's the matter?"

"Oh, nothing," he laughed forcedly. "I'm not very bright to-day. I think it was the sirocco of yesterday that has upset me a little, that's all."

Then, while they were seated at table, Dorise suddenly exclaimed:

"Oh! do you know, mother, that young French lady over yonder, Madame Jacomet, has just told me something. There's a whisper that the mysterious woman, Mademoiselle of Monte Carlo, was shot during the night by a discarded lover!"

"Shot!" exclaimed Lady Ranscomb. "Dear me! How very dreadful. What really happened?"

"I don't know. Madame Jacomet was told by her husband, who heard it in Ciro's this morning."

"How terrible!" remarked Hugh, striving to remain calm.

"Yes. But women of her class invariably come to a bad end," remarked the widow. "How pleased I am, Dorise, that you never spoke to her. She's a most dreadful person, they say."

"Well, she evidently knows how to win money at the tables, mother," said the girl, lifting her clear blue eyes to those of her lover.

"Yes. But I wonder what the scandal is all about?" said the widow of the great engineer.

"Oh! don't trouble to inquire Lady Ranscomb," Hugh hastened to remark. "One hears scandal on every hand in Monte Carlo."

"Yes. I suppose so," replied the elder woman, and then the subject was dropped.

So the ugly affair was being rumoured. It caused Hugh a good deal of apprehension, for he feared that his name would be associated with that of the mysterious Mademoiselle. Evidently one or other of the servants at the Villa Amette had been indiscreet.

At that moment, in his private room at the bureau of police down in Monaco, Superintendent Ogier was carefully perusing a dossier of official papers which had been brought to him by the archivist.

Between his thin lips was a long, thin, Swiss cigar—his favorite smoke—and with his gold-rimmed pince-nez poised upon his aquiline nose he was reading a document which would certainly have been of considerable interest to Hugh Henfrey and his friend Walter Brock could they have seen it.

Upon the pale yellow paper were many lines of typewriting in French—a carbon copy evidently.

It was headed: "Republique Francaise. Department of Herault. Prefecture of Police. Bureau of the Director of Police. Reference Number 20197.B.," and was dated nearly a year before.

It commenced:

"Copy of an 'information' in the archives of the Prefecture of the Department of Herault concerning the woman Marie Mignot, or Leullier, now passing under the name of Yvonne Ferad and living at the Villa Amette at Monte Carlo.

"The woman in question was born in 1884 at Number 45 Rue des Etuves, in Montpellier, and was the daughter of one Doctor Rigaud, a noted toxicologist of the Faculty of Medicine, and curator of the University Library. At the age of seventeen, after her father's death, she became a school teacher at a small school in the Rue Morceau, and at nineteen married Charles Leullier, a good-looking young scoundrel who posed as being well off, but who was afterwards proved to be an expert international thief, a member of a gang of dangerous thieves who committed robberies in the European express trains.

"This fact was unknown to the girl, therefore at first all went smoothly, until the wife discovered the truth and left him. She then joined the chorus of a revue at the Jardin de Paris, where she met a well-to-do Englishman named Bryant. The pair went to England, where she married him, and they resided in the county of Northampton. Six months later Bryant died, leaving her a large sum of money. In the meantime Leullier had been arrested by the Italian police for a daring robbery with violence in a train traveling between Milan and Turin and been sentenced to ten years on the penal island of Gorgona. His wife, hearing of this from an Englishman named Houghton, who, though she was unaware of it, was following the same profession as her husband, returned to France. She rented an apartment in Paris, and afterwards played at Monte Carlo, where she won a considerable sum, with the proceeds of which she purchased the Villa Amette, which she now occupies each season."

"Extracts of reports concerning Marie Leullier, alias Yvonne Ferad, are herewith appended:

"Criminal Investigation Department, New Scotland Yard, London—to the Prefecture of Police, Paris.

"Mademoiselle Yvonne Ferad rented a furnished house at Hove, near Brighton, in June, 1918. Afterwards moved to Worthing and to Exeter, and later took a house in the Cromwell Road, London, in 1919. She was accompanied by an Italian manservant named Cataldi. Her conduct was suspicious, though she was undoubtedly possessed of considerable means. She was often seen at the best restaurants with various male acquaintances, more especially with a man named Kenworthy. Her association with this person, and with another man named Percy Stendall, was curious, as both men were habitual criminals and had served several terms of penal servitude each. Certain suspicions were aroused, and observation was kept, but nothing tangible was discovered. It is agreed, however, that some mystery surrounds this woman in question. She left London quite suddenly, but left no debts behind."

"Information from the Borough Police Office, Worthing, to the Prefecture of Police, Department of Herault.

"Mademoiselle Yvonne Ferad has been identified by the photograph sent as having lived in Worthing in December, 1918. She rented a small furnished house facing the sea, and was accompanied by an Italian manservant and a French maid. Her movements were distinctly mysterious. A serious fracas occurred at the house on the evening of December 18th, 1918. A middle-aged gentleman, whose name is unknown, called there about seven o'clock and a violent quarrel ensued between the lady and her visitor, the latter being very seriously assaulted by the Italian. The constable on duty was called in, but the visitor refused to prosecute, and after having his injuries attended to by a doctor left for London. Three days later Mademoiselle disappeared from Worthing. It is believed by the Chief Constable that the woman is of the criminal class."

Then Charles Ogier, inspector of the detective police of Monaco, smiled, laid down his cigar, and took up another and even more interesting document.

V

On the Hog's Back

Three days later. On a cold afternoon just as the wintry light was fading a tall, dark, middle-aged, rather handsome man with black hair and moustache, and wearing a well-cut, dark-grey overcoat and green velour hat, alighted from the train at the wayside station of Wanborough, in Surrey, and inquired of the porter the way to Shapley Manor.

"Shapley, sir? Why, take the road there yonder up the hill till you get to the main road which runs along the Hog's Back from Guildford to Farnborough. When you get on the main road, turn sharp to the left past the old toll-gate, and you'll find the Manor on the left in among a big clump of trees."

"How far?"

"About a mile, sir."

The stranger, the only passenger who had alighted, slipped sixpence into the man's hand, buttoned his coat, and started out to walk in the direction indicated, breasting the keen east wind.

He was well-set-up, and of athletic bearing. He took long strides as with swinging gait he went up the hill. As he did so, he muttered to himself:

"I was an infernal fool not to have come down in a car! I hate these beastly muddy country roads. But Molly has the telephone—so I can ring up for a car to fetch me—which is a consolation, after all."

And with his keen eyes set before him, he pressed forward up the steep incline to where, for ten miles, ran the straight broad highway over the high ridge known as the Hog's Back. The road is very popular with motorists, for so high is it that on either side there stretches a wide panorama of country, the view on the north being towards the Thames Valley and London, while on the south Hindhead with the South Downs in the blue distance show beyond.

Having reached the high road the stranger paused to take breath, and incidentally to admire the magnificent view. Indeed, an expression of admiration fell involuntarily from his lips. Then he went along for another half-mile in the teeth of the cutting wind with the twilight rapidly coming on, until he came to the clump of dark firs and presently walked up a gravelled drive to a large, but somewhat inartistic, Georgian house of red brick with long square windows. In parts the ivy was trying to hide its terribly ugly architecture for around the deep porch it grew thickly and spread around one corner of the building.

A ring at the door brought a young manservant whom the caller addressed as Arthur, and, wishing him good afternoon, asked if Mrs. Bond were at home.

"Yes, sir," was the reply.

"Oh! good," said the caller. "Just tell her I'm here." And he proceeded to remove his coat and to hang it up in the great flagged hall with the air of one used to the house.

The Manor was a spacious, well-furnished place, full of good pictures and much old oak furniture.

The servant passed along the corridor, and entering the drawing-room, announced:

"Mr. Benton is here, ma'am."

"Oh! Mr. Benton! Show him in," cried his mistress enthusiastically. "Show him in at once!"

Next moment the caller entered the fine, old-fashioned room, where a well-preserved, fair-haired woman of about forty was taking her tea alone and petting her Pekinese.

"Well, Charles? So you've discovered me here, eh?" she exclaimed, jumping up and taking his hand.

"Yes, Molly. And you seem to have very comfortable quarters," laughed Benton as he threw himself unceremoniously into a chintz-covered armchair.

"They are, I assure you."

"And I suppose you're quite a great lady in these parts—eh?—now that you live at Shapley Manor. Where's Louise?"

"She went up to town this morning. She won't be back till after dinner. She's with her old school-fellow—that girl Bertha Trench."

"Good. Then we can have a chat. I've several things to consult you about and ask your opinion."

"Have some tea first," urged his good-looking hostess, pouring him some into a Crown Derby cup.

"Well," he commenced. "I think you've done quite well to take this place, as you've done, for three years. You are now safely out of the way. The Paris Surete are making very diligent inquiries, but the Surrey

　　　　　　　　　　　　WILLIAM LE QUEUX

Constabulary will never identify you with the lady of the Rue Racine. So you are quite safe here."

"Are you sure of that, Charles?" she asked, fixing her big grey eyes upon him.

"Certain. It was the wisest course to get back here to England, although you had to take a very round-about journey."

"Yes. I got to Switzerland, then to Italy, and from Genoa took an Anchor Line steamer across to New York. After that I came over to Liverpool, and in the meantime I had become Mrs. Bond. Louise, of course, thought we were travelling for pleasure. I had to explain my change of name by telling her that I did not wish my divorced husband to know that I was back in England."

"And the girl believed it, of course," he laughed.

"Of course. She believes anything I tell her," said the clever, unscrupulous woman for whom the Paris police were in active search, whose real name was Molly Maxwell, and whose amazing career was well known to the French police.

Only recently a sum of a quarter of a million francs had fallen into her hands, and with it she now rented Shapley Manor and had set up as a country lady. Benton gazed around the fine old room with its Adams ceiling and its Georgian furniture, and reflected how different were Molly's present surroundings from that stuffy little flat *au troisieme* in the Rue Racine.

"Yes," he said. "You had a very narrow escape, Molly. I dared not come near you, but I knew that you'd look after the girl."

"Of course. I always look after her as though she were my own child."

Benton's lip curled as he sipped his China tea, and said:

"Because so much depends upon her—eh? I'm glad you view the situation from a fair and proper stand-point. We're now out for a big thing, therefore we must not allow any little hitch to prevent us from bringing it off successfully."

"I quite agree, Charles. Our great asset is Louise. But she must be innocent of it all. She must know absolutely nothing."

"True. If she had an inkling that we were forcing her to marry Hugh she would fiercely resent it. She's a girl of spirit, after all."

"My dear Charles, I know that," laughed the woman. "Ever since she came home from school I've noticed how independent she is. She certainly has a will of her own. But she likes Hugh, and we must encourage it. Recollect that a fortune is at stake."

"I have not overlooked that," the man said. "But of late I've come to fear that we are treading upon thin ice. I don't like the look of affairs at the present moment. Young Henfrey is head over ears in love with that girl Dorise Ranscomb, and—"

"Bah! It's only a flirtation, my dear Charles," laughed the woman. "When just a little pressure is put upon the boy, and a sly hint to Lady Ranscomb, then the affair will soon be off, and he'll fall into Louise's arms. She's really very fond of him."

"She may be, but he takes no notice of her. She told me so the other day. He's gone to the Riviera—followed Dorise, I suppose," Benton said.

"Yvonne wrote me a few days ago to say that he was there with a friend of his named Walter Brock. Who's he?"

"Oh! a naval lieutenant-commander who served in the war and was invalided out after the Battle of Jutland. He got the D.S.O. over the Falklands affair, and has now some post at the Admiralty. He was in command of a torpedo boat which sank a German cruiser, and was afterwards blown up."

"They are both out at Monte Carlo, Yvonne says. And Henfrey is with Dorise daily," remarked the woman.

"Yvonne is always apprehensive lest young Henfrey should learn the secret of the old fellow's end," said Benton. "But I don't see how the truth of the—well, rather ugly affair can ever come out, except by an indiscretion by one or other of us."

"And that is scarcely likely, Charles, is it?" his hostess laughed as she pushed across to him a big silver box of cigarettes and then reclined lazily among her cushions.

"No. It would certainly be a very sensational affair if the newspapers got hold of the facts, my dear Molly. But don't let us anticipate such a thing. Fortunately Louise, in her girlish innocence, knows nothing. Old Henfrey left his money to his son upon certain conditions, one of which is that Hugh shall marry Louise. And that marriage must, at all hazards, take place. After that, we care for nothing."

The handsome woman who was rolling a cigarette between her well-manicured fingers hesitated. Her countenance assumed a strange look as she reflected. She was far too clever to express any off-hand opinion. She had outwitted the police of Paris, Brussels, and Rome in turn. Her whole career had been a criminal one, punctuated by periods of pretended high respectability—while the funds to support it had

WILLIAM LE QUEUX

lasted. And upon her hands had been placed Louise Lambert, the child Charles Benton had adopted ten years before.

"We shall have to exercise a good deal of discretion and caution in regard to Louise," she declared. "The affair is not at all so plain sailing as I at first believed."

"No. It is a serious contretemps that you had to leave Paris, Molly," agreed her well-dressed visitor. "The young American was a fool, of course, but I think—"

"Paris was flooded by rich young men from the United States who came over to fight the Boche and to spend their money like water when on leave in Paris. Frank was only one of them."

Benton was silent. The affair was a distinctly unsavoury one. Frank van Geen, the son of the Dutch-American millionaire cocoa manufacturer of Chicago, had, by reason of his association with Molly, found himself the poorer by nearly a quarter of a million francs, and his body had been found in the Seine between the Pont d'Auteuil and the Ile St. Germain. At the inquiry some ugly disclosures were made, but already the lady of the Rue Racine and her supposed niece had left Paris; and though the affair was one of suicide, the police raised a hue and cry, and the frontiers had been watched, but the pair had disappeared.

That was several months ago. And now Molly Maxwell the adventuress in Paris had been transformed into the wealthy and highly respectable widow Mrs. Bond, who having presented such excellent references had become tenant of that well-furnished mansion, Shapley Manor, and the beautiful grounds adjoining. For nearly two centuries it had been the home of the Puttenhams, but Sir George Puttenham, Baronet, the present owner, had found himself ruined by war-taxation, and as one of the new poor he had been glad to let the place and live upon the rent obtained for it. His case, indeed, was only one of thousands of others in England, where adventurers and war-profiteers were ousting the landed gentry.

"Yvonne is evidently keeping a good watch upon young Hugh," remarked Benton presently, as he blew a ring of cigarette smoke towards the ceiling.

"Yes," replied the woman, her eyes fixed out of the big window which commanded a glorious view of Gibbet Hill, at Hindhead, and the blue South Downs towards the English Channel. But all was dark and lowering in the winter twilight, now fast darkening into night.

In old-world Guildford, the county town of Surrey, with its steep High Street containing many seventeenth-century houses, its old inns, and its balconied Guildhall—the scene of so many unseemly wrangles among the robed and cocked-hatted borough councillors who are, *par excellence*, outstanding illustrations of the provincial petty jealousies of bumbledom—Mrs. Bond was welcomed by the trades-people who vied with each other to "serve her." Almost daily she went up and down the High Street in her fine Rolls-Royce driven by Mead, an ex-soldier and a worthy fellow whom she had engaged through an advertisement in the *Surrey Advertiser*. He had been in the Queen's West Surrey, and his home being in Guildford, Molly knew that he would serve as a testimonial to her high respectability. Molly Maxwell was an outstandingly clever woman. She never let a chance slip by that might be taken advantageously.

Mead, who went on his "push-bike" every evening along the Hog's Back to Guildford, was never tired of singing the praises of his generous mistress.

"She's a real good sort," he would tell his friends in the bar of the Lion or the Angel. "She knows how to treat a man. She's a widow, and good-looking. I suppose she'll marry again. Nearly all the best people about here have called on her within the last week or two. Magistrates and their wives, retired generals, and lots of the gentry. Yes, my job isn't to be sneezed at, I can tell you. It's better than driving a lorry outside Ypres!"

Mrs. Bond treated Mead extremely well, and paid him well. She knew that by so doing she would secure a good advertisement. She had done so before, when four or five years ago she had lived at Keswick.

"Do you know, Charles," she said presently, "I'm really very apprehensive regarding the present situation. Yvonne is, no doubt, keeping a watchful eye upon the young fellow. But what can she do if he has followed the Ranscomb girl and is with her each day? Each day, indeed, must bring the pair closer together, and—"

"That's what we must prevent, my dear Molly!" exclaimed the lady's visitor. "Think of all it means to us. You are quite safe here—as safe as I am to-day. But we can't last out without money—either of us. We must have cash-money—and cash-money always."

"Yes. That's so. But Yvonne is wonderful—amazing."

"She hasn't the same stake in the affair as we have."

"Why not?" asked the woman for whom the European police were in search.

"Well, because she is rich—she's won pots of money at the tables—and we—well, both of us have only limited means. Yours, Molly, are larger than mine—thanks to Frank. But I must have money soon. My expenses in town are mounting up daily."

"But your rooms don't cost you very much! Old Mrs. Evans looks after things as she has always done."

"Yes. But everything is going up in price, and remember, I dare not cross the Channel just now. At Calais, Boulogne, Cherbourg, and other places, they have my photograph, and they are waiting for me to fall into the trap. But the rat, once encaged, is shy! And I am very shy just now," he added with a light laugh.

"You'll stay and have dinner, won't you?" urged his hostess.

Benton hesitated.

"If I do Louise may return, and just now I don't want to meet her. It is better not."

"But she won't be back till the last train to Guildford. Mead is meeting her. Yes—stay."

"I must get a car to take me back to town. I have to go to Glasgow by the early train in the morning."

"Well, we're order one from one of the garages in Guildford. You really must stay, Charles. There's lots we have to talk over—a lot of things that are of vital consequence to us both."

At that moment there came a rap at the door and the young manservant entered, saying:

"You're wanted on the telephone, ma'am."

Mrs. Bond rose from the settee and went to the telephone in the library, where she heard the voice of a female telephone operator.

"Is that Shapley Manor?" she asked. "I have a telegram for Mrs. Bond. Handed in at Nice at two twenty-five, received here at four twenty-eight. 'To Bond, Shapley Manor, near Guildford. Yvonne shot by some unknown person while with Hugh. In grave danger.—S.' That is the message. Have you got it please?"

Mrs. Bond held her breath.

"Yes," she gasped. "Anything else?"

"No, madam," replied the telephone operator at the Guildford Post Office. "Nothing else. I will forward the duplicate by post."

And she switched off.

VI

Facing the Unknown

That the police were convinced that Hugh Henfrey had shot Mademoiselle was plain.

Wherever he went an agent of detective police followed him. At the Cafe de Paris as he took his aperitif on the *terrasse* the man sat at a table near, idly smoking a cigarette and glancing at an illustrated paper on a wooden holder. In the gardens, in the Rooms, in the Galerie, everywhere the same insignificant little man haunted him.

Soon after luncheon he met Dorise and her mother in the Rooms. With them were the Comte d'Autun, an elegant young Frenchman, well known at the tables, and Madame Tavera, a very chic person who was one of the most admired visitors of that season. They were only idling and watching the players at the end table, where a stout, bearded Russian was making some sensational coups *en plein*.

Presently Hugh succeeded in getting Dorise alone.

"It's awfully stuffy here," he said. "Let's go outside—eh?"

Together they descended the red-carpeted steps and out into the palm-lined Place, at that hour thronged by the smartest crowd in Europe. Indeed, the war seemed to have led to increased extravagance and daring in the dress of those gay Parisiennes, those butterflies of fashion who were everywhere along the Cote d'Azur.

They turned the corner by the Palais des Beaux Arts into the Boulevard Peirara.

"Let's walk out of the town," he suggested to the girl. "I'm tired of the place."

"So am I, Hugh," Dorise admitted. "For the first fortnight the unceasing round of gaiety and the novelty of the Rooms are most fascinating, but, after that, one seems cooped up in an atmosphere of vicious unreality. One longs for the open air and open country after this enervating, exotic life."

So when they arrived at the little church of Ste. Devote, the patron saint of Monaco, that little building which everyone knows standing at the entrance to that deep gorge the Vallon des Gaumates, they descended the steep, narrow path which runs beside the mountain torrent and were soon alone in the beautiful little valley where the grey-green olives overhang the rippling stream. The little valley was delightfully quiet and rural after the garish scenes in Monte Carlo, the cosmopolitan chatter, and the vulgar display of the war-rich. The old habitue of pre-war days lifts his hands as he watches the post-war life around the Casino and listens to the loud uneducated chatter of the profiteer's womenfolk.

As the pair went along in the welcome shadows, for the sun fell strong upon the tumbling stream, Hugh was remarking upon it.

He had been at Monte Carlo with his father before the war, and realized the change.

"I only wish mother would move on," Dorise exclaimed as they strolled slowly together.

She presented a dainty figure in cream gabardine and a broad-brimmed straw hat which suited her admirably. Her clothes were made by a certain famous *couturiere* in Hanover Square, for Lady Ranscomb had the art of dressing her daughter as well as she did herself. Gowns make the lady nowadays, or the fashionable dressmakers dare not make their exorbitant charges.

"Then you also are tired of the place?" asked Hugh, as he strolled slowly at her side in a dark-blue suit and straw hat. They made a handsome pair, and were indeed well suited to each other. Lady Ranscomb liked Hugh, but she had no idea that the young people had fallen so violently in love with each other.

"Yes," said the girl. "Mother promised to spend Easter in Florence. I've never been there and am looking forward to it so much. The Marchesa Ruggeri, whom we met at Harrogate last summer, has a villa there, and has invited us for Easter. But mother said this morning that she preferred to remain here."

"Why?"

"Oh! Somebody in the hotel has put her off. An old Englishwoman who lives in Florence told her that there's nothing to see beyond the Galleries, and that the place is very catty."

Hugh laughed and replied:

"All British colonies in Continental cities are catty, my dear Dorise. They say that for scandal Florence takes the palm. I went there for two seasons in succession before the war, and found the place delightful."

"The Marchesa is a charming woman. Her husband was an attache at the Italian Embassy in Paris. But he has been transferred to Washington, so she has gone back to Florence. I like her immensely, and I do so want to visit her."

"Oh, you must persuade your mother to take you," he said. "She'll be easily persuaded."

"I don't know. She doesn't like travelling in Italy. She once had her dressing-case stolen from the train between Milan and Genoa, so she's always horribly bitter against all Italians."

"There are thieves also on English railways, Dorise," Hugh remarked. "People are far too prone to exaggerate the shortcomings of foreigners, and close their eyes to the faults of the British."

"But everybody is not so cosmopolitan as you are, Hugh," the girl laughed, raising her eyes to those of her lover.

"No," he replied with a sigh.

"Why do you sigh?" asked the girl, having noticed a change in her companion ever since they had met in the Rooms. He seemed strangely thoughtful and preoccupied.

"Did I?" he asked, suddenly pulling himself together. "I didn't know," he added with a forced laugh.

"You don't look yourself to-day, Hugh," she said.

"I've been told that once before," he replied. "The weather—I think! Are you going over to the *bal blanc* at Nice to-night?"

"Of course. And you are coming also. Hasn't mother asked you?" she inquired in surprise.

"No."

"How silly! She must have forgotten. She told me she intended to ask you to have a seat in the car. The Comte d'Autun is coming with us."

"Ah! He admires you, Dorise, hence I don't like him," Hugh blurted forth.

"But, surely, you're not jealous, you dear old thing!" laughed the girl, tantalizing him. Perhaps she would not have uttered those words which cut deeply into his heart had she known the truth concerning the tragedy at the Villa Amette.

"I don't like him because he seems to live by gambling," Hugh declared. "I know your mother likes him very much—of course!"

"And she likes you, too, dear."

"She may like me, but I fear she begins to suspect that we love each other, dearest," he said in a hard tone. "If she does, she will take care in future to keep us apart, and I—I shall lose you, Dorise!"

WILLIAM LE QUEUX

"No—no, you won't."

"Ah! But I shall! Your mother will never allow you to marry a man who has only just sufficient to rub along with, and who is already in debt to his tailor. What hope is there that we can ever marry?"

"My dear Hugh, you are awfully pessimistic to-day," the girl cried. "What is up with you? Have you lost heavily at the tables—or what?"

"No. I have been thinking of the future," he said in a hard voice so very unusual to him. "I am thinking of your mother's choice of a husband for you—George Sherrard."

"I hate him—the egotistical puppy!" exclaimed the girl, her fine eyes flashing with anger. "I'll never marry him—*never*!"

But Hugh Henfrey made no reply, and they went on together in silence.

"Cannot you trust me, Hugh?" asked the girl at last in a low earnest tone.

"Yes, dearest. I trust you, of course. But I feel certain that your mother, when she knows our secret, will forbid your seeing me, and press on your marriage with Sherrard. Remember, he's a rich man, and your mother adores the Golden Calf."

"I know she does. If people have money she wants to know them. Her first inquiry is whether they have money."

It was on the tip of Hugh's tongue to remark with sarcasm that such ideals might well be expected of the wife of a jerry-builder in Golder's green. But he hesitated. Lady Ranscomb was always well disposed towards him, and he had had many good times at her house and on the grouse moor she rented in Scotland each year for the benefit of her intimate friends. Though she had been the wife of a small builder and had commenced her married life in an eight-roomed house on the fringe of Hampstead Heath, yet she had picked up society manners marvellously well, being a woman of quick intelligence and considerable wit. Nevertheless, she had no soul above money, and gaiety was as life to her. She could not live without it. Dorise had been given an excellent education, and after three years at Versailles was now voted one of the prettiest and most charming girls in London society. Hence mother and daughter were sought after everywhere, and their doings were constantly being chronicled in the newspapers.

"Yes," he said. "Your mother has not asked me over to Nice to-night because she believes you and I have been too much together of late."

"No," declared Dorise. "I'm sure it's not that, Hugh—I'm quite sure! It's simply an oversight. I'll see about it when we get back. We leave the hotel at half-past nine. It is the great White Ball of the Nice season."

"Please don't mention it to her on any account, Dorise," Hugh urged. "If you did it would at once show her that you preferred my company to that of the Count. Go with him. I shan't be jealous! Besides, in view of my financial circumstances, what right have I to be jealous? You can't marry a fellow like myself, Dorise. It wouldn't be fair to you."

The girl halted. In her eyes shone the light of unshed tears.

"Hugh! What do you mean? What are you saying?" she asked in a low, faltering voice. "Have I not told you that whatever happens I shall never love another man but yourself?"

He drew a long breath, and without replying placed his strong arms around her and, drawing her to him, kissed her passionately upon the lips.

"Thank you, my darling," he murmured. "Thank you for those words. They put into me a fresh hope, a fresh determination, and a fearlessness—oh! you—you don't know!" he added in a low, earnest voice.

"All I know, Hugh, is that you love me," was the simple response as she reciprocated his fierce caress.

"Love you, darling!" he cried. "Yes. You are mine—mine!"

"True, Hugh. I love no other man. I hate that tailor's dummy, George Sherrard, and as for the Count—well, he's an idiotic Frenchman—the 'hardy annual of Monte Carlo' I heard him called the other day. No, Hugh, I assure you that you have no cause for jealousy."

And she smiled sweetly into his eyes.

They were standing together beneath a twisted old olive tree through the dark foliage of which the sun shone in patches, while by their feet the mountain torrent from the high, snow-clad Alps rippled and splashed over the great grey boulders towards the sea.

"I know it, darling! I know it," Hugh said in a stifled voice. He was thinking of the tragedy of that night, but dare not disclose to her his connexion with it, because he knew the police suspected him of making that murderous attack upon the famous "Mademoiselle."

"Forgive me, Hugh," exclaimed the girl, still clasped in her lover's arms. "But somehow you don't seem your old self to-day. What is the matter? Can't you tell me?"

He drew a long breath.

"No, darling. Excuse me. I—I'm a bit upset that's all."

"Why?"

"I'm upset because for the last day or two I have begun to realize that our secret must very soon come out, and then—well, your mother will forbid me the house because I have no money. You know that she worships Mammon always—just as your father did—forgive me for my words."

"I do forgive you because you speak the truth," Dorise replied. "I know that mother wants me to marry a rich man, and—"

"And she will compel you to do so, darling. I am convinced of that."

"She won't!" cried the girl. "I will never marry a man I do not love!"

"Your mother, if she doesn't suspect our compact, will soon do so," he said. "She's a clever woman. She is on the alert, because she intends you to marry soon, and to marry a rich man."

"Mother is far too fond of society, I admit. She lives only for her gay friends now that father is dead. She spends lavishly upon luncheons and dinners at the Ritz, the Carlton, and Claridge's; and by doing so we get to know all the best people. But what does it matter to me? I hate it all because—"

And she looked straight into his eyes as she broke off.

"Because," she whispered, "because—because I love you, Hugh!"

"Ah! darling! You have never been so frank with me before," he said softly. "You do not know how much those words of yours mean to me! You do not know how all my life, all my hopes, all my future, is centred in your own dear self!" and clasping her again tightly in his arms he pressed his lips fondly to hers in a long passionate embrace.

Yet within the stout heart of Hugh Henfrey, who was so straight, honest and upright a young fellow as ever trod the Broad at Oxford, lay that ghastly secret—indeed, a double secret—that of his revered father's mysterious end and the inexplicable attack upon Yvonne Ferad at the very moment when he had been about to learn the truth.

They lingered there beside the mountain stream for a long time, until the sun sank and the light began to fail. Again and again he told her of his great love for her, but he said nothing of the strange clause in his father's will. She knew Louise Lambert, having met her once walking in the park with her lover. Hugh had introduced them, and had afterwards explained that the girl was the adopted daughter of a great friend of his father.

Dorise little dreamed that if her lover married her he would inherit the remainder of old Mr. Henfrey's fortune.

"Do come over to the ball at Nice to-night," the girl urged presently as they stood with hands clasped gazing into each other's eyes. "It will be nothing without you."

"Ah! darling, that's very nice of you to say so, but I think we ought to be discreet. Your mother has invited the Count to go with you."

"I hate him!" Dorise declared. "He's all elegance, bows and flattery. He bores me to death."

"I can quite understand that. But your mother is fond of his society. She declares that he is so amusing, and in Paris he knows everyone worth knowing."

"Oh, yes. He gave us an awfully good time in Paris last season—took us to Longchamps, and we afterwards went to Deauville with him. He wins and loses big sums on the turf."

"A born gambler. Everyone knows that. I heard a lot about him in the Travellers' Club, in Paris."

"But if mother telephones to you, you'll come with us—won't you?" entreated the girl again.

The young man hesitated. His mind was full of the tragic affair of the previous night. He was wondering whether the end had come— whether Mademoiselle's lips were already sealed by Death.

He gave an evasive reply, whereupon Dorise, taking his hand in hers, said:

"What is your objection to going out with us to-night, Hugh? Do tell me. If you don't wish me to go, I'll make an excuse to mother and she can take the Count."

"I have not the slightest objection," he declared at once. "Go, dearest—only leave me out of it. The *bal blanc* is always good fun."

"I shall not go if you refuse to go," she said with a pout.

Therefore in order to please her he consented—providing Lady Ranscomb invited him.

They had wandered a long way up the narrow, secluded valley, but had met not a soul. All was delightful and picturesque, the profusion of wild flowers, the huge grey moss-grown boulders, the overhanging ilexes and olives, and the music of the tumbling current through a crooked course worn deep by the waters of primeval ages.

It was seldom that in the whirl of society the pair could get a couple of hours together without interruption. And under the blue Riviera sky they were indeed fraught with bliss to both.

When they returned to the town the dusk was already falling, and the great arc lamps along the terrace in front of the Casino were already lit. Hugh took her as far as the entrance to the Metropole and then, after wishing her au revoir and promising to go with her to Nice if invited, he hastily retraced his steps to the Palmiers. Five minutes later he was speaking to the old Italian at the Villa Amette.

"Mademoiselle is still unconscious, m'sieur," was the servant's reply to his eager inquiry. "The doctors have been several times this afternoon, but they hold out no hope."

"I wonder if I can be of any assistance?" Hugh asked in French.

"I think not, m'sieur. What assistance can any of us give poor Mademoiselle?"

Ah, what indeed, Hugh thought as he put down the receiver.

Yet while she lived, there was still a faint hope that he would be able to learn the secret which he anticipated would place him in such a position that he might defy those who had raised their hands against his father and himself.

His marriage with Dorise, indeed his whole future, depended upon the disclosure of the clever plot whereby Louise Lambert was to become his wife.

His friend Brock was not in the hotel, so he went to his room to dress for dinner. Ten minutes later a page brought a message from Lady Ranscomb inviting him to go over to Nice to the ball.

He drew a long breath. He was in no mood for dancing that night, for he was far too perturbed regarding the critical condition of the notorious woman who had turned his friend.

On every hand there were whispers and wild reports concerning the tragedy at the Villa Amette. He had heard about it from a dozen people, though not a word was in the papers. Yet nobody dreamed that he, of all men, had been present when the mysterious shot was fired, or that he was, indeed, the cause of the secret attack.

He dressed slowly, and having done so, descended to the *salle a manger*. The big white room was filled with a gay, reckless cosmopolitan crowd—the crowd of well-dressed moths of both sexes which eternally flutters at night at Monte Carlo, attracted by the candle held by the great god Hazard.

Brock was not there, and he seated himself alone at their table near the long-curtained window. He was surprised at his friend's absence. Perhaps, however, he had met friends and gone over to Beaulieu, Nice, or Mentone with them.

He had but little appetite. He ate a small portion of langouste with an exquisite salad, and drank a single glass of chablis. Then he rose and quitted the chattering, laughing crowd of diners, whose gossip was mainly upon a sensational run on the red at five o'clock that evening. One woman, stout and of Hebrew type, sitting with three men, was wildly merry, for she had won the equivalent to sixty thousand pounds.

All that recklessness jarred upon the young man's nerves. He tried to close his ears to it all, and ascended again to his room, where he sat in silent despondency till it was time for him to go round to the Metropole to join Lady Ranscomb and Dorise.

He had brushed his hair and rearranged his tie, and was about to put on the pierrot's costume of white satin with big buttons of black velvet which he had worn at the *bal blanc* at Mentone about a week before, when the page handed him another note.

Written in a distinctly foreign hand, it read:

"Instantly you receive this get into a travelling-suit and put what money and valuables you have into your pockets. Then go to a dark-green car which will await you by the reservoir in the Boulevard du Midi. Trust the driver. You must get over the frontier into Italy at the earliest moment. Every second's delay is dangerous to you. Do not trouble to find out who sends you this warning! *Bon voyage!*"

Hugh Henfrey read it and re-read it. The truth was plain. The police of Monaco suspected him, and intended that he should be arrested on suspicion of having committed the crime.

But who was his unknown friend?

He stood at the window reflecting. If he did not keep his appointment with Dorise she would reproach him for breaking his word to her. On the other hand, if he motored to Nice he would no doubt be arrested on the French frontier a few miles along the Corniche road.

Inspector Ogier suspected him, hence discretion was the better part of valour. So, after brief consideration, he threw off his dress clothes and assumed a suit of dark tweed. He put his money and a few articles of jewellry in his pockets, and getting into his overcoat he slipped out of the hotel by the back entrance used by the staff.

Outside, he walked in the darkness along the Boulevard du Nord, past the Turbie station, until he came to the long blank wall behind which lay the reservoir.

At the kerb he saw the dim red rear-light of a car, and almost at the same moment a rough-looking Italian chauffeur approached him.

"Quick, signore!" he whispered excitedly. "Every moment is full of danger. There is a warrant out for your arrest! The police know that you intended to go to Nice and they are watching for you on the Corniche road. But we will try to get into Italy. You are an invalid, remember! You'll find in the car a few things with which you can make up to look the part. You are an American subject and a cripple, who cannot leave the car when the customs officers search it. Now, signore, let's be off and trust to our good fortune in getting away. I will tell the officers of the *dogana* at Ventimiglia a good story—trust me! I haven't been smuggling backwards and forwards for ten years without knowing the ropes!"

"But where are we going?" asked Hugh bewildered.

"You, signore, are going to prison if we fail on this venture, I fear," was the rough-looking driver's reply.

So urged by him Hugh got into the car, and then they drove swiftly along the sea-road of the littoral towards the rugged Italian frontier.

Hugh Henfrey was going forth to face the unknown.

VII

From Dark to Dawn

In the darkness the car went swiftly through Mentone and along the steep winding road which leads around the rugged coast close to the sea—the road over the yellow rocks which Napoleon made into Italy.

Presently they began to ascend a hill, a lonely, wind-swept highway with the sea plashing deep below, when, after a sudden bend, some lights came into view. It was the wayside Italian Customs House.

They had arrived at the frontier.

Hugh, by the aid of a flash-lamp, had put on a grey moustache and changed his clothes, putting his own into the suit case wherein he had found the suit already prepared for him. He had wrapped himself up in a heavy travelling-rug, and by his side reposed a pair of crutches, so that when they drew up before the little roadside office of the Italian *dogana* he was reclining upon a cushion presenting quite a pathetic figure.

But who had made all these preparations for his flight?

He held his breath as the chauffeur sounded his horn to announce his arrival. Then the door opened, shedding a long ray of light across the white dusty road.

"*Buona sera, signore!*" cried the chauffeur merrily, as a Customs officer in uniform came forward. "Here's my driving licence and papers for the car. And our two passports."

The man took them, examined them by the light of his electric torch, and told the chauffeur to go into the office for the visas.

"Have you anything to declare?" he added in Italian.

"Half a dozen very bad cigarettes," replied the other, laughing. "They're French! And also I've got a very bad cold! No duty on that, I suppose?"

The officer laughed, and then turned his attention to the petrol tank, into which he put his measuring iron to see how much it contained, while the facetious chauffeur stood by.

During this operation two other men came out of the building, one an Italian carabineer in epaulettes and cocked hat, while the other, tall and shrewd-faced, was in mufti. The latter was the agent of French police who inspects all travellers leaving France by road.

The chauffeur realized that the moment was a critical one.

He was rolling a cigarette unconcernedly, but bending to the Customs officer, he said in a low voice:

"My *padrone* is an *Americano*. An invalid, and a bit eccentric. Lots of money. A long time ago he injured his spine and can hardly move. He fell down a few days ago, and now I've got to take him to Professor Landrini, in Turin. He's pretty bad. We've come from Hyeres. His doctor ordered me to take him to Turin at once. We don't want any delay. He told me to give you this," and he slipped a note for a hundred lire into the man's hand.

The officer expressed surprise, but the merry chauffeur of the rich American exclaimed:

"Don't worry. The *Americano* is very rich; I only wish there were more of his sort about. He's the great Headon, the meat-canner of Chicago. You see his name on the tins."

The man recognized the name, and at once desisted in his examination.

Then to the two police officers who came to his side, he explained:

"The American gentleman inside is an invalid, going to Turin to Professor Landrini. He wants to get off at once, for he has a long journey over the Alps."

The French agent of police grunted suspiciously. Both the French and Italian police are very astute, but money always talks. It is the same at a far-remote frontier station as in any circle of society.

Here was a well-known American—the Customs officer had mentioned the name of Headon, which both police officers recognized—an invalid sent with all haste to the famous surgeon in Turin. It was not likely that he would be carrying contraband, or be an escaping criminal.

Besides, the chauffeur, in full view of the two police agents, slipped a second note into the hand of the Customs officer, and said:

"So all is well, isn't it, signori? Just visa my papers, and we'll get along. It looks as though we're to have a bad thunderstorm, and, if so, we shall catch it up on the Col di Tenda!"

Thus impelled, the quartette went back to the well-lit little building, where the beetle-browed driver again chaffed the police-agents, while the Customs officer placed his rubber stamp upon the paper, scribbled his initials and charged three-lire-twenty as fee.

All this was being watched with breathless anxiety by the supposed invalid reclining against the cushion with his crutches at his side.

Again the mysterious chauffeur reappeared, and with him the French police officer in plain clothes.

"We are keeping watch for a young Englishman from Monte Carlo who has shot a woman," remarked the latter.

"Oh! But they arrested him to-night in Mentone," replied the driver. "I heard it half an hour ago as I came through."

"Are you sure?"

"Well, they told me so at the Garage Grimaldi. He shot a woman known as Mademoiselle of Monte Carlo—didn't he?"

"Yes, that's the man! But they have not informed us yet. I'll telephone to Mentone." Then he added: "As a formality I'll just have a peep at your master."

The chauffeur held his breath.

"He's pretty bad, I think. I hope we shall be in Turin early in the morning."

Advancing to the car, the police officer opened the door and flashed his torch upon the occupant.

He saw a pale, elderly man, with a grey moustache, wearing a golf cape and reclining uneasily upon the pillow, with his leg propped up and wrapped with a heavy travelling-rug. Upon the white countenance was an expression of pain as he turned wearily, his eyes dazzled by the sudden light.

"Where are we?" he asked faintly in English.

"At the Italian *douane*, m'sieur," was the police officer's reply, as for a few seconds he gazed upon the invalid's face, seconds that seemed hours to Hugh. He was, of course, unaware of the cock-and-bull story which his strange chauffeur had told, and feared that at any moment he might find himself under arrest.

While the door remained open there was danger. At last, however, the man reclosed it.

Hugh's heart gave a great bound. The chauffeur had restarted the engine, and mounting to the wheel shouted a merry:

"*Buona notte, signori!*"

Then the car moved away along the winding road and Hugh knew that he was on Italian soil—that he had happily escaped from France.

But why had he escaped, he reflected? He was innocent. Would not his flight lend colour to the theory that Yvonne Ferad had been shot by his hand?

Again, who was his unknown friend who had warned him of his

peril and made those elaborate arrangements for his escape? Besides, where was Walter?

His brain was awhirl. As they tore along in the darkness ever beside the sea over that steep and dangerous road along the rock coast, Hugh Henfrey fell to wondering what the motive of it all could be. Why had Yvonne been shot just at that critical moment? It was evident that she had been closely watched by someone to whom her silence meant a very great deal.

She had told him that his father had been a good man, and she was on the point of disclosing to him the great secret when she had been struck down.

What was the mystery of it all? Ay, what indeed?

He recalled every incident of that fateful night, her indignation at his presence in her house, and her curious softening of manner towards him, as though repentant and ready to make amends.

Then he wondered what Dorise would think when he failed to put in an appearance to go with her to the ball at Nice. He pictured the car waiting outside the hotel, Lady Ranscomb fidgeting and annoyed, the count elegant and all smiles and graces, and Dorise, anxious and eager, going to the telephone and speaking to the concierge at the Palmiers. Then inquiry for Monsieur Henfrey, and the discovery that he had left the hotel unseen.

So far Dorise knew nothing of Hugh's part in the drama of the Villa Amette, but suddenly he was horrified by the thought that the police, finding he had escaped, would question her. They had been seen together many times in Monte Carlo, and the eyes of the police of Monaco are always very wide open. They know much, but are usually inactive. When one recollects that all the *escrocs* of Europe gather at the *tapis vert* in winter and spring, it is not surprising that they close their eyes to such minor crimes as theft, blackmail and false pretences.

In his excited and unnerved state, he pictured Ogier calling upon Lady Ranscomb and questioning her closely concerning her young English friend who was so frequently seen with her daughter. That would, surely, end their friendship! Lady Ranscomb would never allow her daughter to associate further with a man accused of attempting to murder a notorious woman after midnight!

The car presently descended the steep rocky road which wound up over the promontory and back again down to the sea, until they passed through the little frontier town of Ventimiglia.

It was late, and few people were about in the narrow, ill-lit streets.

Suddenly, a couple of Italian carabineers stopped the car.

Hugh's heart beat quickly. Had they at the *dogana* discovered the trick and telephoned from the frontier?

Instantly the fugitive reassumed his role of invalid, and no sooner had he settled himself than the second man in a cocked hat and heavy black cloak opened the door and peered within.

Another lamp was flashed upon his face.

The carabineer asked in Italian:

"What is your name, signore?"

But Hugh, pretending that he did not understand the language, asked:

"Eh? What?"

"Here are our papers, signore," interrupted the ever-ready chauffeur, and he produced the papers for the officer's inspection.

He looked at them, bending to read them by the light of the torch which his companion held.

Then, after an officious gesture, he handed them back, saying:

"*Benissimo*! You may pass!"

Again Hugh was free! Yet he wondered if that examination had been consequent upon the hue and cry set up now that he had escaped from Monaco.

They passed out of the straggling town of Ventimiglia, but instead of turning up the valley by that long road which winds up over the Alps until it reaches the snow and then passes through the tunnel on the Col di Tenda and on to Cuneo and Turin, the mysterious driver kept on by the sea-road towards Bordighera.

Hugh realised that his guide's intention was to go in the direction of Genoa.

About two miles out of Ospedaletti, on the road to San Remo, Henfrey rapped at the window, and the chauffeur, who was travelling at high speed, pulled up.

Hugh got out and said in French:

"Well, so far we've been successful. I admire your ingenuity and your pluck."

The man laughed and thanked him.

"I have done what I was told to do," he replied simply. "Monsieur is, I understand, in a bit of a scrape, and it is for all of us to assist each other—is it not?"

"Of course. But who told you to do all this?" Hugh inquired, standing in the dark road beside the car. The pair could not see each other's faces, though the big head-lamps glared far ahead over the white road.

"Well—a friend of yours, m'sieur."

"What is his name?"

"Pardon, I am not allowed to say."

"But all this is so very strange—so utterly mysterious!" cried Hugh. "I have not committed any crime, and yet I am hunted by the police! They are anxious to arrest me for an offence of which I am entirely innocent."

"I know that, m'sieur," was the fellow's reply. "At the *dogana*, however, we had a narrow escape. The man who looked at you was Morain, the chief inspector of the Sureté of the Alpes-Maritimes, and he was at the outpost especially to stop you!"

"Again I admire your perfect nonchalance and ingenuity," Hugh said. "I owe my liberty entirely to you."

"Not liberty, m'sieur. We are not yet what you say in English 'out of the wood.'"

"Where are we going now?"

"To Genoa. We ought to be there by early morning," was the reply. "Morain has, no doubt, telephoned to Mentone and discovered that my story is false. So if later, on, they suspect the American invalid they will be looking out for him on the Col di Tenda, in Cuneo, and in Turin."

"And what shall we do in Genoa?"

"Let us get there first—and see."

"But I wish you would tell me who you are—and why you take such a keen interest in my welfare," Hugh said.

The man gave vent to an irritating laugh.

"I am not permitted to disclose the identity of your friend," he answered. "All I know is that you are innocent."

"Then perhaps you know the guilty person?" Hugh suggested.

"Ah! Let us talk of something else, signore," was the mysterious chauffeur's reply.

"But I confess to you that I am bent upon solving the mystery of Mademoiselle's assailant. It means a very great deal to me."

"How?" asked the man.

Hugh hesitated.

"Well," he replied. "If the culprit is found, then there would no longer be any suspicion against myself."

"Probably he never will be found," the man said.

"But tell me, how did you know about the affair, and why are you risking arrest by driving me to-night?"

"I have reasons," was all he would say. "I obey the demands of those who are your friends."

"Who are they?"

"They desire to conceal their identity. There is a strong reason why this should be done."

"Why?"

"Are they not protecting one who is suspected of a serious crime? If discovered they would be punished," was the quiet response.

"Ah! There is some hidden motive behind all this!" declared the young Englishman. "I rather regret that I did not remain and face the music."

"It would have been far too dangerous, signore. Your enemies would have contrived to convict you of the crime."

"My enemies—but who are they?"

"Of that, signore, I am ignorant. Only I have been told that you have enemies, and very bitter ones."

"But I have committed no crime, and yet I am a fugitive from justice!" Hugh cried.

"You escaped in the very nick of time," the man replied. "But had we not better be moving again? We must be in Genoa by daybreak."

"But do, I beg of you, tell me more," the young man implored. "To whom do I owe my liberty?"

"As I have already told you, signore, you owe it to those who intend to protect you from a false charge."

"Yes. But there is a lady in the case," Hugh said. "I fear that if she hears that I am a fugitive she will misjudge me and believe me to be guilty."

"Probably so. That is, I admit, unfortunate—but, alas! it cannot be avoided. It was, however, better for you to get out of France."

"But the French police, when they know that I have escaped, will probably ask the Italian police to arrest me, and then apply for my extradition."

"If they did, I doubt whether you would be surrendered. The police of my country are not too fond of assisting those of other countries. Thus if an Italian commits murder in a foreign country and gets back to Italy, our Government will refuse to give him up. There have been many such cases, and the murderer goes scot free."

"Then you think I am safe in Italy?"

"Oh, no, not by any means. You are not an Italian subject. No, you must not be very long in Italy."

"But what am I to do when we get to Genoa?" Hugh asked.

"The signore had better wait until we arrive there," was the driver's enigmatical reply.

Then the supposed invalid re-entered the car and they continued on their way along the bleak, storm-swept road beside the sea towards that favourite resort of the English, San Remo.

The night had grown pitch dark, and rain had commenced to fall. Before the car the great head-lamps threw long beams of white light against which Hugh saw the silhouette of the muffled-up mysterious driver, with his keen eyes fixed straight before him, and driving at such a pace that it was apparent that he knew every inch of the dangerous road.

What could it all mean? What, indeed?

VIII

The White Cavalier

While Hugh Henfrey was travelling along that winding road over high headlands and down steep gradients to the sea which stretched the whole length of the Italian Riviera, Dorise Ranscomb in a white silk domino and black velvet mask was pretending to enjoy herself amid the mad gaiety at the Casino in Nice.

The great *bal blanc* is always one of the most important events of the Nice season, and everyone of note wintering on the Riviera was there, yet all carefully masked, both men and women.

"I wonder what prevented Hugh from coming with us, mother?" the girl remarked as she sat with Lady Ranscomb watching the merriment and the throwing of serpentines and confetti.

"I don't know. He certainly ought to have let me know, and not have kept me waiting nearly half an hour, as he did," her mother snapped.

The girl did not reply. The truth was that while her mother and the Count had been waiting for Hugh's appearance, she had gone to the telephone and inquired for Mr. Henfrey. Walter Brock had spoken to her.

"I'm awfully sorry, Miss Ranscomb," he had replied. "But I don't know where Hugh can be. I've just been up to his room, but his fancy dress is there, flung down as though he had suddenly discarded it and gone out. Nobody noticed him leave. The page at the door is certain that he did not go out. So he must have left by the staff entrance."

"That's very curious, isn't it?" Dorise remarked.

"Very. I can't understand it."

"But he promised to go with us to the ball at Nice to-night!"

"Well, Miss Ranscomb, all I can think is that something—something very important must have detained him somewhere."

Walter knew that his friend was suspected by the police, but dared not tell her the truth. Hugh's disappearance had caused him considerable anxiety because, for aught he knew, he might already be arrested.

So Dorise, much perplexed, but resolving not to say to her mother that she had telephoned to the Palmiers, rejoined the Count in the hotel lounge, where they waited a further ten minutes. Then they entered the car and drove along to Nice.

There are few merrier gatherings in all Europe than the *bal blanc*. The Municipal Casino, at all times the center of revelry, of mild gambling, smart dresses and gay suppers, is on that night an amazing spectacle of black and white. The carnival colours—the two shades of colour chosen yearly by the International Fetes Committee—are abandoned, and only white is worn.

When the trio entered the fun was already in full swing. The gay crowd disguised by their masks and fancy costumes were revelling as happily as school children. A party of girls dressed as clowns were playing leap-frog. Another party were dancing in a great and ever-widening ring. Girls armed with jesters' bladders were being carried high on the shoulders of their male acquaintances, and striking all and sundry as they passed, staid, elderly folk were performing grotesque antics for persons of their age. The very air of the Riviera seems to be exhilarating to both old and young, and the constant church-goers at home quickly become infected by the spirit of gaiety, and conduct themselves on the Continental Sabbath in a manner which would horribly disgust their particular vicar.

"Hugh must have been detained by something very unexpected, mother," Dorise said. "He never disappoints us."

"Oh, yes, he does. One night we were going to the Embassy Club—don't you recollect it—and he never turned up."

"Oh, well, mother. It was really excusable. His cousin arrived from New York quite unexpectedly upon some family business. He phoned to you and explained," said the girl.

"Well, what about that night when I asked him to dinner at the Ritz to meet the Courtenays and he rang up to say he was not well? Yet I saw him hale and hearty next day at a matinee at the Comedy."

"He may have been indisposed, mother," Dorise said. "Really I think you judge him just a little too harshly."

"I don't. I take people as I find them. Your father always said that, and he was no fool, my dear. He made a fortune by his cleverness, and we now enjoy it. Never associate with unsuccessful persons. It's fatal!"

"That's just what old Sir Dudley Ash, the steel millionaire, told me the other day when we were over at Cannes, mother. Never associate with the unlucky. Bad luck, he says, is a contagious malady."

"And I believe it—I firmly believe it," declared Lady Ranscomb. "Your poor father pointed it out to me long ago, and I find that what he said is too true."

"But we can't all be lucky, mother," said the girl, watching the revelry before her blankly as she reflected upon the mystery of Hugh's absence.

"No. But we can, nevertheless, be rich, if we look always to the main chance and make the best of our opportunities," her mother said meaningly.

At that moment the Count d'Autun approached them. He was dressed as a pierrot, but being masked was only recognizable by the fine ruby ring upon his finger.

"Will mademoiselle do me the honour?" he said in French, bowing elegantly. "They are dancing in the theatre. Will you come, Mademoiselle Dorise?"

"Delighted," she said, with an inward sigh, for the dressed-up Parisian always bored her. She rose quickly, and promising her mother to be back soon, she linked her arm to that of the notorious gambler and passed through the great palm-court into the theatre.

Then, a few moments later, she found herself carried around amid the mad crowd of revellers, who laughed merrily as the coloured serpentines thrown from the boxes fell upon them.

To lift one's *loup* was a breach of etiquette. Everyone was closely masked. British members of Parliament, French senators, Italian members of the Camera, Spanish grandees and Russian princes, all with their womenfolk, hob-nobbed with cocottes, *escrocs*, and the most notorious adventurers and adventuresses in all Europe. Truly, it was a never-to-be-forgotten scene of cosmopolitan fun.

The Count, who was a bad dancer, collided with a slim, well-dressed French girl, but did not apologize.

"Oh! la la!" cried the girl to her partner, a stout figure in Mephistophelian garb. "An exquisitely polite gentleman that, mon cher Alphonse! I believe he must really be the Pork King from Chicago—eh?"

The Count heard it, and was furious. Dorise, however, said nothing. She was thinking of Hugh's strange disappearance, and how he had broken his word to her.

Meanwhile, Lady Ranscomb, secretly very glad that Hugh had been prevented from accompanying them, and centring all her hopes upon her daughter's marriage with George Sherrard, sat chattering with a Mrs. Down, the fat wife of a war-profiteer, whose acquaintance she had made in Paris six months before.

Dorise made pretense of enjoying the dance though eager to get back again to Monte Carlo in order to learn the reason of her lover's absence. She was devoted to Hugh. He was all in all to her.

She danced with several partners, having first made a rendezvous with her mother at midnight at a certain spot under one of the great palms in the promenade. At masked balls the chaperon is useless, and everyone, being masked, looks so much alike that mistakes are easy.

About half-past one o'clock a big motor-car drew up in the Place before the Casino, and a tall man in a white fancy dress of a cavalier, with wide-brimmed hat and staggering plume, stepped from it and, presenting his ticket, passed at once into the crowded ball-room. For a full ten minutes he stood watching the crowd of revellers intently, eyeing each of them keenly, though the expression on his countenance was hidden by the strip of black velvet.

His eyes, shining through the slits in the mask, were, however, dark and brilliant. In them could be seen alertness and eagerness, for it was apparent that he had come there hot-foot in search of someone. In any case he had a difficult task, for in the whirling, laughing, chattering crowd each person resembled the other save for their feet and their stature.

It was the feet of the dancers that the tall masked man was watching. He stood in the crowd near the doorway with his hand upon his sword-hilt, a striking figure remarked by many. His large eyes were fixed upon the shoes of the dancers, until, of a sudden, he seemed to discover that for which he was in search, and made his way quickly after a pair who, having finished a dance, were walking in the direction of the great hall.

The stranger never took his eyes off the pair. The man was slightly taller than the woman, and the latter wore upon her white kid shoes a pair of old paste buckles. It was for those buckles that he had been searching.

"Yes," he muttered in English beneath his breath. "That's she—without a doubt!"

He drew back to near where the pair had halted and were laughing together. The girl with the glittering buckles upon her shoes was Dorise Ranscomb. The man with her was the Count d'Autun.

The white cavalier pretended to take no interest in them, but was, nevertheless, watching intently. At last he saw the girl's partner bow, and leaving her, he crossed to greet a stout Frenchwoman in a plain domino. In a moment the cavalier was at the girl's side.

"Please do not betray surprise, Miss Ranscomb," he said in a low, refined voice. "We may be watched. But I have a message for you."

"For me?" she asked, peering through her mask at the man in the plumed hat.

"Yes. But I cannot speak to you here. It is too public. Besides, your mother yonder may notice us."

"Who are you?" asked the girl, naturally curious.

"Do not let us talk here. See, right over yonder in the corner behind where they are dancing in a ring—under the balcony. Let us meet there at once. *Au revoir*."

And he left her.

Three minutes later they met again out of sight of Lady Ranscomb, who was still sitting at one of the little wicker tables talking to three other women.

"Tell me, who are you?" Dorise inquired.

The white cavalier laughed.

"I'm Mr. X," was his reply.

"Mr. X? Who's that?"

"Myself. But my name matters nothing, Miss Ranscomb," he said. "I have come here to give you a confidential message."

"Why confidential—and from whom?" she asked, standing against the wall and surveying the mysterious masker.

"From a gentleman friend of yours—Mr. Henfrey."

"From Hugh?" she gasped. "Do you know him?"

"Yes."

"I expected him to come with us to-night, but he has vanished from his hotel."

"I know. That is why I am here," was the reply.

There was a note in the stranger's voice which struck her as somehow familiar, but she failed to recognize the individual. She was as quick at remembering voices as she was at recollecting faces. Who could he be, she wondered?

"You said you had a message for me," she remarked.

"Yes," he replied. "I am here to tell you that a serious contretemps has occurred, and that Mr. Henfrey has escaped from France."

"Escaped!" she echoed. "Why?"

"Because the police suspect him of a crime."

"Crime! What crime? Surely he is innocent?" she cried.

"He certainly is. His friends know that. Therefore, Miss Ranscomb, I beg of you to betray no undue anxiety even if you do not hear from him for many weeks."

"But will he write to me?" she asked in despair. "Surely he will not keep me in suspense?"

"He will not if he can avoid it. But as soon as the French police realize that he has got away a watch will be kept upon his correspondence." Then, lowering his voice, he urged her to move away, as he thought that an idling masker was trying to overhear their conversation.

"You see," he went on a few moments later, "it might be dangerous if he were to write to you."

Dorise was thinking of what her mother would say when the truth reached her ears. Hugh was a *fugitive*!

"Of what crime is he suspected?" asked the girl.

"I—well, I don't exactly know," was the stranger's faltering response. "I was told by a friend of his that it was a serious one, and that he might find it extremely difficult to prove himself innocent. The circumstantial evidence against him is very strong."

"Do you know where he is now?"

"Not in the least. All I know is that he is safely across the frontier into Italy," was the reply of the tall white cavalier.

"I wish I could see your face," declared Dorise frankly.

"And I might express a similar desire, Miss Ranscomb. But for the present it is best as it is. I have sought you here to tell you the truth in secret, and to urge you to remain calm and patient."

"Is that a message from Hugh?"

"No—not exactly. It is a message from one who is his friend."

"You are very mysterious," she declared. "If you do not know where he is at the moment, perhaps you know where we can find him later."

"Yes. He is making his way to Brussels. A letter addressed to Mr. Godfrey Brown, Poste Restante, Brussels, will eventually find him. Recollect the name," he added. "Disguise your handwriting on the envelope, and when you post it see that you are not observed. Recollect that his safety lies in your hands."

"Trust me," she said. "But do let me know your name," she implored.

"Any old name is good enough for me," he replied. "Call me Mr. X."

"Don't mystify me further, please."

"Well, call me Smith, Jones, Robinson—whatever you like."

"Then you refuse to satisfy my curiosity—eh?"

"I regret that I am compelled to do so—for certain reasons."

"Are you a detective?" Dorise suddenly inquired.

The stranger laughed.

"If I were a police officer I should scarcely act as an intermediary between Mr. Henfrey and yourself, Miss Ranscomb."

"But you say he is innocent. Are you certain of that? May I set my mind at rest that he never committed this crime of which the police suspect him?" she asked eagerly.

"Yes. I repeat that he is entirely innocent," was the earnest response. "But I would advise you to affect ignorance. The police may question you. If they do, you know nothing, remember—absolutely nothing. If you write to Mr. Henfrey, take every precaution that nobody sees you post the letter. Give him a secret address in London, or anywhere in England, so that he can write to you there."

"But how long will it be before I can see him again?"

"Ah! That I cannot tell. There is a mystery underlying it all that even I cannot fathom, Miss Ranscomb."

"What kind of mystery?"

The white cavalier shrugged his shoulders.

"You must ask Mr. Henfrey. Or perhaps his friend Brock knows. Yet if he does, I do not suppose he would disclose anything his friend may have told him in confidence."

"I am bewildered!" the girl declared. "It is all so very mysterious—Hugh a fugitive from justice! I—I really cannot believe it! What can the mystery be?"

"Of that I have no means of ascertaining, Miss Ranscomb. I am here merely to tell you what has happened and to give you in secret the name and address to which to send a letter to him," the masked man said very politely. "And now I think we must part. Perhaps if ever we meet again—which is scarcely probable—you will recognize my voice. And always recollect that should you or Mr. Henfrey ever receive a message from 'Silverado' it will be from myself." And he spelt the name.

"Silverado. Yes, I shall not forget you, my mysterious friend."

"*Au revoir!*" he said as, bowing gracefully, he turned and left her.

The sun was rising from the sea when Dorise entered her bedroom at the hotel. Her maid had retired, so she undressed herself, and putting on a dressing-gown, she pulled up the blinds and sat down to write a letter to Hugh.

She could not sleep before she had sent him a reassuring message.

In the frenzy of her despair she wrote one letter and addressed it, but having done so she changed her mind. It was not sufficiently reassuring, she decided. It contained an element of doubt. Therefore she tore it up

WILLIAM LE QUEUX

and wrote a second one which she locked safely in her jewel case, and then pulled the blinds and retired.

It was nearly noon next day before she left her room, yet almost as soon as she had descended in the lift the head *femme de chambre*, a stout Frenchwoman in a frilled cap, entered the room, and walking straight to the waste-paper basket gathered up the contents into her apron and went back along the corridor with an expression of satisfaction upon her full round face.

IX

Concerns the Sparrow

With the rosy dawn rising behind them the big dusty car tore along over the white road which led through Pegli and Cornigliano, with their wealth of olives and palms, into the industrial suburbs of old-world Genoa. Then, passing around by the port, the driver turned the car up past Palazzo Doria and along that street of fifteenth-century palaces, the Via Garibaldi, into the little piazza in front of the Annunziata Church.

There he pulled up after a run of two hours from the last of the many railway crossings, most of which they had found closed.

When Hugh got out, the mysterious man, whose face was more forbidding in the light of day, exclaimed:

"Here I must leave you very shortly, signore. But first I have certain instructions to give you, namely, that you remain for the present in a house in the Via della Maddalena to which I shall take you. The man and the woman there you can trust. It will be as well not to walk about in the daytime. Remain here for a fortnight, and then by the best means, without, of course, re-entering France, you must get to Brussels. There you will receive letters at the Poste Restante in the name of Godfrey Brown. That, indeed, is the name you will use here."

"Well, all this is very strange!" remarked Hugh, utterly bewildered as he glanced at the forbidding-looking chauffeur and the dust-covered car.

"I agree, signore," the man laughed. "But get in again and I will drive to the Via della Maddalena."

Five minutes later the car pulled up at the end of a narrow stuffy ancient street of high houses with closed wooden shutters. From house to house across the road household linen was flying in the wind, for the neighbourhood was certainly a poverty-stricken one.

The place did not appeal to Hugh in the least. He, however, recollected that he was about to hide from the police. Italians are early risers, and though it was only just after dawn, Genoa was already agog with life and movement.

Leaving the car, the mysterious chauffeur conduced the young

Englishman along the street, where women were calling to each other from the windows of their apartments and exchanging salutations, until they came to an entrance over which there was an old blue majolica Madonna. The house had no outer door, but at the end of the passage was a flight of stone steps leading up to the five storeys above.

At the third flight Hugh's conductor paused, and finding a piece of cord protruding from a hole in a door, pulled it. A slight tinkle was heard within, and a few moments later the sound of wooden shoes was heard upon the tiles inside.

The door opened, revealing an ugly old woman whose face was sallow and wrinkled, and who wore a red kerchief tied over her white hair.

As soon as she saw the chauffeur she welcomed him, addressing him as Paolo, and invited them in.

"This is the English signore," explained the man. "He has come to stay with you."

"The signore is welcome," replied the old woman as she clattered into the narrow, cheaply furnished little sitting-room, which was in half darkness owing to the *persiennes* being closed.

Truly, it was an uninviting place, which smelt of garlic and of the paraffin oil with which the tiled floors had been rubbed.

"You will require another certificate of identity, signore," said the man, who admitted that he had been engaged in smuggling contraband across the Alps. And delving into his pocket he produced an American passport. It was blank, though the embossed stamp of the United States Government was upon it. The places were ready for the photograph and signature. With it the man handed him a large metal disc, saying:

"When you have your picture taken and affixed to it, all you have to do is to damp the paper slightly and impress this stamp. It will then defy detection."

"Where on earth did you get this from?" asked Hugh, noticing that it was a replica of the United States consular seal.

The man smiled, replying:

"They make passports of all countries in Spain. You pay for them, and you can get them by the dozen. The embossing stamps are extra. There is a big trade in them now owing to the passport restrictions. Besides, in every country there are passport officers who are amenable to a little baksheesh!" And he grinned.

What he said was true. At no period has it ever been more easy for a criminal to escape than it is to-day, providing, of course, that he is a cosmopolitan and has money.

Hugh took the passport and the disc, adding:

"How am I to repay you for all this?"

"I want no payment, signore. All I ask you is to conform to the suggestions of the worthy Signore Ravecca and his good wife here. You are not the first guest they have had for whom the police searched in vain."

"No," laughed the old woman. "Do you recollect the syndic of Porticello, how we had him here for nearly three years, and then he got safely away to Argentina and took the money, three million lire, with him?"

"Yes," was the man's reply. "I recollect it, signora. But the Signore Inglese must be very careful—very careful. He must never go out in the daytime. You can buy him English papers and books of Luccoli, in the Via Bosco. They will serve to while away the time."

"I shall, no doubt, pass the time very pleasantly," laughed Hugh, speaking in French.

Then the old crone left them and returned with two cups of excellent *cafe nero*, that coffee which, roasted at home one can get only in Italy.

It was indeed refreshing after that long night drive.

Hugh stood there without luggage, and with only about thirty pounds in his pocket.

Suddenly the man who had driven him looked him curiously in the face, and said:

"Ah! I know you are wondering what your lady friend in Monte Carlo will think. Well, I can tell you this. She already knows that you have escaped, and she had been told to write to you in secret at the Poste Restante at Brussels."

Hugh started.

"Who has told her? Surely she knows nothing of the affair at the Villa Amette?"

"She will not be told that. But she has been told that you are going to Brussels, and that in future your name is Monsieur Godfrey Brown."

"But why have all these elaborate arrangements been made for my security?" Hugh demanded, more than ever nonplussed.

"It is useless to take one precaution unless the whole are taken," laughed the sphinx-like fellow whose cheerful banter had so successfully passed them through the customs barrier.

WILLIAM LE QUEUX

Then, swallowing his coffee, he wished Hugh, "buon viaggio" and was about to depart, when Hugh said:

"Look here. Is it quite impossible for you to give me any inkling concerning this astounding affair? I know that some unknown friend, or friends, are looking after my welfare. But why? To whom am I indebted for all this? Who has warned Miss Ranscomb and told her of my alias and my journey to Brussels?"

"A friend of hers and of yourself," was the chauffeur's reply. "No, please do not question me, signore," he added. "I have done my best for you. And now my journey is at an end, while yours is only beginning. Pardon me—but you have money with you, I suppose? If you have not, these good people here will trust you."

"But what is this house?"

The man laughed. Then he said:

"Well, really it is a bolt-hole used by those who wish to evade our very astute police. If one conforms to the rules of Signora Ravecca and her husband, then one is quite safe and most comfortable."

Hugh realized that he was in a hiding-place used by thieves. A little later he knew that the ugly old woman's husband paid toll to a certain *delegato* of police, hence their house was never searched. While the criminal was in those shabby rooms he was immune from arrest. The place was, indeed, one of many hundreds scattered over Europe, asylums known to the international thief as places ever open so long as they can pay for their board and lodging and their contribution towards the police bribes.

A few moments later the ugly, uncouth man who had brought him from Monte Carlo lit a cigarette, and wishing the old woman a merry "addio" left and descended the stairs.

The signora then showed Hugh to his room, a small, dispiriting and not overclean little chamber which looked out upon the backs of the adjoining houses, all of which were high and inartistic. Above, however, was a narrow strip of brilliantly blue sunlit sky.

A quarter of an hour later he made the acquaintance of the woman's husband, a brown-faced, sinister-looking individual whose black bushy eyebrows met, and who greeted the young Englishman familiarly in atrocious French, offering him a glass of red wine from a big rush-covered flask.

"We only had word of your coming late last night," the man said. "You had already started from Monte Carlo, and we wondered if you would get past the frontier all right."

"Yes," replied Hugh, sipping the wine out of courtesy. "We got out of France quite safely. But tell me, who made all these arrangements for me?"

"Why, Il Passero, of course," replied the man, whose wife addressed him affectionately as Beppo.

"Who is Il Passero, pray?"

"Well, you know him surely. Il Passero, or The Sparrow. We call him so because he is always flitting about Europe, and always elusive."

"The police want him, I suppose."

"I should rather think they do. They have been searching for him for these past five years, but he always dodges them, first in France, then here, then in Spain, and then in England."

"But what is this mysterious and unknown friend of mine?"

"Il Passero is the chief of the most daring of all the gangs of international thieves. We all work at his direction."

"But how did he know of my danger?" asked Hugh, mystified and dismayed.

"Il Passero knows many strange things," he replied with a grin. "It is his business to know them. And besides, he has some friends in the police—persons who never suspect him."

"What nationality is he?"

The man Beppo shrugged his shoulders.

"He is not Italian," he replied. "Yet he speaks the *lingua Toscano* perfectly and French and English and *Tedesco*. He might be Belgian or German, or even English. Nobody knows his true nationality."

"And the man who brought me here?"

"Ah! that was Paolo, Il Passero's chauffeur—a merry fellow—eh?"

"Remarkable," laughed Hugh. "But I cannot see why The Sparrow has taken such a paternal interest in me," he added.

"He no doubt has, for he has, apparently, arranged for your safe return to England."

"You know him, of course. What manner of man is he?"

"A signore—a great signore," replied Beppo. "He is rich, and is often on the Riviera in winter. He's probably there now. Nobody suspects him. He is often in England, too. I believe he has a house in London. During the war he worked for the French Secret Service under the name of Monsieur Franqueville, and the French Government never suspected that they actually had in their employ the famous Passero for whom the Sureté were looking everywhere."

"You have no idea where he lives in London?"

"I was once told that he had a big house somewhere in what you call the West End—somewhere near Piccadilly. I have, however, only seen him once. About eighteen months ago he was hard pressed by the police and took refuge here for two nights, till Paolo called for him in his fine car and he passed out of Italy as a Swiss hotel-proprietor."

"Then he is head of a gang—is he?"

"Yes," was the man's reply. "He is marvellous, and has indeed well earned his sobriquet 'Il Passero.'"

A sudden thought flitted through Hugh's mind.

"I suppose he is a friend of Mademoiselle of Monte Carlo?"

"Ah, signore, I do not know. Il Passero had many friends. He is rich, prosperous, well-dressed, and has influential friends in France, in Italy and in England who never suspect him to be the notorious king of the thieves."

"Now, tell me," urged young Henfrey. "What do you know concerning Mademoiselle of Monte Carlo?"

The Italian looked at him strangely.

"Nothing," he replied, still speaking bad French.

"You are not speaking the truth."

"Why should I tell it to you? I do not know you!" was the quick retort.

"But you are harbouring me."

"At the orders of Il Passero."

"You surely can tell me what you know of Mademoiselle," Hugh persisted after a brief pause. "We are mutually her friends. The attempt to kill her is outrageous, and I, for one, intend to do all I can to trace and punish the culprit."

"They say that you shot her."

"Well—you know that I did not," Henfrey said. "Have you yourself ever met Mademoiselle?"

"I have seen her. She was living for a time at Santa Margherita last year. I had a friend of hers living here with me and I went to her with a message. She is a very charming lady."

"And a friend of Il Passero?"

The Italian shrugged his shoulders with a gesture of ignorance.

Hugh Henfrey had certainly learned much that was curious. He had never before heard of the interesting cosmopolitan thief known as The Sparrow, but it seemed evident that the person in question had suddenly become interested in him for some obscure and quite unaccountable reason.

As day followed day in that humble place of concealment, Beppo told him many things concerning the famous criminal Il Passero, describing his exploits in terms of admiration. Hugh learnt that it was The Sparrow who had planned the great jewel robbery at Binet's, in the Rue de la Paix, when some famous diamonds belonging to the Shah of Persia, which had been sent to Paris to be reset, were stolen. It was The Sparrow, too, who had planned the burglary at the art gallery of Evans and Davies in Bond Street and stolen Raphael's famous Madonna.

During the daytime Hugh, anxious to get away to Brussels, but compelled to obey the order of the mysterious Passero, spent the time in smoking and reading books and newspapers with which Beppo's wife provided him, while at night he would take long walks through the silent city, with its gloomy old palaces, the courtyards of which echoed to his footsteps. At such times he was alone with his thoughts and would walk around the port and out upon the hills which surrounded the bay, and then sit down and gaze out to the twinkling lights across the sea and watch the long beams of the great lighthouse searching in the darkness.

His host and hostess were undoubtedly criminals. Indeed, they did not hide the fact. Both were paid by The Sparrow to conceal and provide for anyone whom he sent there.

He had been there four weary, anxious days when one evening a pretty, well-dressed young French girl called, and after a short chat with Beppo's wife became installed there as his fellow-guest. He did not know her name and she did not tell him.

She was known to them as Lisette, and Hugh found her a most vivacious and interesting companion. Truly, he had been thrown into very queer company, and he often wondered what his friends would say if they knew that he was guest in a hiding-place of thieves.

X

A Lesson in Argot

Late one evening the dainty girl thief, Lisette, went out for a stroll with Hugh, but in the Via Roma they met an agent of police.

"Look!" whispered the girl in French, "there's a *pince sans rire*! Be careful!"

She constantly used the argot of French thieves, which was often difficult for the young Englishman to understand. And the dark-haired girl would laugh, apologize, and explain the meaning of her strange expressions.

Outside the city they were soon upon the high road which wound up the deep green valley of the Bisagno away into the mountains, ever ascending to the little hill-town of Molassana. The scene was delightful in the moonlight as they climbed the steep hill and then descended again into the valley, Lisette all the time gossiping on in a manner which interested and amused him.

Her arrival had put an end to his boredom, and, though he was longing to get away from his surroundings, she certainly cheered him up.

They had walked for nearly an hour, when, declaring she felt tired, they sat upon a rock to rest and eat the sandwiches with which they had provided themselves.

Two carabineers in cloaks and cocked hats who met them on the road put them down as lovers keeping a clandestine tryst. They never dreamed that for both of them the police were in search.

"Now tell me something concerning yourself, mademoiselle," Hugh urged presently.

"Myself! Oh! la la!" she laughed. "What is there to tell? I am just of *la haute pegre*—a *truqueuse*. Ah! you will not know the expression. Well—I am a thief in high society. I give indications where we can make a coup, and afterwards *bruler le pegriot*—efface the trace of the affair."

"And why are you here?"

"*Malheureusement*! I was in Orleans and a *friquet* nearly captured me. So Il Passero sent me here for a while."

"You help Il Passero—eh?"

"Yes. Very often. Ah! m'sieur, he is a most wonderful man—English, I think. *Girofle* (genteel and amiable), like yourself."

"No, no, mademoiselle," Hugh protested, laughing.

"But I mean it. Il Passero is a real gentleman—but—*maquiller son truc*, and he is marvellous. When he exercises his wonderful talent and forms a plan it is always flawless."

"Everyone seems to hold him in high esteem. I have never met him," Hugh remarked.

"He was in Genoa on the day that I arrived. Curious that he did not call and see Beppo. I lunched with him at the Concordia, and he paid me five thousand francs, which he owed me. He has gone to London now with his *ecrache-tarte*."

"What is that, pray?"

"His false passport. He has always a good supply of them for anyone in need of one. They are printed secretly in Spain. But m'sieur," she added, "you are not of our world. You are in just a little temporary trouble. Over what?"

In reply he was perfectly frank with her. He told her of the suspicion against him because of the affair of the Villa Amette.

"Ah!" she replied, her manner changing, "I have heard that Mademoiselle was shot, but I had no idea that you had any connexion with that ugly business."

"Yes. Unfortunately I have. Do you happen to know Yvonne Ferad?"

"Of course. Everyone knows her. She is very charming. Nobody knows the truth."

"What truth?" inquired Hugh quickly.

"Well—that she is a *marque de ce*."

"A *marque de ce*—what is that?" asked Hugh eagerly.

"Ah! *non*, m'sieur. I must not tell you anything against her. You are her friend."

"But I am endeavouring to find out something about her. To me she is a mystery."

"No doubt. She is to everybody."

"What did you mean by that expression?" he demanded. "Do tell me. I am very anxious to know your opinion of her, and something about her. I have a very earnest motive in trying to discover who and what she really is."

"If I told you I should offend Il Passero," replied the girl simply. "It is evident that he wishes you should remain in ignorance."

"But surely, you can tell me in confidence? I will divulge nothing."

"No," answered the girl, whose face he could not see in the shadow. "I am sorry, M'sieur Brown"—she had not been told his Christian name—"but I am not permitted to tell you anything concerning Mademoiselle Yvonne."

"She is a very remarkable person—eh?" said Henfrey, again defeated.

"Remarkable! Oh, yes. She is of the *grande monde*."

"Is that still your argot?" he asked.

"Oh no. Mademoiselle Yvonne is a lady. Some say she is the daughter of a rich Englishman. Others say she is just a common adventuress."

"The latter is true, I suppose?"

"I think not. She has *le clou* for the *eponge d'or*."

"I do not follow that."

"Well," she laughed, "she has the attraction for those who hold the golden sponge—the Ministers of State. Our argot is difficult for you, m'sieur—eh?"

"I see! Your expressions are a kind of cipher, unintelligible to the ordinary person—eh?"

"That is so. If I exclaim, *par exemple, tarte*, it means false; if I say *gilet de flanelle*, it is lemonade; if I say *frise*, it means a Jew; or *casserole*, which is in our own tongue a police officer. So you see it is a little difficult—is it not? To us *tire-jus* is a handkerchief, and we call the ville de Paris *Pantruche*."

Hugh sat in wonder. It was certainly a strange experience to be on a moonlight ramble with a girl thief who had, according to her own confession, been born in Paris the daughter of a man who was still one of Il Passero's clever and desperate band.

"Yes, m'sieur," she said a few moments later. "They are all dangerous. They do not fear to use the knife or automatic pistol when cornered. For myself, I simply move about Europe and make discoveries as to where little affairs can be negotiated. I tell Il Passero, and he then works out the plans. *Dieu*! But I had a narrow escape the other day in Orleans!"

"Do tell me about Mademoiselle of Monte Carlo. I beg of you to tell me something, Mademoiselle Lisette," Hugh urged, turning to the girl of many adventures who was seated at his side upon the big rock overlooking the ravine down which the bright moon was shining.

"I would if I were permitted," she replied. "Mademoiselle Yvonne is charming. You know her, so I need say nothing, but—"

"Well—what?"

"She is clever—very clever," said the girl. "As Il Passero is clever, so is she."

"Then she is actively associated with him—eh?"

"Yes. She is cognizant of all his movements, and of all his plans. While she moves in one sphere—often in a lower sphere, like myself—yet in society she moves in the higher sphere, and she 'indicates,' just as I do."

"So she is one of The Sparrow's associates?" Hugh said.

"Yes," was the reply. "From what you have told me I gather that Il Passero knew by one of his many secret sources of information that you were in danger of arrest, and sent Paolo to rescue you—which he did."

"No doubt that is so. But why should he take all this interest in me? I don't know and have never even met him."

"Il Passero is always courteous. He assists the weak against the strong. He is like your English bandit Claude Duval of the old days. He always robs with exquisite courtesy, and impresses the same trait upon all who are in his service. And I may add that all are well paid and all devoted to their great master."

"I have heard that he has a house in London," Hugh said. "Do you know where it is situated?"

"Somewhere near Piccadilly. But I do not know exactly where it is. He is always vague regarding his address. His letters he receives in several names at a newspaper shop in Hammersmith and at the Poste Restante at Charing Cross."

"What names?" asked Hugh, highly interested.

"Oh! a number. They are always being changed," the French girl replied.

"Where do you write when you want to communicate with him?"

"Generally to the Poste Restante in the Avenue de l'Opera, in Paris. Letters received there are collected for him and forwarded every day."

"And so clever is he that nobody suspects him—eh?"

"Exactly, m'sieur. His policy is always '*Rengraciez!*' and he cares not a single *rotin* for *La Reniffe*," she replied, dropping again into the slang of French thieves.

"Of course he is on friendly terms with Mademoiselle of Monte Carlo?" Hugh remarked. "He may have been at Monte Carlo on the night of the tragic affair."

"He may have been. He was, no doubt, somewhere on the Riviera, and he sent Paolo in one of the cars to rescue you from the police."

"In that case, he at least knows that I am innocent."

"Yes. And he probably knows the guilty person. That would account for the interest he takes in you, though you do not know him," said Lisette. "I have known Il Passero perform many kindly acts to persons in distress who have never dreamed that they have received money from a notorious international thief."

"Well, in my case he has, no doubt, done me signal service," young Henfrey replied. "But," he added, "why cannot you tell me something more concerning Mademoiselle? What did you mean by saying that she was a *marque de ce*? I know it is your slang, but won't you explain what it means? You have explained most of your other expressions."

But the girl thief was obdurate. She was certainly a *chic* and engaging little person, apparently well educated and refined, but she was as sly as her notorious employer, whom she served so faithfully. She was, she had already told Hugh, the daughter of a man who had made jewel thefts his speciality and after many convictions was now serving ten years at the convict prison at Toulon. She had been bred in the Montmartre, and trained and educated to a criminal life. Il Passero had found her, and, after several times successfully "indicating" where coups could be made, she had been taken into his employment as a decoy, frequently travelling on the international *wagon-lits* and restaurants, where she succeeded in attracting the attention of men and holding them in conversation with a mild flirtation while other members of the gang investigated the contents of their valises. From one well-known diamond dealer travelling between Paris and Amsterdam, she and the man working with her had stolen a packet containing diamonds of the value of two hundred thousand francs, while from an English business man travelling from Boulogne to Paris, two days later, she had herself taken a wallet containing nearly four thousand pounds in English bank-notes. It was her share of the recent robbery that Il Passero had paid her three days before at the Concordia Restaurant in the Via Garibaldi, in Genoa.

Hugh pressed her many times to tell him something concerning the mysterious Mademoiselle, but he failed to elicit any further information of interest.

"Her fortune at the Rooms is wonderful, they say," Lisette said. "She must be very rich."

"But she is one of Il Passero's assistants—eh?"

The girl laughed lightly.

"Perhaps," was her enigmatical reply. "Who knows? It is, however, evident that Il Passero is seriously concerned at the tragic affair at the Villa Amette."

"Have you ever been there?"

She hesitated a few moments, then said: "Yes, once."

"And you know the old Italian servant Cataldi?"

She replied in the affirmative. Then she added:

"I know him, but I do not like him. She trusts him, but—"

"But what?"

"I would not. I should be afraid, for to my knowledge he is a *saigneur a musique*."

"And what is that?"

"An assassin."

"What?" cried Henfrey. "Is he guilty of murder—and Mademoiselle knows it?"

"Mademoiselle may not know about it. She is probably in ignorance, or she would not employ him."

Her remark was of considerable interest, inasmuch as old Cataldi had seemed to be most devoted to his mistress, and entirely trusted by her.

"Do you know the circumstances?" asked Hugh.

"Yes. But it is not our habit to speak of another's—well, shortcomings," was her reply.

"Surely, Mademoiselle should have been told the truth! Does not Il Passero know?" he asked.

There flitted across his mind at that moment the recollection of Dorise. What could she think of his disappearance? He longed to write to her, but The Sparrow's chauffeur had impressed upon him the serious danger he would be running if he wrote to her while she was at Monte Carlo.

"I question whether he does know. But if he does he would say nothing."

"Ah!" sighed Hugh. "Yours is indeed a queer world, mademoiselle. And not without interest."

"It is full of adventure and excitement, of ups and downs, of constant travel and change, and of eternal apprehension of arrest," replied the girl, with a laugh.

"I wish you would tell me something about Yvonne Ferad," he repeated.

"Alas! m'sieur, I am not permitted," was her obdurate reply. "I am truly sorry to hear of the dastardly attack upon her. She once did me a very kind and friendly action at a moment when I was in sore need of a friend."

"Who could have fired the shot, do you think?" Henfrey asked. "You know her friends. Perhaps you know her enemies?"

Mademoiselle Lisette was silent for some moments.

"Yes," she replied reflectively. "She has enemies, I know. But who has not?"

"Is there any person who, to your knowledge, would have any motive to kill her?"

Again she was silent.

"There are several people who hate her. One of them might have done it out of revenge. You say you saw nobody?"

"Nobody."

"Why did you go and see her at that hour?" asked the girl.

"Because I wanted her to tell me something—something of greatest importance to me."

"And she refused, of course? She keeps her own secrets."

"No. On the other hand, she was about to disclose to me the information I sought when someone fired through the open window."

"The shot might have been intended for you—eh?"

Hugh paused.

"It certainly might," he admitted. "But with what motive?"

"To prevent you from learning the truth."

"She was on the point of telling me what I wanted to know."

"Exactly. And what more likely than someone outside, realizing that Mademoiselle was about to make a disclosure, fired at you."

"But you said that Mademoiselle had enemies."

"So she has. But I think my theory is the correct one," replied the girl. "What was it that you asked her to reveal to you?"

"Well," he replied, after a brief hesitation, "my father died mysteriously in London some time ago, and I have reason to believe that she knows the truth concerning the sad affair."

"Where did it happen?"

"My father was found in the early morning lying in a doorway in Albemarle Street, close to Piccadilly. The only wound found was a slight scratch in the palm of the hand. The police constable at first thought he was intoxicated, but the doctor, on being called, declared that my father was suffering from poison. He was at once taken to St. George's Hospital, but an hour later he died without recovering consciousness."

"And what was your father's name?" asked Lisette in a strangely altered voice.

"Henfrey."

"Henfrey!" gasped the girl, starting up at mention of the name. "*Henfrey*! And—and are—you—*his son*?"

"Yes," replied Hugh. "Why? You know about the affair, mademoiselle! Tell me all you know," he cried. "I—the son of the dead man—have a right to demand the truth."

"Henfrey!" repeated the girl hoarsely in a state of intense agitation. "Monsieur Henfrey! And—and to think that I am here—with you—*his son*! Ah! forgive me!" she gasped. "I—I—Let us return."

"But you shall tell me the truth!" cried Hugh excitedly. "You know it! You cannot deny that you know it!"

All, however, he could get from her were the words:

"You—Monsieur Henfrey's son! *Surely Il Passero does not know this*!"

XI

More About the Sparrow

A month of weary anxiety and nervous tension had gone by.

Yvonne Ferad had slowly struggled back to health, but the injury to the brain had, alas! seriously upset the balance of her mind. Three of the greatest French specialists upon mental diseases had seen her and expressed little hope of her ever regaining her reason.

It was a sad affair which the police of Monaco had, by dint of much bribery and the telling of many untruths, successfully kept out of the newspapers.

The evening after Hugh's disappearance, Monsieur Ogier had called upon Dorise Ranscomb—her mother happily being away at the Rooms at the time. In one of the sitting-rooms of the hotel the official of police closely questioned the girl, but she, of course made pretense of complete ignorance. Naturally Ogier was annoyed at being unable to obtain the slightest information, and after being very rude, he told the girl the charge against her lover and then left the hotel in undisguised anger.

Lady Ranscomb was very much mystified at Hugh's disappearance, though secretly she was very glad. She questioned Brock, but he, on his part, expressed himself very much puzzled. A week later, however, Walter returned to London, and on the following night Lady Ranscomb and her daughter took the train-de-luxe for Boulogne, and duly arrived home.

As day followed day, Dorise grew more mystified and still more anxious concerning Hugh. What was the truth? She had written to Brussels three times, but her letters had elicited no response. He might be already under arrest, for aught she knew. Besides, she could not rid herself of the recollection of the white cavalier, that mysterious masker who had told her of her lover's escape.

In this state of keen anxiety and overstrung nerves she was compelled to meet almost daily, and be civil to, her mother's friend, the odious George Sherrard.

Lady Ranscomb was for ever singing the man's praises, and never weary of expressing her surprise at Hugh's unforgivable behaviour.

"He simply disappeared, and nobody has heard a word of him since!" she remarked one day as they sat at breakfast. "I'm quite certain he's done something wrong. I've never liked him, Dorise."

"You don't like him, mother, because he hasn't money," remarked the girl bitterly. "If he were rich and entertained you, you would call him a delightful man!"

"Dorise! What are you saying? What's the good of life without money?" queried the widow of the great contractor.

"Everyone can't be rich," the girl averred simply. "I think it's positively hateful to judge people by their pockets."

"Well, has Hugh written to you?" snapped her mother.

Dorise replied in the negative, stifling a sigh.

"And he isn't likely to. He's probably hiding somewhere. I wonder what he's done?"

"Nothing. I'm sure of that!"

"Well, I'm not so sure," was her mother's response. "I was chatting about it to Mr. Sherrard last night, and he's promised to make inquiry."

"Let Mr. Sherrard inquire as much as he likes," cried the girl angrily. "He'll find nothing against Hugh, except that he's poor."

"H'm! And he's been far too much in your company of late, Dorise. People were beginning to talk at Monte Carlo."

"Oh! Let them talk, mother! I don't care a scrap. I'm my own mistress!"

"Yes, but I tell you frankly that I'm very glad that we've seen the last of the fellow."

"Mother! You are really horrid!" cried the girl, rising abruptly and leaving the table. When out of the room she burst into tears.

Poor girl, her heart was indeed full.

Now it happened that early on that same morning Hugh Henfrey stepped from a train which had brought him from Aix-la-Chapelle to the Gare du Nord, in Brussels. He had spent three weeks with the Raveccas, in Genoa, whence he had travelled to Milan and Bale, and on into Belgium by way of Germany.

From Lisette he had failed to elicit any further facts concerning his father's death, though it was apparent that she knew something about it—something she dared not tell.

On the day following their midnight stroll, he had done all in his power to induce her to reveal something at least of the affair, but, alas! to no avail. Then, two days later, she had suddenly left—at orders of The Sparrow, she said.

Before Hugh left Ravecca had given him eighty pounds in English notes, saying that he acted at Il Passero's orders, for Hugh would no doubt need the money, and it would be most dangerous for him to write to his bankers.

At first Henfrey protested, but, as his funds were nearly exhausted, he had accepted the money.

As he left the station in Brussels on that bright spring morning and crossed the busy Place, he was wondering to what hotel he should go. He had left his scanty luggage in the *consigne*, intending to go out on foot and search for some cheap and obscure hotel, there being many such in the vicinity of the station. After half an hour he chose a small and apparently clean little place in a narrow street off the Place de Brouckere, and there, later on, he carried his handbag. Then, after a wash, he set out for the Central Post Office in the Place de la Monnaie.

He had not gone far along the busy boulevard when he was startled to hear his name uttered from behind, and, turning, encountered a short, thick-set little man wearing a brown overcoat.

The man, noticing the effect his words had upon him, smiled reassuringly, and said in broken English: "It is all right! I am not a police officer, Monsieur Henfrey. Cross the road and walk down that street yonder. I will follow in a few moments."

And then the man walked on, leaving Hugh alone.

Much surprised, Hugh did as he was bid, and a few minutes later the Belgian met him again.

"It is very dangerous for us to be seen together," he said quickly, scarcely pausing as he walked. "Do not go near the Post Office, but go straight to 14 Rue Beyaert, first floor. I shall be there awaiting you. I have a message for you from a friend. You will find the street close to the Porte de Hal."

And the man continued on his way, leaving Hugh in wonder. He had been on the point of turning from the boulevard into the Place de la Monnaie to obtain Dorise's long looked for letter. Indeed, he had been hastening his footsteps full of keen apprehension when the stranger had accosted him.

But in accordance with the man's suggestion, he turned back towards the station, where he entered a taxi and drove across the city to the corner of Rue Beyaert, a highly respectable thoroughfare. He experienced no difficulty in finding the house indicated, and on ascending the stairs, found the stranger awaiting him.

"Ah!" he cried. "Come in! I am glad that I discovered you! I have been awaiting your arrival from Italy for the past fortnight. It is indeed fortunate that I found you in time to warn you not to go to the Poste Restante." He spoke in French, and had shown his visitor into a small but well furnished room.

"Why?" asked Hugh. "Is there danger in that quarter?"

"Yes, Monsieur Henfrey. The French police have, by some unknown means, discovered that you were coming here, and a strict watch is being kept for anyone calling for letters addressed to Godfrey Brown."

"But how could they know?" asked Hugh.

"Ah! That is the mystery! Perhaps your lady friend has been indiscreet. She was told in strict confidence, and was warned that your safety was in her hands."

"Surely, Dorise would be most careful not to betray me!" cried the young Englishman.

"Well, somebody undoubtedly has."

"I presume you are one of Il Passero's friends?" Hugh said with a smile.

"Yes. Hence I am your friend," was the reply.

"Have you heard of late how Mademoiselle Yvonne is progressing?"

The man, who told his visitor his name was Jules Vervoort, shook his head.

"She is no better. I heard last week that the doctors have said that she will never recover her mental balance."

"What! Is she demented?"

"Yes. The report I had was that she recognized nobody, except at intervals she knows her Italian manservant and calls him by name. I was ordered to tell you this."

"Ordered by Il Passero—eh?"

The man Vervoort nodded in the affirmative. Then he went on to warn his visitor that the Brussels police were on the eager watch for his arrival. "It is fortunate that you were not recognized when you came this morning," he said. "I had secret warning and was at the station, but I dared not approach you. You passed under the very nose of two detectives, but luckily for you, their attention had been diverted to a woman who is a well-known pickpocket. I followed you to your hotel and then waited for you to go to the Poste Restante."

"But I want my letters," said Hugh.

"Naturally, but it is far too dangerous to go near there. You, of course, want news of your lady friend. That you will have by special messenger very soon. Therefore remain patient."

"Why are all these precautions being taken to prevent my arrest?" Hugh asked. "I confess I don't understand it."

"Neither do I. But when Il Passero commands we all obey."

"You are, I presume, his agent in Brussels?"

"His friend—not his agent," Vervoort replied with a smile.

"Do you know Mademoiselle Lisette?" Hugh asked. "She was with me in Genoa."

"Yes. We have met. A very clever little person. Il Passero thinks very highly of her. She has been educated in the higher schools, and is perhaps one of our cleverest decoys."

Hugh Henfrey paused.

"Now look here, Monsieur Vervoort," he exclaimed at last, "I'm very much in the dark about all this curious business. Lisette knows a lot concerning Mademoiselle Yvonne."

"Admitted. She acted once as her maid, I believe, in some big affair. But I don't know much about it."

"Well, you know what happened at the Villa Amette that night? Have you any idea of the identity of the person who shot poor Mademoiselle—the lady they call Mademoiselle of Monte Carlo?"

"Not in the least," was the reply. "All I know is that Il Passero has some very keen and personal interest in the affair. He has sent further orders to you. It is imperative, he says, that you should get away from Brussels. The police are too keen here."

"Where shall I go?"

"I suggest that you go at once to Malines. Go to Madame Maupoil, 208 Rue de Stassart, opposite the Military Hospital. It is far too dangerous for you to remain here in Brussels. I have already written that you are coming. Her house is one of the sanctuaries of the friends of Il Passero. Remember the name and address."

"The Sparrow seems to be ubiquitous," Hugh remarked.

"He is. No really great robbery can be accomplished unless he plans and finances it."

"I cannot think why he takes so keen an interest in me."

"He often does in persons who are quite ignorant of his existence."

"That is my own case. I never heard of him until I was in Genoa, a fugitive," said Hugh. "But you told me I shall receive a message from Miss Ranscomb by special messenger. When?"

"When you are in Malines."

"But all this is very strange. Will the mysterious messenger call upon Miss Ranscomb in London?"

"Of course. Il Passero has several messengers who travel to and fro in secret. Mademoiselle Lisette was once one of them. She has travelled many times the length and breadth of Europe. But nowadays she is an indicator—and a very clever one indeed," he added with a laugh.

"I suppose I had better get away to Malines without delay?" Hugh remarked.

"Yes. Go to your hotel, pay them for your room and get your valise. I shall be waiting for you at noon in a car in the Rue Gretry, close to the Palais d'Ete. Then we can slip away to Malines. Have you sufficient money? If not, I can give you some. Il Passero has ordered me to do so."

"Thanks," replied Hugh. "I have enough for the present. My only desire is to be back again in London."

"Ah! I am afraid that is not possible for some time to come."

"But I shall hear from Miss Ranscomb?"

"Oh, yes. The messenger will come to you in Malines."

"Who is the messenger?"

"Of that I have no knowledge," was Vervoort's reply. He seemed a very refined man, and was no doubt an extremely clever crook. He said little of himself, but sufficient to cause Hugh to realize that his was one of the master minds of underground Europe.

The young Englishman was naturally eager to further penetrate the veil of mystery surrounding Mademoiselle Yvonne, but he learned little or nothing. Vervoort either knew nothing, or else refused to disclose what he knew. Which, Hugh could not exactly decide.

Therefore, in accordance with the Belgian's instructions, he left the house and at noon carried his valise to the Rue Gretry, where he found his friend awaiting him in a closed car, which quickly moved off out of the city by the Laeken road. Travelling by way of Vilvorde they were within an hour in old-world Malines, famous for its magnificent cathedral and its musical carillon. Crossing the Louvain Canal and entering by the Porte de Bruxelles, they were soon in an inartistic cobbled street under the shadow of St. Rombold, and a few minutes later Hugh was introduced to a short, stout Belgian woman, Madame Maupoil. The place was meagrely furnished, but scrupulously clean. The floor of the room to which Hugh was shown shone with beeswax, and the walls were whitewashed.

"I hope monsieur will make himself quite comfortable," madame said, a broad smile of welcome upon her round face.

"You will be comfortable enough under madame's care," Vervoort assured him. "She has had some well-known guests before now."

"True, monsieur. More than one of them have been world-famous and—well—believed to be perfectly honest and upright."

"Yes," laughed Vervoort. "Do you remember the English ex-member of Parliament?"

"Ah! He was with me nearly four months when supposed to be in South America. There was a warrant out for him on account of some great financial frauds—all of which was, of course, hushed up. But he stayed here in strict concealment and his friends managed to get the warrant withdrawn. He was known to Il Passero, and the latter aided him—in return for certain facilities regarding the English police."

"What do you think of the English police, madame?" Hugh asked. The fat woman grinned expressively and shrugged her broad shoulders.

"Since the war they have been effete as regards serious crime. At least, that is what Il Passero told me when he was here a month ago."

"Someone is coming here to meet Monsieur Henfrey," Vervoort said. "Who is it?"

"I don't know. I only received word of it the day before yesterday. A messenger from London, I believe."

"Well, each day I become more and more mystified," Hugh declared. "Why Il Passero, whom I do not know, should take all this interest in me, I cannot imagine."

"Il Passero very often assists those against whom a false charge is laid," the woman remarked. "There is no better friend when one is in trouble, for so clever and ubiquitous is he, and so many friends in high quarters does he possess, that he can usually work his will. His is the master-mind, and we obey without question."

XII

The Stranger in Bond Street

As Dorise walked up Bond Street, smartly dressed, next afternoon, on her way to her dressmaker's, she was followed by a well-dressed young girl in black, dark-eyed, with well-cut, refined features, and apparently a lady.

From Piccadilly the stranger had followed Dorise unseen, until at the corner of Maddox Street she overtook her, and smiling, uttered her name.

"Yes," responded Doris in surprise. "But I regret—you have the advantage of me?"

"Probably," replied the stranger. "Do you recollect the *bal blanc* at Nice and a certain white cavalier? I have a message from him to give you in secret."

"Why in secret?" Dorise asked rather defiantly.

"Well—for certain reasons which I think you can guess," answered the girl in black, as she strolled at Dorise's side.

"Why did not you call on me at home?"

"Because of your mother. She would probably have been a little inquisitive. Let us go into some place—a tea-room—where we can talk," she suggested. "I have come to see you concerning Mr. Henfrey."

"Where is he?" asked Dorise, in an instant anxious.

"Quite safe. He arrived in Malines yesterday—and is with friends."

"Has he had my letters?"

"Unfortunately, no. But do not let us talk here. Let's go in yonder," and she indicated the Laurel Tea Rooms, which, the hour being early, they found, to their satisfaction, practically deserted.

At a table in the far corner they resumed their conversation.

"Why has he not received my letters?" asked Dorise. "It is nearly a month ago since I first wrote."

"By some mysterious means the police got to know of your friend's intended visit to Brussels to obtain his letters. Therefore, it was too dangerous for him to go to the Poste Restante, or even to send anyone there. The Brussels police were watching constantly. How they have gained their knowledge is a complete mystery."

"Who sent you to me?"

"A friend of Mr. Henfrey. My instructions are to see you, and to convey any message you may wish to send to Mr. Henfrey to him direct in Malines."

"I'm sure it's awfully good of you," Dorise replied. "Does he know you are here?"

"Yes. But I have not met him. I am simply a messenger. In fact, I travel far and wide for those who employ me."

"And who are they?"

"I regret, but they must remain nameless," said the girl, with a smile.

Dorise was puzzled as to how the French police could have gained any knowledge of Hugh's intentions. Then suddenly, she became horrified as a forgotten fact flashed across her mind. She recollected how, early in the grey morning, after her return from the ball at Nice, she had written and addressed a letter to Hugh. On reflection, she had realized that it was not sufficiently reassuring, so she had torn it up and thrown it into the waste-paper basket instead of burning it.

She had, she remembered, addressed the envelope to Mr. Godfrey Brown, at the Poste Restante in Brussels.

Was it possible that the torn fragments had fallen into the hands of the police? She knew that they had been watching her closely. Her surmise was, as a matter of fact, the correct one. Ogier had employed the head chambermaid to give him the contents of Dorise's waste-paper basket from time to time, hence the knowledge he had gained.

"Are you actually going to Malines?" asked Dorise of the girl.

"Yes. As your messenger," the other replied with a smile. "I am leaving to-night. If you care to write him a letter, I will deliver it."

"Will you come with me over to the Empress Club, and I will write the letter there?" Dorise suggested, still entirely mystified.

To this the stranger agreed, and they left the tea-shop and walked together to the well-known ladies' club, where, while the mysterious messenger sipped tea, Dorise sat down and wrote a long and affectionate letter to her lover, urging him to exercise the greatest caution and to get back to London as soon as he could.

When she had finished it, she placed it in an envelope.

"I would not address it," remarked the other girl. "It will be safer blank, for I shall give it into his hand."

And ten minute later the mysterious girl departed, leaving Dorise to reflect over the curious encounter.

So Hugh was in Malines. She went to the telephone, rang up Walter Brock, and told him the reassuring news.

"In Malines?" he cried over the wire. "I wonder if I dare go there to see him? What a dead-alive hole!"

Not until then did Dorise recollect that the girl had not given her Hugh's address. She had, perhaps, purposely withheld it.

This fact she told Hugh's friend, who replied over the wire:

"Well, it is highly satisfactory news, in any case. We can only wait, Miss Ranscomb. But this must relieve your mind, I feel sure."

"Yes, it does," admitted Dorise, and a few moments later she rang off.

That evening Il Passero's *chic* messenger crossed from Dover to Ostend, and next morning she called at Madame Maupoil's, in Malines, where she delivered Dorise's note into Hugh's own hand. She was an expert and hardened traveller.

Hugh eagerly devoured its contents, for it was the first communication he had had from her since that fateful night at Monte Carlo. Then, having thanked the girl again, and again, the latter said:

"If you wish to write back to Miss Ranscomb do so. I will address the envelope, and as I am going to Cologne to-night I will post it on my arrival."

Hugh thanked her cordially, and while she sat chatting with Madame Maupoil, sipping her *cafe au lait*, he sat down and wrote a long letter to the girl he loved so deeply—a letter which reached its destination four days later.

One morning about ten days afterwards, when the sun shone brightly upon the fresh green of the Surrey hills, Mrs. Bond was sitting before a fire in the pretty morning room at Shapley Manor, a room filled with antique furniture and old blue china, reading an illustrated paper. At the long, leaded window stood a tall, fair-faced girl in a smart navy-suit. She was decidedly pretty, with large, soft grey eyes, dimpled cheeks, and a small, well-formed mouth. She gazed abstractedly out of the window over the beautiful panorama to where Hindhead rose abruptly in the blue distance. The view from the moss-grown terrace at Shapley, high upon the Hog's back, was surely one of the finest within a couple of hundred miles of London.

Since Mrs. Bond's arrival there she had had many callers among the *nouveau riche*, those persons who, having made money at the expense of our gallant British soldiers, have now ousted half the county families from their solid and responsible homes. Mrs. Bond, being wealthy, had displayed her riches ostentatiously. She had subscribed lavishly to charities both in Guildford and in Farnham, and hence, among her callers there had been at least three magistrates and their flat-footed wives, as well as a plethoric alderman, and half a dozen insignificant persons possessing minor titles.

The display of wealth had always been one of Molly Maxwell's games. It always paid. She knew that to succeed one must spend, and now, with her recently acquired "fortune," she spent to a very considerable tune.

"I do wish you'd go in the car to Guildford and exchange those library books, Louise," exclaimed the handsome woman, suddenly looking up from her paper. "We've got those horrid Brailsfords coming to lunch. I was bound to ask them back."

"Can't you come, too?" asked the girl.

"No. I expect Mr. Benton this morning."

"I didn't know he was back from Paris. I'm so glad he's coming," replied the girl. "He'll stay all the afternoon, of course?"

"I hope so. Go at once and get back as soon as you can, dear. Choose me some nice new books, won't you?"

Louise Lambert, Benton's adopted daughter, turned from the leaded window. In the strong morning light she looked extremely charming, but upon her countenance there was a deep, thoughtful expression, as though she were entirely preoccupied.

"I've been thinking of Hugh Henfrey," the woman remarked suddenly. "I wonder why he never writes to you?" she added, watching the girl's face.

Louise's cheeks reddened slightly, as she replied with affected carelessness:

"If he doesn't care to write, I shall trouble no longer."

"He's still abroad, is he not? The last I heard of him was that he was at Monte Carlo with that Ranscomb girl."

Mention of Dorise Ranscomb caused the girl's cheeks to colour more deeply.

"Yes," she said, "I heard that also."

"You don't seem to care very much, Louise," remarked the woman. "And yet, he's such an awfully nice young fellow."

"You've said that dozens of times before," was Louise's abrupt reply.

"And I mean it. You could do a lot worse than to marry him, remember, though he is a bit hard-up nowadays. But things with him will right themselves before long."

"Why do you suggest that?" asked the girl resentfully.

"Well—because, my dear, I know that you are very fond of him," the woman laughed. "Now, you can't deny it—can you?"

The girl, who had travelled so widely ever since she had left school, drew a deep breath and, turning her head, gazed blankly out of the window again.

What Mrs. Bond had said was her secret. She was very fond of Hugh. They had not met very often, but he had attracted her—a fact of which both Benton and his female accomplice were well aware.

"You don't reply," laughed the woman for whom the Paris Sureté was searching everywhere; "but your face betrays the truth, my dear. Don't worry," she added in a tone of sympathy. "No doubt he'll write as soon as he is back in England. Personally, I don't believe he really cares a rap for the Ranscomb girl. It's only a matter of money—and Dorise has plenty."

"I don't wish to hear anything about Mr. Henfrey's love affairs!" cried the girl petulantly. "I tell you that they do not interest me."

"Because you are piqued that he does not write, child. Ah, dear, I know!" she laughed, as the girl left the room.

A quarter of an hour later Louise was seated in the car, while Mead drove her along the broad highway over the Hog's Back into Guildford. The morning was delightful, the trees wore their spring green, and all along in the fields, as they went over the high ridge, the larks were singing gaily the music of a glad morning of the English spring, and the view spread wide on either side.

Life in Surrey was, she found, much preferable to that on the Continent. True, in the Rue Racine they had entertained a great deal, and she had, during the war, met many very pleasant young English and American officers; but the sudden journey to Switzerland, then on into Italy, and across to New York, had been a whirl of excitement. Mrs. Maxwell had changed her name several times, because she said that she did not want her divorced husband, a ne'er-do-well, to know of her whereabouts. He was for ever molesting her, she had told Louise, and for that reason she had passed in different names.

The girl was in complete ignorance of the truth. She never dreamed that the source of the woman's wealth was highly suspicious, or that the constant travelling was in order to evade the police.

As she was driven along, she sat back reflecting. Truth to tell, she was much in love with Hugh. Benton had first introduced him one night at the Spa in Scarborough, and after that they had met several times on the Esplanade, then again in London, and once in Paris. Yet while she, on her part, became filled with admiration, he was, apparently, quite unconscious of it.

At last she had heard of Hugh's infatuation for Dorise Ranscomb, the daughter of the great engineer who had recently died, and indeed she had met her once and been introduced to her.

Of the conditions of old Mr. Henfrey's will she was, of course, in ignorance. The girl had no idea of the great plot which had been formed by her foster father and his clever female friend.

The world is a strange one beneath the surface of things. Those who passed the imposing gates of the beautiful old English manor-house never dreamed that it sheltered one of the most notorious female criminals in Europe. And the worshipful magistrates and their wives who visited her would have received a rude shock had they but known. But many modern adventuresses have been able to bamboozle the mighty. Madame Humbert of Paris, in whose imagination were "The Humbert Millions," used to entertain Ministers of State, aristocrats, financiers, and others of lower degree, and show them the sealed-up safe in which she declared reposed millions' worth of negotiable securities which might not see the light of day until a certain date. The avaricious, even shrewd, bankers advanced loans upon things they had never seen, and the Humberts were the most sought-after family in Paris until the bubble burst and they fled and were afterwards arrested in Spain.

Molly Maxwell was a marvel of ingenuity, of criminal foresight, and of amazing elusiveness. Louise, young and unsuspicious, looked upon her as a mother. Benton she called "Uncle," and was always grateful to him for all he did for her. She understood that they were cousins, and that Benton advised Mrs. Maxwell in her disastrous matrimonial affairs.

Yet the life she had led ever since leaving school had been a truly adventurous one. She had been in half the watering places of Europe, and in most of its capitals, leading, with the woman who now called herself Mrs. Bond, a most extravagant life at hotels of the first order.

The car at last ran into the station yard at Guildford, and at the bookstall Louise exchanged her books with the courteous manager.

She was passing through the booking-office back to the car, when a voice behind her called:

"Hallo, Louise!"

Turning, she found her "uncle," Charles Benton, who, wearing a light overcoat and grey velour hat, grasped her hand.

"Well, dear," he exclaimed. "This is fortunate. Mead is here, I suppose?"

"Yes, uncle," replied the girl, much gratified at meeting him.

"I was about to engage a taxi to take me up to the Manor, but now you can take me there," said the rather handsome man. "How is Mrs. Bond?" he asked, calling her by her new name.

"Quite well. She's expecting you to lunch. But she has some impossible people there to-day—the Brailsfords, father, mother, and son. He made his money in motor-cars during the war. They live over at Dorking in a house with forty-nine bedrooms, and only fifteen years ago Mrs. Brailsford used to do the housework herself. Now they're rolling in money, but can't keep servants."

"Ah, my dear, it's the same everywhere," said Benton as he entered the car after her. "I've just got back from Madrid. It is the same there. The world is changing. Crooks prosper while white men starve. Honesty spells ruin in these days."

They drove over the railway bridge and up the steep hill out of Guildford seated side by side. Benton had been her "uncle" ever since her childhood days, and a most kind and considerate one he had always proved.

Sometimes when at school she did not see him for periods of a year or more and she had no home to go to for holidays. Her foster-father was abroad. Yet her school fees were paid regularly, her allowance had been ample, and her clothes were always slightly better than those of the other girls. Therefore, though she called him "uncle," she looked upon Benton as her father and obeyed all his commands.

Just about noon the car swung into the gates of Shapley, and soon they were indoors. Benton threw off his coat, and in an abrupt manner said to the servant:

"I want to see Mrs. Bond at once."

Then, turning to Louise, he exclaimed:

"I want to see Molly privately. I have some urgent business to discuss with her before your profiteer friends arrive."

"All right," replied the girl cheerily. "I'll leave you alone," and she ascended the broad oak staircase, the steps of which were worn thin by the tramp of many generations.

A few moments later Charles Benton stood in the morning-room, where Mrs. Bond still sat before the welcome log fire.

"Back again, Charles!" she exclaimed, rising to greet him. "Well, how goes it?"

"Not too well," was his reply as he closed the door. "I only got back last night. Five days ago I saw The Sparrow at the Palace Hotel in Madrid. He's doing all he can in young Henfrey's interests, but he is not too hopeful."

"Why?"

"I can't make out," said the man, apparently much perturbed. "He wired me to go to Madrid, and I went. But it seems that I've been on a fool's errand."

"That's very unsatisfactory," said the woman.

"It is, my dear Molly! From his attitude it seemed to me that he is protecting Henfrey from some secret motive of his own—one that is not at all in accordance with our plans."

"But he is surely acting in our interests!"

"Ah! I'm not so sure about that."

"You surprise me. He knows our intentions and approved of them!"

"His approval has, I think, been upset by the murderous attack upon Yvonne."

"But he surely will not act against us! If he does—"

"If he does—then we may as well throw up the sponge, Molly."

"We could give it all away to the police," remarked the woman.

"And by so doing give ourselves away!" answered Benton. "The Sparrow has many friends in the police, recollect. Abroad, he distributes a quantity of annual *douceurs*, and hence he is practically immune from arrest."

"I wish we were," laughed the handsome adventuress.

"Yes. We have only to dance to his tune," said he. "And the tune just now is not one which is pleasing to us—eh?"

"You seem strangely apprehensive."

"I am. I believe that The Sparrow, while making pretence of supporting our little affair, is in favour of Hugh's marriage with Dorise Ranscomb."

The woman looked him straight in the face.

"He could never go back on his word!" she declared.

"The Sparrow is a curious combination of the crook—chivalrous and philanthropic—as you already know."

"But surely, he wouldn't let us down?"

Benton paused. He was thinking deeply. A certain fact had suddenly occurred to him.

"If he does, then we must, I suppose, do our best to expose him. I happen to know that he has quarrelled with Henri Michaux, the under-secretary of the Surete in Paris, who has declared that his payment is not sufficient. Michaux is anxious to get even with him. A word from us would result in The Sparrow's arrest."

"Excellent!" exclaimed Molly. "If we fail we can, after all, have our revenge. But," she added, "would not he suspect us both, and, in turn, give us away?"

"No. He will never suspect, my dear Molly. Leave it to me. Are we not his dearest and most trusted friends?" and the man, who was as keenly sought by the police of Europe, grinned sardonically and took a cigarette from the big silver box on the little table at his elbow.

XIII

POISONED LIPS

Week after week passed.

Spring was slowly developing into summer and the woods around Blairglas, the fine estate in Perthshire which old Sir Richard Ranscomb had left to his wife, were delightful.

Blairglas Castle, a grand old turreted pile, was perched on the edge of a wooded glen through which flowed a picturesque burn well known to tourists in Scotland. Once Blairglas Burn had been a mighty river which had, in the bygone ages, worn its way deep through the grey granite down to the broad Tay and onward to the sea. On the estate was some excellent salmon-fishing, as well as grouse on Blairglas Moor, and trout in Blairglas Loch. Here Lady Ranscomb entertained her wealthy Society friends, and certainly she did so lavishly and well. Twice each year she went up for the fishing and for the shooting. Old Sir Richard, notwithstanding his gout, had been fond of sport, and for that reason he had given a fabulous price for the place, which had belonged to a certain Duke who, like others, had become impoverished by excessive taxation and the death duties.

Built in the fifteenth century as a fortress, it was, for a time, the home of James V. after his marriage with Mary of Guise. It was to Blairglas that, after his defeat on Solway Moss, he retired, subsequently dying of a broken heart. Twenty years later Darnley, the elegant husband of Mary Stuart, had lived there, and on the level bowling green he used to indulge in his favourite sport.

The grim old place, with its towers, its dimly-lit long stone corridors, cyclopean ivy-clad walls, narrow windows, and great panelled chambers, breathed an atmosphere of the long ago. So extensive was it that only one wing—that which looked far down the glen to the blue distant mountains—had been modernised; yet that, in itself, was sufficiently spacious for the entertainment of large house-parties.

One morning, early in June, Dorise, in a rough tweed suit and a pearl-grey suede tam-o'shanter, carrying a mackintosh across her shoulder, and accompanied by a tall, dark-haired, clean-shaven man of thirty-two, with rather thick lips and bushy eyebrows, walked down through the woods to the river. The man, who was in fishing clothes, sauntered at her side, smoking a cigarette; while behind them came old Sandy Murray, the grizzled, fair-bearded head keeper, carrying the salmon rods, the gaff, creel, and luncheon basket.

"The spate is excellent for us," exclaimed George Sherrard. "We ought to kill a salmon to-day, Dorise."

"I sincerely hope so," replied the girl; "but somehow I never have any luck in these days."

"No, you really don't! But Marjorie killed a twelve-pounder last week, your mother tells me."

"Yes. She went out with Murray every day for a whole fortnight, and then on the day before she went back to town she landed a splendid fish."

On arrival at the bank of the broad shallow Tay, Murray stepped forward, and in his pleasant Perthshire accent suggested that a trial might be made near the Ardcraig, a short walk to the left.

After fixing the rods and baiting them, the head keeper discreetly withdrew, leaving the pair alone. In the servants' hall at Blairglas it was quite understood that Miss Dorise and Mr. Sherrard were to marry, and that the announcement would be made in due course.

"What a lovely day—and what a silent, delightful spot," Sherrard remarked, as he filled his pipe preparatory to walking up-stream, while the girl remained beside the dark pool where sport seemed likely.

"Yes," she replied, inwardly wishing to get rid of her companion so as to be left alone with her own thoughts. "I'll remain here for a little and then go down-stream to the end of our water."

"Right oh!" he replied cheerily as he moved away.

Dorise breathed more freely when he had gone.

George Sherrard had arrived from London quite unexpectedly at nine o'clock on the previous morning. She had been alone with her mother after the last guest of a gay house-party had departed, when, unknown to Dorise, Lady Ranscomb had telegraphed to her friend George to "run up for a few days' fishing."

Lady Ranscomb's scheme was to throw the pair into each other's society as much as possible. She petted George, flattered him, and in every way tried to entertain him with one sole object, namely, to induce him to propose to Dorise, and so get the girl "off her hands."

On the contrary, the girl's thoughts were for ever centred upon Hugh, even though he remained under that dark cloud of suspicion.

To her the chief element in the affair was the mystery why her lover had gone on that fateful night to the Villa Amette, the house of that notorious Mademoiselle. What had really occurred?

Twice she had received letters from him brought to her by the mysterious girl-messenger from Belgium. From them she knew how grey and dull was his life, hiding there from those who were so intent upon his arrest.

Indeed, within her blouse she carried his last letter which she had received three weeks before when in London—a letter in which he implored her not to misjudge him, and in which he promised that, as soon as he dared to leave his hiding-place and meet her, he would explain everything. In return, she had again written to him, but though three weary weeks had passed, she had received no word in reply. She could neither write by post, nor could she telegraph. It was far too dangerous. In addition, his address had been purposely withheld from her.

Walter Brock had tried to ascertain it. He had even seen the mysterious messenger on her last visit to England, but she had refused point-blank, declaring that she had been ordered to disclose nothing. She was merely a messenger.

That her correspondence was still being watched by the police, Dorise was quite well aware. Her maid, Duncan, had told her in confidence quite recently that while crossing Berkeley Square one evening she had been accosted by a good-looking young man who, having pressed his attentions upon her, had prevailed upon her to meet him on the following evening.

He then took her to dinner to a restaurant in Soho, and to the pictures afterwards. They had met half a dozen times, when he began to cleverly question her concerning her mistress, asking whether she had letters from her gentleman friends. At this Duncan had grown suspicious, and she had not met the young fellow since.

That, in itself, showed her that the police were bent on discovering and arresting Hugh.

The great mystery of it all was why Hugh should have gone deliberately and clandestinely to the Villa Amette on the night of the tragic affair.

Dorise was really an expert in casting a fly; also she excelled in several branches of sport. She was a splendid tennis-player, she rode well to hounds, and was very fair at golf. But that morning she had no heart for fishing, and especially in such company. She despised George Sherrard as a prig, fond of boasting of his means, and, indeed, so terribly self-conscious was he that in many circles he was declared impossible. Men disliked him for his swagger and conceit, and women despised him for his superior attitude towards them.

For a full hour Dorise continued making casts, but in vain. She changed her flies once or twice, until at last, by a careless throw, she got her tackle hooked high in a willow, with the result that, in endeavouring to extricate it, she broke off the hook. Then with an exclamation of impatience, she wound up her line and threw her rod upon the grass.

"Hallo, Dorise!" cried a voice. "No luck, eh?"

Sherrard had returned and had witnessed her outbreak of impatience.

"None!" she snapped, for the loss of her fly annoyed her. She knew that she had been careless, because under old Murray's careful tuition she had become quite expert with the rod, both with trout and salmon.

"Never mind," he said, "I've had similar luck. I've just got hooked up in a root and lost a fly. Let's have lunch—shall we?"

Dorise was in no mood to lunch with her mother's visitor, but, nevertheless, was compelled to be polite.

After washing their hands in the stream, they sat down together upon a great, grey boulder that had been worn smooth by the action of the water, and, taking out their sandwiches, began to eat them.

"Oh, I say!" exclaimed Sherrard suddenly, after they had been gossiping for some time. "Have you heard from your friend Henfrey lately?"

"Not lately," replied the girl, a trifle resentful that he should obtrude upon her private affairs.

"I only ask because—well, because there are some jolly queer stories going about town of him."

"Queer stories!" she echoed quickly. "What are they? What do people say?"

"Oh! They say lots of extraordinary things. I think your mother has done very well to drop him."

"Has mother dropped him?" asked the girl in pretence of ignorance.

"She told me so last night, and I was extremely glad to hear it—though he is your friend. It seems that he's hardly the kind of fellow you should know, Dorise."

"Why do you say that?" his companion asked, her eyes flashing instantly.

"What! Haven't you heard?"

WILLIAM LE QUEUX

"Heard what?"

"The story that's going round the clubs. He's missing, and has been so for quite a long time. You haven't seen him—have you?"

The girl was compelled to reply in the negative.

"But what do they say against him?" she demanded breathlessly.

"There's a lot of funny stories," was Sherrard's reply. "They say he's hiding from the police because he attempted to murder a notorious woman called Mademoiselle of Monte Carlo. Do you know about it?"

"It's a wicked lie!" blurted forth the girl. "Hugh never attempted to kill the woman!"

Sherrard looked straight into her blue eyes, and asked:

"Then why was he in her room at midnight? They say the reason Henfrey is hard-up is because he spent all he possessed upon the woman, and on going there that night she laughed him to scorn and told him she had grown fond of a rich Austrian banker. After mutual recriminations, Henfrey, knowing the woman had ruined him, drew out a revolver and shot her."

"I tell you it's an abominable lie! Hugh is not an assassin!" cried the girl fiercely.

"I merely repeat what I have heard on very good authority," replied the smug-faced man with the thick red lips.

"And you have of course told my mother that—eh?"

"I didn't think it was any secret," he said. "Indeed, I think it most fortunate we all know the truth. The police must get him one day—before long."

For a few moments Dorise remained silent, her eyes fixed across the broad river to the opposite bank.

"And if they do, he will most certainly clear himself, Mr. Sherrard," she said coldly.

"Ah! You still have great faith in him," he laughed airily. "Well—we shall see," and he grinned.

"Yes, Mr. Sherrard. I still have faith in Mr. Henfrey. I know him well enough to be certain that he is no assassin."

"Then I ask you, Dorise, why is he hiding?" said her companion. "If he is innocent, what can he fear?"

"I know he is innocent."

"Of course. You must remain in that belief until he is found guilty."

"You already condemn him!" the girl cried in anger. "By what right do you do this, I ask?"

"Well, common sense shows that he is in fear lest the truth should come to light," was Sherrard's lame reply. "He escaped very cleverly from Monte Carlo the moment he heard that the police suspected him, but where is he now? Nobody knows. Haynes, of Scotland Yard, who made the inquiries when my flat in Park Lane was broken into, tells me they have had a description of him from the Paris police, and that a general hue-and-cry has been circulated."

"But the woman is still alive, is she not?"

"Yes. She's a hopeless idiot, Haynes tells me. She had developed homicidal mania as a result of the bullet wound in the head, and they have had to send her to a private asylum at Cannes. She's there in close confinement."

Dorise paused. Her anger had risen, and her cheeks were flushed. The sandwich she was eating choked her, so she cast it into the river.

Then she rose abruptly, and looking very straight into the man's eyes, said:

"I consider, Mr. Sherrard, that you are absolutely horrid. Mr. Henfrey is a friend of mine, and whatever gossip there is concerning him I will not believe until I hear his story from his own lips."

"I merely tell you of the report from France to Scotland Yard," said Sherrard.

"You tell me this in order to prejudice me against Hugh—to—to—"

"Hugh! Whom you love—eh?" sneered Sherrard.

"Yes. I *do* love him," the girl blurted forth. "I make no secret of it. And if you like you can tell my mother that! You are very fond of acting as her factotum!"

"It is to be regretted, Dorise, that you have fallen in love with a fellow who is wanted by the police," he remarked with a sigh.

"At any rate, I love a genuine man," she retorted with bitter sarcasm. "I know my mother's intention is that I shall marry you. But I tell you here frankly—as I stand here—I would rather kill myself first!"

George Sherrard with his dark bushy brows and thick lips only laughed at her indignation. This incensed her the more.

"Yes," she went on. "You may be amused at my distress. You have laughed at the distress of other women, Mr. Sherrard. Do not think that I am blind. I have watched you, and I know more concerning your love affairs of the past than you ever dream. So please leave Blairglas as soon as you can with decency excuse yourself, and keep away from me in future."

"But really, Dorise—!" he cried, advancing towards her.

"I mean exactly what I say. Let me get back. When I go fishing I prefer to go alone," the girl said.

"But what am I to say to Lady Ranscomb?"

"Tell her that I love Hugh," laughed the girl defiantly. "Tell her that I intend to defeat all her clever intrigues and sly devices!"

His countenance now showed that he was angry. He and Lady Ranscomb thoroughly understood each other. He admired the girl, and her mother had assured him her affection for Hugh Henfrey was but a passing fancy. This stubborn outburst was to him a complete revelation.

"I have no knowledge of any intrigue, Dorise," he said in that bland, superior manner which always irritated her. She knew that a dozen mothers with eligible feminine encumbrances were trying to angle him, and that Lady Ranscomb was greatly envied by them. But to be the wife of the self-conscious ass—well, as she has already bluntly told him, she would die rather than become Mrs. George Sherrard.

"Intrigue!" the girl retorted. "Why, from first to last the whole thing is a plot between my mother and yourself. Please give me credit for just a little intelligence. First, I despise you as a coward. During the war you crept into a little clerkship in the Home Office in order to save your precious skin, while Hugh went to the front and risked his life flying a 'bomber' over the enemy's lines. You were a miserable stay-at-home, hiding in your little bolt-hole in Whitehall when the Zepps came over, while Hugh Henfrey fought for his King and for Britain. Now I am quite frank, Mr. Sherrard. That's why I despise you!" and the girl's pale face showed two pink spots in the centre of her cheeks.

"Really," he said in that same superior tone which he so constantly assumed. "I must say that you are the reverse of polite, Miss Dorise," and his colour heightened.

"I am! And I intend to be so!" she cried in a frenzy, for all her affection for Hugh had in those moments been redoubled. Her lover was accused and had no chance of self-defence. "Go back to my mother," she went on. "Tell her every word I have said and embroider it as much as you like. Then you can both put your wits together a little further. But, remember, I shall exert my own woman's wits against yours. And as soon as you feel it practicable, I hope you will leave Blairglas. And further, if you have not left by noon to-morrow, I will tell my maid, Duncan, the whole story of this sinister plot to part me from Hugh.

She will spread it, I assure you. Maids gossip—and to a purpose when their mistresses will it so."

"But Dorise—"

"Enough! Mr. Sherrard. I prefer to walk up to the Castle by myself. Murray will bring up the rods. Please tell my mother what I say when you get back," she added. "The night train from Perth to London leaves at nine-forty to-night," she said with biting sarcasm.

Then turning, she began to ascend the steep path which led from the river bank into a cornfield and through the wood, while the man stood and bit his lip.

"H'm!" he growled beneath his breath. "We shall see!—yes, we shall see!"

XIV

Red Dawn

That night when Dorise, in a pretty, pale-blue evening gown, entered the great, old panelled dining-room rather late for dinner, her mother exclaimed petulantly:

"How late you are, dear! Mr. Sherrard has had a telegram recalling him to London. He has to catch the nine-something train from Perth."

"Have you?" she asked the man who was odious to her. "I'm so sorry I'm late, but that Mackenzie girl called. They are getting up a bazaar for the old people down in the village, and we have to help it, I suppose. Oh! these bazaars, sales of work, and other little excuses for extracting shillings from the pockets of everybody! They are most wearying."

"She called on me last week," said Lady Ranscomb. "Newte told her I was not at home."

The old-fashioned butler, John Newte, a white-haired, rosy-faced man, who had seen forty years' service with the ducal owner of Blairglas, served the dinner in his own stately style. Sir Richard had been a good master, but things had never been the same since the castle had passed into its new owner's hands.

Dorise endeavoured to be quite affable to the smooth-haired man seated before her, expressing regret that he was called away so suddenly, while he, on his part, declared that it was "awful hard luck," as he had been looking forward to a week's good sport on the river.

"Do come back, George," Lady Ranscomb urged. "Get your business over and get back here for the weekend."

"I'll try," was Sherrard's half-hearted response, whereat Newte entered to announce that the car was ready.

Then he bade mother and daughter adieu, and went out.

Dorise could see that her mother was considerably annoyed at her plans being so abruptly frustrated.

"We must ask somebody else," she said, as they lingered over the dessert. "Whom shall we ask?"

"I really don't care in the least, mother. I'm quite happy here alone. It is a rest. We shall have to be back in town in a fortnight, I suppose."

"George could quite well have waited for a day or two," Lady Ranscomb declared. "I went out to see the Muirs, at Forteviot, and when I got back he told me he had just had a telegram telling him that it was imperative he should be in town to-morrow morning. I tried to persuade him to stay, but he declared it to be impossible."

"An appointment with a lady, perhaps," laughed Dorise mischievously.

"What next, my dear! You know he is over head and ears in love with you!"

"Oh! That's quite enough, mother. You've told me that lots of times before. But I tell you quite frankly his love leaves me quite cold."

"Ah! dear. That reply is, after all, but natural. You, of course, won't confess the truth," her mother laughed.

"I do, mother. I'm heartily glad the fellow has gone. I hate his supercilious manner, his superior tone, and his unctuous bearing. He's simply odious! That's my opinion."

Her mother looked at her severely across the table.

"Please remember, Dorise, that George is my friend."

"I never forget that," said the girl meaningly, as she rose and left the table.

Half an hour later, when she entered her bedroom, she found Duncan, her maid, awaiting her.

"Oh! I've been waiting to see you this half hour, miss," she said. "I couldn't get you alone. Just before eight o'clock, as I was about to enter the park by the side gate near Bervie Farm, a gentleman approached me and asked if my name was Duncan. I told him it was, and then he gave me this to give to you in secret. He also gave me a pound note, miss, to say nothing about it." And the prim lady's maid handed her young mistress a small white envelope upon which her name was written.

Opening it, she found a plain visiting card which bore the words in a man's handwriting:

Would it be possible for you to meet me to-night at ten at the spot where I have given this to your maid? Urgent.

SILVERADO

Dorise held her breath. It was a message from the mysterious white cavalier who had sought her out at the *bal blanc* at Nice, and told her of Hugh's peril!

Duncan was naturally curious owing to the effect the card had had upon her mistress, but she was too well trained to make any comment. Instead, she busied herself at the wardrobe, and a few moments afterwards left the room.

Dorise stood before the long cheval glass, the card still in her hand.

What did it mean? Why was the mysterious white cavalier in Scotland? At least she would now be able to see his face. It was past nine, and the moon was already shining. She had still more than half an hour before she went forth to meet the man of mystery.

She descended to the drawing-room, where her mother was reading, and after playing over a couple of songs as a camouflage, she pretended to be tired and announced her intention of retiring.

"We have to go into Edinburgh to-morrow morning," her mother remarked. "So we should start pretty early. I've ordered the car for nine o'clock."

"All right, mother. Good-night," said the girl as she closed the door.

Then hastening to her room she threw off her dinner gown, and putting on a coat and skirt and the boots which she had worn when fishing that morning, she went out by a door which led from the great old library, with its thousands of brown-backed volumes, on to the broad terrace which overlooked the glen, now a veritable fairyland beneath the light of the moon.

Outside the silence was only broken by the ripple of the burn over its pebbles deep below, and the cry of the night-bird upon the steep rock whereon the historic old castle was built. By a path known to her she descended swiftly, and away into the park by yet another path, used almost exclusively by the servants and the postman, down to a gate which led out into the high road to Perth by one of the farms on the estate, the one known as the Bervie.

As she was about to pass through the small swing gate, she heard a voice which she recognized exclaim:

"Miss Ranscomb! I have to apologize!" And from the dark shadow a rather tall man emerged and barred her path.

"I daresay you will think this all very mysterious," he went on, laughing lightly. "But I do hope I have not inconvenienced you. If so, pray accept my deepest apologies. Will you?"

"Not at all," the girl replied, though somewhat taken aback by the suddenness of the encounter. The man spoke slowly and with evident refinement. His voice was the same she had heard at Nice on that memorable night of gaiety. She recognized it instantly.

As he stood before her, his countenance became revealed in the moonlight, and she saw a well-moulded, strongly-marked face, with a pair of dark, penetrating eyes, set a little too close perhaps, but denoting strong will and keen intelligence.

"Yes," he laughed. "Look at me well, Miss Ranscomb. I am the white cavalier whom you last saw disguised by a black velvet mask. Look at me again, because perhaps you may wish to recognize me later on."

"And you are still Mr. X—eh?" asked the girl, who had halted, and was gazing upon his rather striking face.

"Still the same," he said, smiling. "Or you may call me Brown, Jones, or Robinson—or any of the other saints' names if you prefer."

"You have been very kind to me. Surely I may know your real name?"

"No, Miss Ranscomb. For certain very important reasons I do not wish to disclose it. Pardon me—will you not? I ask that favour of you."

"But will you not satisfy my curiosity?"

"At my personal risk? No. I do not think you would wish me to do that—eh?" he asked in a tone of mild reproof.

Then he went on:

"I'm awfully sorry I could not approach you openly. In London I found out that you were up here, so I thought it best to see you in secret. You know why I have come to you, Miss Ranscomb—eh?"

"On behalf of Mr. Henfrey."

"Yes. He is still in hiding. It has been impossible—through force of circumstances—for him to send you further messages."

"Where is he? I want to see him."

"Have patience, Miss Ranscomb, and I will arrange a meeting between you."

"But why do the police still search for him?"

"Because of an unfortunate fact. The lady, Mademoiselle Ferad, is now confined to a private asylum at Cannes, but all the time she raves furiously about Monsieur Henfrey. Hence the French police are convinced that he shot her—and they are determined upon his arrest."

"But do you think he is guilty?"

"I know he is not. Yet by force of adverse circumstances, he is compelled to conceal himself until such time that we can prove his innocence."

"Ah! But shall we ever be in a position to prove that?"

"I hope so. We must have patience—and still more patience," urged the mysterious man as he stood in the full light of the brilliant moon. "I

WILLIAM LE QUEUX

have here a letter for you which Mr. Henfrey wrote a week ago. It only came into my hands yesterday." And he gave her an envelope.

"Tell me something about this woman, Mademoiselle of Monte Carlo. Who is she?" asked Dorise excitedly.

"Well—she is a person who was notorious at the Rooms, as you yourself know. You have seen her."

"And tell me, why do you take such an interest in Hugh?" inquired the girl, not without a note of suspicion in her voice.

"For reasons best known to myself, Miss Ranscomb. Reasons which are personal."

"That's hardly a satisfactory reply."

"I fear I can give few satisfactory replies until we succeed in ascertaining the truth of what occurred at the Villa Amette," he said. "I must urge you, Miss Ranscomb, to remain patient, and—and not to lose faith in the man who is wrongfully accused."

"But when can I see him?" asked Dorise eagerly.

"Soon. But you must be discreet—and you must ask no questions. Just place yourself in my hands—that is, if you can trust me."

"I do, even though I am ignorant of your name."

"It is best that you remain in ignorance," was his reply. "Otherwise perhaps you would hesitate to trust me."

"Why?"

But the tall, good-looking man only laughed, and then he said:

"My name really doesn't matter at present. Later, Miss Ranscomb, you will no doubt know it. I am only acting in the interests of Henfrey."

Again she looked at him. His face was smiling, and yet was sphinx-like in the moonlight. His voice was certainly that of the white cavalier which she recollected so well, but his personality, so strongly marked, was a little overbearing.

"I know you mistrust me," he went on. "If I were in your place I certainly should do so. A thousand pities it is that I cannot tell you who I am. But—well—I tell you in confidence that I dare not!"

"Dare not! Of what are you afraid?" inquired Dorise. The man she had met under such romantic circumstances interested her keenly. He was Hugh's go-between. Poor Hugh! She knew he was suffering severely in his loneliness, and his incapability to clear himself of the terrible stigma upon him.

"I'm afraid of several things," replied the white cavalier. "The greatest fear I have is that you may not believe in me."

"I do believe in you," declared the girl.

"Excellent!" he replied enthusiastically. "Then let us get to business—pardon me for putting it so. But I am, after all, a business man. I am interested in a lot of different businesses, you see."

"Of what character?"

"No, Miss Ranscomb. That is another point upon which I regret that I cannot satisfy your pardonable curiosity. Please allow your mind to rest upon the one main point—that I am acting in the interests of the man with—the man who is, I believe, your greatest and most intimate friend."

"I understood that when we met in Nice."

"Good! Now I understand that your mother, Lady Ranscomb, is much against your marriage with Hugh Henfrey. She has other views."

"Really! Who told you that?"

"I have ascertained it in the course of my inquiry."

Dorise paused, and then looking the man of mystery straight in the face, asked:

"What do you really know about me?"

"Well," he laughed lightly. "A good deal. Now tell me when could you be free to get away from your mother for a whole day?"

"Why?"

"I want to know. Just tell me the date. When are you returning to London?"

"On Saturday week. I could get away—say—on Tuesday week."

"Very good. You would have to leave London by an early train in the morning—if I fail to send a car for you, which I hope to do. And be back again late at night."

"Why?"

"Why," he echoed. "Because I have a reason."

"I believe you will take me to meet Hugh—eh? Ah! How good you are!" cried the girl in deep emotion. "I shall never be able to thank you sufficiently for all you are doing. I—I have been longing all these weeks to see him again—to hear his explanation why he went to the woman's house at that hour—why—"

"He will tell you everything, no doubt," said her mysterious visitor. "He will tell you everything except one fact."

"And what is that?" she asked breathlessly.

"One fact he will not tell you. But you will know it later. Hugh

Henfrey is a fine manly fellow, Miss Ranscomb. That is why I have done my level best in his interest."

"But why should you?" she asked. "You are, after all, a stranger."

"True. But you will know the truth some day. Meanwhile, leave matters as they are. Do not prejudge him, even if the police are convinced of his guilt. Could you be at King's Cross station at ten o'clock on the morning of Tuesday week? If so, I will meet you there."

"Yes," she replied. "But where are we going?"

"At present I have no idea. When one is escaping from the police one's movements have to be ruled by circumstances from hour to hour. I will do my best on that day to arrange a meeting between you," he added.

She thanked him very sincerely. He was still a mystery, but his face and his whole bearing attracted her. He was her friend. She recollected his words amid that gay revelry at Nice—words of encouragement and sympathy. And he had travelled there, far north into Perthshire, in order to carry the letter which she had thrust into her pocket, yet still holding it in her clenched hand.

"I do wish you would tell me the motive of your extreme kindness towards us both," Dorise urged. "I can't make it out at all. I am bewildered."

"Well—so am I, Miss Ranscomb," replied the tall, elegant man who spoke with such refinement, and was so shrewd and alert. "There are certain facts—facts of which I have no knowledge. The affair at the Villa Amette is still, to me, a most profound mystery."

"Why did Hugh go there at all? That is what I fail to understand," she declared.

"Don't wonder any longer. He had, I know, an urgent and distinct motive to call that night."

"But the woman! I hear she is a notorious adventuress."

"And the adventuress, Miss Ranscomb, often has, deep in her soul, the heart of a pure woman," he said. "One must never judge by appearance or gossip. What people may think is the curse of many of our lives. I hope you do not misjudge Mr. Henfrey."

"I do not. But I am anxious to hear his explanation."

"You shall—and before long, too," he replied. "But I want you, if you will, to answer a question. I do not put it from mere idle curiosity, but it very closely concerns you both. Have you ever heard him speak of a girl named Louise Lambert?"

"Louise Lambert? Why, yes! He introduced her to me once. She is, I understand, the adopted daughter of a man named Benton, an intimate friend of old Mr. Henfrey."

"Has he ever told you anything concerning her?"

"Nothing much. Why?"

"He has never told you the conditions of his father's will?"

"Never—except that he has been left very poorly off, though his father died in affluent circumstances. What are the conditions?"

The mysterious stranger paused for a moment.

"Have you, of late, formed an acquaintance of a certain Mrs. Bond, a widow?"

"I met her recently in South Kensington, at the house of a friend of my mother, Mrs. Binyon. Why?"

"How many times have you met her?"

"Two—or I think three. She came to tea with us the day before we came up here."

"H'm! Your mother seems rather prone to make easy acquaintanceships—eh? The Hardcastles were distinctly undesirable, were they not?—and the Jameses also?"

"Why, what do you know about them?" asked the girl, much surprised, as they were two families who had been discovered to be not what they represented.

"Well," he laughed. "I happen to be aware of your mother's charm—that's all."

"You seem to know quite a bit about us," she remarked. "How is it?"

"Because I have made it my business to know, Miss Ranscomb," he replied. "Further, I would urge upon you to have nothing to do with Mrs. Bond."

"Why not? We found her most pleasant. She is the widow of a wealthy man who died abroad about two years ago, and she lives somewhere down in Surrey."

"I know all about that," he answered in a curious tone. "But I repeat my warning that Mrs. Bond is by no means a desirable acquaintance. I tell you so for your own benefit."

Inwardly he was angry that the woman should have so cleverly made the acquaintance of the girl. It showed him plainly that Benton and she were working on a set and desperate plan, while the girl before him was entirely ignorant of the plot.

"Now, Miss Ranscomb," he added, "I want you to please make me a promise—namely, that you will say nothing to a single soul of what I have said this evening—not even to your friend, Mr. Henfrey. I have very strong reasons for this. Remember, I am acting in the interests of you both, and secrecy is the essence of success."

"I understand. But you really mystify me. I know you are my friend," she said, "but why are you doing all this for our benefit?"

"In order that Hugh Henfrey may return to your side, and that hand in hand you may be able to defeat your enemies."

"My enemies! Who are they?" asked the girl.

"One day, very soon, they must reveal themselves. When they do, and you find yourself in difficulties, you have only to call upon me, and I will further assist you. Advertise in the *Times* newspaper at any time for an appointment with 'Silverado.' Give me seven days, and I will keep it."

"But do tell me your name!" she urged, as they moved together from the pathway along the road in the direction of Perth. "I beg of you to do so."

"I have already begged a favour of you, Miss Ranscomb," he answered in a soft, refined voice. "I ask you not to press your question. Suffice it that I am your sincere friend."

"But when shall I see Hugh?" she cried, again halting. "I cannot bear this terrible suspense any longer—indeed I can't! Can I go to him soon?"

"No!" cried a voice from the shadow of a bush close beside them as a dark alert figure sprang forth into the light. "It is needless. I am here, dearest!—*at last*!"

And next second she found herself clasped in her lover's strong embrace, while the stranger, utterly taken aback, stood looking on, absolutely mystified.

XV

The Nameless Man

"Who is this gentleman, Dorise?" asked Hugh, when a moment later the girl and her companion had recovered from their surprise.

"I cannot introduce you," was her reply. "He refuses to give his name."

The tall man laughed, and said:

"I have already told you that my name is X."

Hugh regarded the stranger with distinct suspicion. It was curious that he should discover them together, yet he made but little comment.

"We were just speaking about you, Mr. Henfrey," the tall man went on. "I believed that you were still in Belgium."

"How did you know I was there?"

"Oh!—well, information concerning your hiding-place reached me," was his enigmatical reply. "I am, however, glad you have been able to return to England in safety. I was about to arrange a meeting between you. But I advise you to be most careful."

"You seem to know a good deal concerning me," Hugh remarked resentfully, looking at the stern, rather handsome face in the moonlight.

"This is the gentleman who sought me out in Nice, and first told me of your peril, Hugh. I recognize his voice, and have to thank him for a good deal," the girl declared.

"Really, Miss Ranscomb, I require no thanks," the polite stranger assured her. "If I have been able to render Mr. Henfrey a little service it has been a pleasure to me. And now that you are together again I will leave you."

"But who are you?" demanded Hugh, filled with curiosity.

"That matters not, now that you are back in England. Only I beseech of you to be very careful," said the tall man. Then he added: "There are pitfalls into which you may very easily fall—traps set by your enemies."

"Well, sir, I thank you sincerely for what you have done for Miss Ranscomb during my absence," said the young man, much mystified at finding Dorise strolling at that hour with a man of whose name even she was ignorant. "I know I have enemies, and I shall certainly heed your warning."

"Your enemies must not know you are in England. If they do, they will most certainly inform the police."

"I shall take care of that," was Hugh's reply. "I shall be compelled to go into hiding again—but where, I do not know."

"Yes, you must certainly continue to lie low for a time," the man urged. "I know how very dull it must have been for you through all those weeks. But even that is better than the scandal of arrest and trial."

"Ah! I know of what you are accused, Hugh!" cried the girl. "And I also know you are innocent!"

"Mr. Henfrey is innocent," said the tall stranger. "But there must be no publicity, hence his only chance of safety lies in strict concealment."

"It is difficult to conceal oneself in England," replied Hugh.

The stranger laughed, as he slowly answered:

"There are certain places where no questions are asked—if you know where to look for them. But first, I am very interested to know how you got over here."

"I went to Ostend, and for twenty pounds induced a Belgian fisherman to put me ashore at night near Caister, in Norfolk. I went to London at once, only to discover that Miss Ranscomb was at Blairglas— and here I am. But I assure you it was an adventurous crossing, for the weather was terrible—a gale blew nearly the whole time."

"You are here, it is true, Mr. Henfrey. But you mustn't remain here," the stranger declared. "Though I refuse to give you my name, I will nevertheless try to render you further assistance. Go back to London by the next train you can get, and then call upon Mrs. Mason, who lives at a house called 'Heathcote,' in Abingdon Road, Kensington. She is a friend of mine, and I will advise her by telegram that she will have a visitor. Take apartments at her house, and remain there in strict seclusion. Will you remember the address—shall I write it down?"

"Thanks very much indeed," Hugh replied. "I shall remember it. Mrs. Mason, 'Heathcote,' Abingdon Road, Kensington."

"That's it. Get there as soon as ever you can," urged the stranger. "Recollect that your enemies are still in active search of you."

Hugh looked his mysterious friend full in the face.

"Look here!" he said, in a firm, hard voice. "Are you known as Il Passero?"

"Pardon me," answered the stranger. "I refuse to satisfy your curiosity as to who I may be. I am your friend—that is all that concerns you."

"But the famous Passero—The Sparrow—is my unknown friend," he said, "and I have a suspicion that you and he are identical!"

"I have a motive in not disclosing my identity," was the man's reply in a curious tone. "Get to Mrs. Mason's as quickly as you can. Perhaps one day soon we may meet again. Till then, I wish both of you the best of luck. *Au revoir!*"

And, raising his hat, he turned abruptly, and, leaving them, set off up the high road which led to Perth.

"But, listen, sir—one moment!" cried Hugh, as he turned away.

Nevertheless the stranger heeded not, and a few seconds later his figure was lost in the shadow of the high hedgerow.

"Well," said Hugh, a few moments later, "all this is most amazing. I feel certain that he is either the mysterious Sparrow himself, or one of his chief accomplices."

"The Sparrow? Who is he—dear?" asked Dorise, her hand upon her lover's shoulder.

"Let's sit down somewhere, and I will tell you," he said. Then, re-entering the park by the small iron gate, Dorise led him to a fallen tree where, as they sat together, he related all he had been told concerning the notorious head of a criminal gang known to his confederates, and the underworld of Europe generally, as Il Passero, or The Sparrow.

"How very remarkable!" exclaimed Dorise, when he had finished, and she, in turn, had told him of the encounter at the White Ball at Nice, and the coming and going of the messenger from Malines. "I wonder if he really is the notorious Sparrow?"

"I feel convinced he is," declared Hugh. "He sent me a message in secret to Malines a fortnight ago forbidding me to attempt to leave Belgium, because he considered the danger too great. He was, no doubt, much surprised to-night when he found me here."

"He certainly was quite as surprised as myself," the girl replied, happy beyond expression that her lover was once again at her side.

In his strong arms he held her in a long, tight embrace, kissing her upon the lips in a frenzy of satisfaction—long, sweet kisses which she reciprocated with a whole-heartedness that told him of her devotion. There, in the shadow, he whispered to her his love, repeating what he had told her in London, and again in Monte Carlo.

Suddenly he put a question to her:

"Do you really believe I am innocent of the charge against me, darling?"

"I do, Hugh," she answered frankly.

"Ah! Thank you for those words," he said, in a broken voice. "I feared that you might think because of my flight that I was guilty."

"I know you are not. Mother, of course, says all sorts of nasty things—that you must have done something very wrong—and all that."

"My escape certainly gives colour to the belief that I am in fear of arrest. And so I am. Yet I swear that I never attempted to harm the lady at the Villa Amette."

"But why did you go there at all, dear?" the girl asked. "You surely knew the unenviable reputation borne by that woman!"

"I know it quite well," he said. "I expected to meet an adventuress—but, on the contrary, I met a real good woman!"

"I don't understand you, Hugh," she said.

"No, darling. You, of course, cannot understand!" he exclaimed. "I admit that I followed her home, and I demanded an interview."

"Why?"

"Because I was determined she should divulge to me a secret of her own."

"What secret?"

"One that concerns my whole future."

"Cannot you tell me what it is?" she asked, looking into his face, which in the moonlight she saw was much changed, for it was unusually pale and haggard.

"I—well—at the present moment I am myself mystified, darling. Hence I cannot explain the truth," he replied. "Will you trust me if I promise to tell you the whole facts as soon as I have learnt them? One day I hope I shall know all, yet—"

"Yes—yet—what?"

He drew a deep breath.

"The poor unfortunate lady has lost her reason as the result of the attempt upon her life. Therefore, after all, I may never be in a position to know the truth which died upon her lips."

For nearly two hours the pair remained together. Often she was locked in her lover's arms, heedless of everything save her unbounded joy at his return, and of the fierce, passionate caresses he bestowed upon her. Truly, that was a night of supreme delight as they held each other's hands, and their lips met time after time in ecstasy.

He inquired about George Sherrard, but she said little. She hesitated to tell him of the incident while fishing that morning, but merely said:

"Oh! He was up here for two or three days, but had to go back to London on business. And I was very glad."

"Of course, dearest, your mother still presses you to marry him."

"Yes," laughed the girl. "But she will continue to press. She's constantly singing his praises until I'm utterly sick of hearing of all his good qualities."

Hugh sighed, and replied:

"All men who are rich are possessed of good qualities in the estimation of the world. The poor and hard-up are the despised. But, after all, Dorise," he added, in a changed voice, "you have not forgotten what you told me at Monte Carlo—that you love me?"

"I repeat it, Hugh!" declared the girl, deeply in earnest, her hand stealing into his. "I love only you!—*you*!"

Then again he took her in his arms, and imprinted a fierce, passionate kiss upon her ready lips.

"I suppose we must part again," he sighed. "I am compelled to keep away from you because no doubt a watch has been set upon you, and upon your correspondence. Up to the present, I have been able, by the good grace of unknown friends, to slip through the meshes of the net spread for me. But how long this will continue, I know not."

"Oh! do be careful, Hugh, won't you?" urged the girl, as they sat side by side. The only sound was the rippling of the burn deep down in the glen, and the distant barking of a shepherd's dog.

"Yes. I'll get away into the wilds of Kensington—to Abingdon Road. One is safer in a London suburb than in a desert, no doubt. West London is a good hiding-place."

"Recollect the name. Mason, wasn't it? And she lives at 'Heathcote.'"

"That was it. But do not communicate with me, otherwise my place of concealment will most certainly be discovered."

"But can't I see you, Hugh?" implored the girl. "Must we again be parted?"

"Yes. It seems so, according to our mysterious friend, whom I believe most firmly to be the notorious thief known by the Italian sobriquet of Il Passero—The Sparrow."

"Do you think he is a thief?" asked the girl.

"Yes. I am convinced that your friend is none other than the picturesque and romantic criminal whose octopus hand is upon almost every great theft in Europe, and whom the police always fail to catch, so elusive and clever is he."

WILLIAM LE QUEUX

She gave him further details of their first meeting at Nice.

"Exactly. That is one of his methods—secrecy and generosity are his two traits. He and his accomplices rob the wealthy, and assist those wrongly accused. It must be he—or one of his assistants. Otherwise he would not know of the secret hiding-place for those after whom a hue-and-cry has been raised."

He recollected at that moment the girl who had been his fellow-guest in Genoa—the dainty mademoiselle who evidently had some secret knowledge of his father's death, and yet refused to divulge a single word.

Ever since that memorable night at the Villa Amette, he had existed in a mist of suspicion and uncertainty. Yet, after all, he cared little for anything so long as Dorise still believed in his innocence, and she still loved him. His one great object was to clear up the mystery of his father's tragic end, and thus defeat the clever plot of those whose intention it, apparently, was to marry him to Louise Lambert.

On every hand there was mystification. The one woman—notorious as she was—who knew the truth had been rendered mentally incompetent by an assassin's bullet, while he, himself, was accused of the crime.

Hugh Henfrey would have long ago confessed to Dorise the whole facts concerning his father's death, but his delicacy prevented him. He honoured his dead father, and was averse to telling the girl he loved that he had been found in a curious state in a West End street late at night. He was loyal to his poor father's memory, and, until he knew the actual truth, he did not intend that Dorise should be in a position to misconstrue the facts, or to misjudge.

On the face of it, his father's death was exceedingly suspicious. He had left his home in the country and gone to town upon pretence. Why? That a woman was connected with his journey was now apparent. Hugh had ascertained certain facts which he had resolved to withhold from everybody.

But why should the notorious Sparrow, the King of the Underworld, interest himself so actively on his behalf as to travel up there to Perthshire, after making those secret, but elaborate, arrangements for safety? The whole affair was a mystery, complete and insoluble.

It was early morning, after they had rambled for several hours in the moonlight, when Hugh bade his well-beloved farewell.

They had returned through the park and were at a gate quite close to the castle when they halted. It had crossed Hugh's mind that they might be seen by one of the keepers, and he had mentioned this to Dorise.

"What matter?" she replied. "They do not know you, and probably will not recognize me."

So after promising Hugh to remain discreet, she told him they were returning to London in a few days.

"Look here!" he said suddenly. "We must meet again very soon, darling. I daresay I may venture out at night, therefore why not let us make an appointment—say, for Tuesday week. Where shall we meet? At midnight at the first seat on the right on entering the part at the Marble Arch? You remember, we met there once before—about a year ago."

"Yes. I know the spot," the girl replied. "I remember what a cold, wet night it was, too!" and she laughed at the recollection. "Very well. I will contrive to be there. That night we are due at a dance at the Gordons' in Grosvenor Gardens. But I'll manage to be there somehow—if only for five minutes."

"Good," he exclaimed, again kissing her fondly. "Now I must make all speed to Kensington and there go once more into hiding. When—oh, when will this wearying life be over!"

"You have a friend, as I have, in the mysterious white cavalier," she said. "I wonder who he really is?"

"The Sparrow—without a doubt—the famous 'Il Passero' for whom the police of Europe are ever searching, the man who at one moment lives in affluence and the highest respectability in a house somewhere near Piccadilly, and at another is tearing over the French, Spanish, or Italian roads in his powerful car directing all sorts of crooked business. It's a strange world in which I find myself, Dorise, I assure you! Good-bye, darling—good-bye!" and he took her in a final embrace. "Good-bye—till Tuesday week."

Then stepping on to the grass, where his feet fell noiselessly, he disappeared in the dark shadow of the great avenue of beeches.

XVI

The Escrocs of London

For ten weary days Hugh Henfrey had lived in the close, frowsy-smelling house in Abingdon Road, Kensington, a small, old-fashioned place, once a residence of well-to-do persons, but now sadly out of repair.

Its occupier was a worthy, and somewhat wizened, widow named Mason, who was supposed to be the relict of an army surgeon who had been killed at the Battle of the Marne. She was about sixty, and suffered badly from asthma. Her house was too large for one maid, a stout, matronly person called Emily, hence the place was not kept as clean as it ought to have been, and the cuisine left much to be desired.

Still, it appeared to be a safe harbour of refuge for certain strange persons who came there, men who looked more or less decent members of society, but whose talk and whose slang was certainly that of crooks. That house in the back street of old-world Kensington, a place built before Victoria ascended the throne, was undoubtedly on a par with the flat of the Reveccas in Genoa, and the thieves' sanctuary in the shadow of the cathedral at Malines.

Adversity brings with it queer company, and Hugh had found himself among a mixed society of men who had been gentlemen and had taken up the criminal life as an up-to-date profession. They all spoke of The Sparrow with awe; and they all wondered what his next great coup would be.

Hugh became more than ever satisfied that Il Passero was one of the greatest and most astute criminals who have graced the annals of our time.

Everyone sang his praise. The queer visitors who lodged there for a day, a couple of days, or more; the guests who came suddenly, and who disappeared just as quickly, were one and all loud in their admiration of Il Passero, though Hugh could discover nobody who had actually seen the arch-thief in the flesh.

On the Tuesday night Hugh had had a frugal and badly-cooked meal with three mysterious men who had arrived as Mrs. Mason's guests during the day. After supper the widow rose and left the room, whereupon the trio, all well-dressed men-about-town, began to chatter openly about a little "deal" in diamonds in which they had been interested. The "deal" in question had been reported in the newspapers on the previous morning, namely, how a Dutch diamond dealer's office in Hatton Garden had been broken into, the safe cut open by the most scientific means, and a very valuable parcel of stones extracted.

"Harry Austen has gone down to Surrey to stay with Molly."

"Molly? Why, I thought she was in Paris!"

"She was—but she went to America for a trip and she finds it more pleasant to live down in Surrey just now," replied the other with a grin. "She has Charlie's girl living with her."

"H'm!" grunted the third man. "Not quite the sort of companion Charlie might choose for his daughter—eh?"

Hugh took but little notice of the conversation. It was drawing near the time when he would go forth to meet Dorise at their trysting place. In anxiety he went into the adjoining room, and there smoked alone until just past eleven o'clock, when he put on his hat and went forth into the dark, deserted street.

Opposite High Street Kensington Station he jumped upon a bus, and at five minutes to midnight alighted at the Marble Arch. On entering the park he quickly found the seat he had indicated as their meeting place, and sat down to wait.

The home-going theatre traffic behind him in the Bayswater Road had nearly ceased as the church clocks chimed the midnight hour. In the semi-darkness of the park dark figures were moving, lovers with midnight trysts like his own. In the long, well-lit road behind him motors full of gaily-dressed women flashed homeward from suppers or theatres, while from the open windows of a ballroom in a great mansion, the house of an iron magnate, came the distant strains of waltz music.

Time dragged along. He strained his eyes down the dark pathway, but could see no approaching figure. Had she at the last moment been prevented from coming? He knew how difficult it was for her to slip away at night, for Lady Ranscomb was always so full of engagements, and Dorise was compelled to go everywhere with her.

At last he saw a female figure in the distance, as she turned into the park from the Marble Arch, and springing to his feet, he went forward to meet her. At first he was not certain that it was Dorise, but as he approached nearer he recognized her gait.

A few seconds later he confronted her and grasped her warmly by the hand. The black cloak she was wearing revealed a handsome jade-coloured evening gown, while her shoes were not those one would wear for promenading in the park.

"Welcome at last, darling!" he cried. "I was wondering if you could get away, after all!"

"I had a little difficulty," she laughed. "I'm at a dance at the Gordons' in Grosvenor Gardens, but I managed to slip out, find a taxi, and run along here. I fear I can't stay long, or they will miss me."

"Even five minutes with you is bliss to me, darling," he said, grasping her ungloved hand and raising it to his lips.

"Ah! Hugh. If you could only return to us, instead of living under this awful cloud of suspicion!" the girl cried. "Every day, and every night, I think of you, dear, and wonder how you are dragging out your days in obscurity down in Kensington. Twice this week I drove along the Earl's Court Road, quite close to you."

"Oh! life is a bit dull, certainly," he replied cheerfully. "But I have papers and books—and I can look out of the window on to the houses opposite."

"But you go out for a ramble at night?"

"Oh! yes," he replied. "Last night I set out at one o'clock and walked up to Hampstead Heath, as far as Jack Straw's Castle and back. The night was perfect. Really, Londoners who sleep heavily all night lose the best part of their lives. London is only beautiful in the night hours and at early dawn. I often watch the sun rise from the Thames Embankment. I have a favourite seat—just beyond Scotland Yard. I've become quite a night-bird these days. I sleep when the sun shines, and with a sandwich box and a flask I go long tramps at night, just as others do who, like myself, are concealing their identity."

"But when will all this end?" queried the girl, as together they strolled in the direction of Bayswater, passing many whispering couples sitting on seats. London lovers enjoy the park at all hours of the twenty-four.

"It will only end when I am able to discover the truth," he said vaguely. "Meanwhile I am not disheartened, darling, because—because I know that you believe in me—that you still trust me."

"That man whom I saw in Nice dressed as a cavalier, and who again came to me in Scotland, is a mystery," she said. "Do you really believe he is the person you suspect?"

"I do. I still believe he is the notorious and defiant criminal 'Il Passero'—the most daring and ingenious thief of the present century."

"But he is evidently your friend."

"Yes. That is the great mystery of it all. I cannot discern his motive."

"Is it a sinister one, do you think?"

"No. I do not believe so. I have heard of The Sparrow's fame from the lips of many criminals, but none has uttered a single word against him. He is, I hear, fierce, bitter, and relentless towards those who are his enemies. To his friends, however, he is staunchly loyal. That is what is said of him."

"But, Hugh, I wish you would be more frank with me," the girl said. "There are several things you are hiding from me."

"I admit it, darling," he blurted forth, holding her hand in the darkness as they walked. The ecstasy and the bliss of that moment held him almost without words. She was as life to him. He pursued that soul-deadening evasion, and lived that grey, sordid life among men and women escaping from justice solely for her sake. If he married Louise Lambert and then cast off the matrimonial shackles he would recover his patrimony and be well-off.

To many men the temptation would have proved too great. The inheritance of his father's fortune was so very easy. Louise was a pretty girl, well educated, bright, vivacious, and thoroughly up to date. Yet somehow, he always mistrusted Benton, though his father, perhaps blinded in his years, had reckoned him his best and most sincere friend. There are many unscrupulous men who pose as dear, devoted friends of those who they know are doomed by disease to die—men who hope to be left executors with attaching emoluments, and men who have some deep game to play either by swindling the orphans, or by advancing one of their own kith and kin in the social scale.

Old Mr. Henfrey, a genuine country landowner of the good old school, a man who lived in tweeds and leggings, and who rode regularly to hounds and enjoyed his days across the stubble, was one of the unsuspicious. Charles Benton he had first met long ago in the Hotel de Russie in Rome while he was wintering there. Benton was merry, and, apparently, a gentleman. He talked of his days at Harrow, and afterwards at Cambridge, of being sent down because of a big "rag" in the Gladstonian days, and of his life since as a fairly well-off bachelor with rooms in London.

Thus a close intimacy had sprung up between them, and Hugh had naturally regarded his father's friend with entire confidence.

"You admit that you are not telling me the whole truth, Hugh," remarked the girl after a long pause. "It is hardly fair of you, is it?"

WILLIAM LE QUEUX

"Ah! darling, you do not know my position," he hastened to explain as he gripped her little hand more tightly in his own. "I only wish I could learn the truth myself so as to make complete explanation. But at present all is doubt and uncertainty. Won't you trust me, Dorise?"

"Trust you!" she echoed. "Why, of course I will! You surely know that, Hugh."

The young man was again silent for some moments. Then he exclaimed:

"Yet, after all, I can see no ray of hope."

"Why?"

"Hope of our marriage, Dorise," he said hoarsely. "How can I, without money, ever hope to make you my wife?"

"But you will have your father's estate in due course, won't you?" she asked quite innocently. "You always plead poverty. You are so like a man."

"Ah! Dorise, I am really poor. You don't understand—*you can't!*"

"But I do," she said. "You may have debts. Every man has them—tailor's bills, restaurant bills, betting debts, jewellery debts. Oh! I know. I've heard all about these things from another. Well, if you have them, you'll be able to settle them out of your father's estate all in due course."

"And if he has left me nothing?"

"Nothing!" exclaimed the handsome girl at his side. "What do you mean?"

"Well—" he said very slowly. "At present I have nothing—that's all. That is why at Monte Carlo I suggested that—that—"

He did not conclude the sentence.

"I remember. You said that I had better marry George Sherrard—that thick-lipped ass. You said that because you are hard-up?"

"Yes. I am hard-up. Very hard-up. At present I am existing in an obscure lodging practically upon the charity of a man upon whom, so far as I can ascertain, I have no claim whatsoever."

"The notorious thief?"

Hugh nodded, and said:

"That fact in itself mystifies me. I can see no motive. I am entirely innocent of the crime attributed to me, and if Mademoiselle were in her right mind she would instantly clear me of this terrible charge."

"But why did you go to her home that night, Hugh?"

"As I have already told you, I went to demand a reply to a single question I put to her," he said. "But please do no let us discuss the affair further. The whole circumstances are painful to me—more painful than you can possibly imagine. One day—and I hope it will be soon—you will fully realize what all this has cost me."

The girl drew a long breath.

"I know, Hugh," she said. "I know, dear—and I do trust you."

They halted, and he bent and impressed upon her lips a fierce caress.

So entirely absorbed in each other were the pair that they failed to notice the slim figure of a man who had followed the girl at some distance. Indeed, the individual in question had been lurking outside the house in Grosvenor Gardens, and had watched Dorise leave. At the end of the street a taxi was drawn up at the kerb awaiting him. Dorise had hailed the man, but his reply was a surly "Engaged."

Then, walking about a couple of hundred yards, she had found another, and entering it, had driven to the Marble Arch. But the first taxi had followed the second one, and in it was the well-set-up man who was silently watching her in the park as she walked with her lover towards the Victoria Gate.

"What can I say to you in reply to your words of hope, darling?" exclaimed Hugh as he walked beside her. "I know full well how much all this must puzzle you. Have you seen Brock?"

"Oh! yes. I saw him two days ago. He called upon mother and had tea. I managed to get five minutes alone with him, and I asked if he had heard from you. He replied that he had not. He's much worried about you."

"Is he, dear old chap? I only wish I dared write to him, and give him my address."

"I told him that you were back in London. But I did not give him your address. You told me to disclose nothing."

"Quite right, Dorise," he said. "If, as I hope one day to do, I can ever clear myself and combat my secret enemies, then there will be revealed to you a state of things of which you little dream. To-day I confess I am under a cloud. In the to-morrow I hope and pray that I may be able to expose the guilty and throw a new light upon those who have conspired to secure my downfall."

They had halted in the dark path, and again their lips met in fond caress. Behind them was the silent watcher, the tall man who had followed Dorise when she had made her secret exit from the house wherein the gay dance was till in progress.

An empty seat was near, and with one accord the lovers sank upon it, Hugh still holding the girl's soft hand.

WILLIAM LE QUEUX

"I must really go," she said. "Mother will miss me, no doubt."

"And George Sherrard, too?" asked her companion bitterly.

"He may, of course."

"Ah! Then he is with you to-night?"

"Yes. Unfortunately, he is. Ah! Hugh! How I hate his exquisite and superior manners. But he is such a close friend of mother's that I can never escape him."

"And he still pesters you with his attentions, of course," remarked Hugh in a hard voice.

"Oh! yes, he is always pretending to be in love with me."

"Love!" echoed Hugh. "Can such a man ever love a woman? Never, Dorise. He does not love you as I love you—with my whole heart and my whole soul."

"Of course the fellow cannot," she replied. "But, for mother's sake, I have to suffer his presence."

"At least you are frank, darling," he laughed.

"I only tell you the truth, dear. Mother thinks she can induce me to marry him because he is so rich, but I repeat that I have no intention whatever of doing so. I love you, Hugh—and only you."

Again he took her in his strong arms and pressed her to him, still being watched by the mysterious individual who had followed Dorise.

"Ah! my darling, these are, indeed, moments of supreme happiness," Hugh exclaimed as he held her tightly in his arms. "I wonder when we dare meet again?"

"Soon, dear—very soon, I hope. Let us make another appointment," she said. "On Friday week mother is going to spend the night with Mrs. Deane down at Ascot. I shall make excuse to stay at home."

"Right. Friday week at the same place and time," he said cheerily.

"I'll have to go now," she said regretfully. "I only wish I could stay longer, but I must get back at once. If mother misses me she'll have a fit."

So he walked with her out of the Victoria Gate into the Bayswater Road and put her into an empty taxi which was passing back to Oxford Street.

Then, when he had pressed her hand and wished her adieu, he continued, towards Notting Hill Gate, and thence returned to Kensington.

But, though he was ignorant of the fact, the rather lank figure which had been waiting outside the house in Grosvenor Gardens now followed him almost as noiselessly as a shadow. Never once did the watcher lose sight of him until he saw him enter the house in Abingdon Road with his latchkey.

Then, when the door had closed, the mysterious watcher passed by and scrutinized the number, after which he hastened back to Kensington High Street, where he found a belated taxi in which he drove away.

XVII

ON THE SURREY HILLS

On the following morning, about twelve o'clock, Emily, Mrs. Mason's stout maid-of-all-work, showed a tall, well-dressed man into Hugh's frowsy little sitting-room where he sat reading.

He sprang to his feet when he recognized his visitor to be Charles Benton.

"Well my boy!" cried his visitor cheerily. "So I've found you at last! We all thought you were on the Continent, lying low somewhere."

"So I have been," replied the young man faintly. "You've heard of that affair at Monte Carlo?"

"Of course. And you are suspected—wanted by the police? That's why I'm here," Benton replied. "This place isn't safe for you. You must get away from it at once," he added, lowering his voice.

"Why isn't it safe?"

"Because at Scotland Yard they know you are somewhere in Kensington, and they're hunting high and low for you."

"How do you know?"

"Because Harpur, one of the assistant Commissioners of Police, happened to be in the club yesterday, and we chatted. So I pumped him as to the suspected person from Monte Carlo, and he declared that you were known to be in this district, and your arrest was only a matter of time. So you must clear out at once."

"Where to?" asked Hugh blankly.

"Well, there's a lady you met once or twice with me, Mrs. Bond. She will be delighted to put you up for a few weeks. She has a charming house down in Surrey—a place called Shapley Manor."

"She might learn the truth and give me away," remarked Hugh dubiously.

"She won't. Recollect, Hugh, that I was your father's friend, and am yours. What advice I give you is for your own good. You can't stay here—it's impossible."

The name of The Sparrow was upon Hugh's lips, and he was about to tell Benton of that mysterious person's efforts on his behalf, but, on reflection, he saw that he had no right to expose The Sparrow's existence to others. The very house in which they were was one of the bolt-holes of the wonderfully organized gang of crooks which Il Passero controlled.

"How did you know that I was here?" asked Hugh suddenly in curiosity.

"That I'm not at liberty to say. It was not a friend of yours, but rather an enemy who told me—hence I tell you that you run the gravest risk in remaining here a moment longer. As soon as I heard you were here, I telephoned to Mrs. Bond, and she has very generously asked us both to stay with her," Benton went on. "If you agree, I'll get a car now, without delay, and we'll run down into Surrey together," he added.

Hugh glanced at the tall, well-dressed man of whom his father had thought so highly. Charles Benton, in spite of his hair tuning grey, was a handsome man, and moved in a very good circle of society. Nobody knew his source of income, and nobody cared. In these days clothes make the gentleman, and a knighthood a lady.

Like many others, old Mr. Henfrey had been sadly deceived by Charles Benton, and had taken him into his family as a friend. Other men had done the same. His geniality, his handsome, open face, and his plausible manner, proved the open sesame to many doors of the wealthy, and the latter were robbed in various ways, yet never dreaming that Benton was the instigator of it all. He never committed a theft himself. He gave the information—and others did the dirty work.

"You recollect Mrs. Bond," said Benton. "But I believe Maxwell, her first husband, was alive then, wasn't he?"

"I have a faint recollection of meeting a Mrs. Maxwell in Paris—at lunch at the Pre Catalan—was it not?"

"Yes, of course. About six years ago. That's quite right!" laughed Benton. "Well, Maxwell died and she married again—a Colonel Bond. He was killed in Mesopotamia, and now she's living up on the Hog's Back, beyond Guildford, on the road to Farnham."

Hugh again reflected. He had come to Abingdon Road at the suggestion of the mysterious White Cavalier. Ought he to leave the place without first consulting him? Yet he had no knowledge of the whereabouts of the man of mystery whom he firmly believed was none other than the elusive Sparrow. Besides, was not Benton, his father's closest friend, warning him of his peril?

The latter thought decided him.

"I'm sure it's awfully good of Mrs. Bond whom I know so slightly to invite me to stay with her."

"Nothing, my dear boy. She's a very old friend of mine. I once did her a rather good turn when Maxwell was alive, and she's never forgotten it. She's one of the best women in the world, I assure you," Benton declared. "I'll run along to a garage I know in Knightsbridge and get a car to take us down to Shapley. It's right out in the country, and as long as you keep clear of the town of Guildford—where the police are unusually wary under one of the shrewdest chief constables in England—then you needn't have much fear. Pack up your traps, Hugh, and I'll call for you at the end of the road in half an hour."

"Yes. But I'll want a dress suit and lots of other things if I'm going to stay at a country house," the young man demurred.

"Rot! You can get all you want in Aldershot, Farnham or Portsmouth. Come just as you are. Mrs. Bond will make all allowances."

"And probably have her suspicions aroused at the same time?"

"No, she won't. This is a sudden trip into the country. I told her you had been taken unwell—a nervous breakdown—and that the doctor had ordered you complete rest at once."

"I wish I had stayed in Monte Carlo and faced the charge against me," declared Hugh fervently. "Being hunted from pillar to post like this is so absolutely nerve-racking."

"Why did you go to that woman's house, Hugh?" Benton asked. "What business had you that led you to call at that hour upon such a notorious person?"

Hugh remained silent. He saw that to tell Benton the truth would be to reopen the whole question of the will and of Louise.

So he merely shrugged his shoulders.

"Won't you tell me what really happened at the Villa Amette, Hugh?" asked the elder man persuasively. "I've seen Brock, but he apparently knows nothing."

"Of course he does not. I was alone," was Hugh's answer. "The least said about that night of horror the better, Benton."

So his father's friend left the house, while Hugh sought Mrs. Mason, settled his bill with her, packed his meagre wardrobe into a suit-case, and half an hour later entered the heavy old limousine which he found at the end of the road.

They took the main Portsmouth road, by way of Kingston, Cobham and Ripley, until in the cold grey afternoon they descended the steep hill through Guildford High Street, and crossing the bridge, instead of continuing along the road to Portsmouth, bore to the right, past the station, and up the steep wide road over that long hill, the Hog's Back, whence a great misty panorama was spread out on either side of the long, high-up ridge which in the sunshine gives such a wonderful view to motorists on their way out of London southward.

Presently the car turned into the gravelled drive, and Hugh found himself at Shapley.

In the chintz-hung, old-world morning-room, lit by the last rays of the declining sun, for the sky had suddenly cleared, Mrs. Bond entered, loud-voiced and merry.

"Why, Mr. Henfrey! I'm so awfully pleased to see you. Charles telephoned to me that you were a bit out of sorts. So you must stay with me for a little while—both of you. It's very healthy up here on the Surrey hills, and you'll soon be quite right again."

"I'm sure, Mrs. Bond, it is most hospitable of you," Hugh said. "London in these after the war days is quite impossible. I always long for the country. Certainly your house is delightful," he added, looking round.

"It's one of the nicest houses in the whole county of Surrey, my boy," Benton declared enthusiastically. "Mrs. Bond was awfully lucky in securing it. The family are unfortunately ruined, as so many others are by excessive taxation and high prices, and she just stepped in at the psychological moment."

"Well, I really don't know how to thank you sufficiently, Mrs. Bond," Hugh declared. "It is really extremely good of you."

"Remember, Mr. Henfrey, we are not strangers," exclaimed the handsome woman. "Do you recollect when we met in Paris, and afterwards in Biarritz, and then that night at the Carlton?"

"I recollect perfectly well. We met before the war, when one could really enjoy oneself contentedly."

"Since then I have been travelling a great deal," said the woman. "I've been in Italy, the South of Spain, the Azores, and over to the States. I got back only a few months ago."

And so after a chat Hugh was shown to his room, a pretty apartment, from the diamond-paned windows of which spread out a lovely view across to Godalming and Hindhead, with the South Downs in the blue far away.

"Now you must make yourselves at home, both of you," the handsome woman urged as they came down into the drawing-room after a wash.

Tea was served, and over it much chatter about people and places.

WILLIAM LE QUEUX

Mrs. Bond was, like her friend Benton, a thorough-going cosmopolitan. Hugh had no idea of her real reputation, or of her remarkable adventures. Neither had he any idea that Molly Maxwell was wanted by the Paris Sureté, just as he himself was wanted.

"Isn't this a charming place?" remarked Benton as, an hour later, they strolled on the long terrace smoking cigarettes before dinner. "Mrs. Bond was indeed fortunate in finding it."

"Beautiful!" declared Hugh in genuine admiration. Since that memorable night in Monte Carlo he had been living in frowsy surroundings, concealed in thieves' hiding-places, eating coarse food, and hearing the slang of the underworld of Europe.

It had been exciting, yet he had been drawn into it against his will—just because he had feared for Dorise's sake, to face the music after that mysterious shot had been fired at the Villa Amette.

Mrs. Bond was most courteous to her guests, and as Hugh and Benton strolled up and down the terrace in the fast growing darkness, the elder man remarked:

"You'll be quite safe here, you know, Hugh. Don't worry. I'm truly sorry that you have landed yourself into this hole, but—well, for the life of me I can't see what led you to seek out that woman, Yvonne Ferad. Why ever did you go there?"

Hugh paused.

"I—I had reasons—private reasons of my own," he replied.

"That's vague enough. We all have private reasons for doing silly things, and it seems that you did an exceptionally silly thing. I hear that Mademoiselle of Monte Carlo, after the doctors operated upon her brain, has now become a hopeless idiot."

"So I've been told. It is all so very sad—so horrible. Though people have denounced her as an adventuress, yet I know that at heart she is a real good woman."

"Is she? How do you know?" asked Benton quickly, for instantly he was on the alert.

"I know. And that is all."

"But tell me, Hugh—tell me in confidence, my boy—what led you to seek her that night. You must have followed her from the Casino and have seen her enter the Villa. Then you rang at the door and asked to see her?"

"Yes, I did."

"Why?"

"I had my own reasons."

"Can't you tell them to me, Hugh?" asked the tall man in a strange, low voice. "Remember, I am an old friend of your father. And I am still your best friend."

Hugh pursued his walk in silence.

"No," he said at last, "I prefer not to discuss the affair. That night is one full of painful memories."

"Very well," answered Benton shortly. "If you don't want to tell me, Hugh, I quite understand. That's enough. Have another cigarette," and he handed the young fellow his heavy gold case.

A week passed. Hugh Henfrey and Charles Benton greatly enjoyed their stay at Shapley Manor. With their hostess they motored almost daily to many points of interest in the neighbourhood, never, by the way, descending into the town of Guildford, where the police were so unusually alert and shrewd.

More than once when alone with Benton, Hugh felt impelled to refer to the mysterious death of his father, but it was a very painful subject. The last time Hugh had referred to it, about a month before his visit to Monte Carlo, Benton had been greatly upset, and had begged the young man not to mention the tragic affair.

Constantly, however, Benton, on his part, would put cunning questions to him concerning Yvonne Ferad, as to what he knew concerning her, and how he had managed to escape over the frontier into Italy.

Late one night as they sat together in the billiard-room after their final game, Benton, removing the cigar from his lips, exclaimed:

"Oh! I quite forgot to tell you, Mrs. Bond has been awfully good to Louise. She took her from Paris with her and they went quite a long tour, first to Spain and other places, and then to New York and back."

"Has she?" exclaimed Hugh in surprise. Only once before had Benton mentioned Louise's name, then he had casually remarked that she was on a visit to some friends in Yorkshire.

"Yes. She's making her home with Mrs. Bond for the present. She returns here to-morrow."

As he said this, he watched the young man's face. It was sphinx-like.

"Oh! That's jolly!" he replied, with well assumed satisfaction. "It seems such an age since we last met—nearly a year before my father's death, I believe."

In his heart he had no great liking for the girl, although she was bright, vivacious and extremely good company.

Next afternoon the pair met in the hall after the car had brought her from Guildford station.

"Hallo, Hugh!" she cried as she grasped his hand. "Uncle wrote and told me you were here! How jolly, isn't it? Why—you seem to have grown older," she laughed.

"And you younger," he replied, bending over her hand gallantly. "I hear you've been all over the world of late!"

"Yes. Wasn't it awfully good of Mrs. Bond? I had a ripping time. I enjoyed New York ever so much. I find this place a bit dull after Paris though, so I'm often away with friends."

And he followed her into the big morning-room where Mrs. Bond, alias Molly Maxwell, was awaiting her.

That afternoon there had been several callers; a retired admiral and his wife, and two county magistrates with their womenfolk, for since her residence at Shapley Mrs. Bond had been received in a good many smart houses, especially by the *nouveau riche* who abound in that neighbourhood. But the callers had left and they were now alone.

As Louise sat opposite the woman who had taken her under her charge, Hugh gazed at her furtively and saw that there was no comparison between her and the girl he loved so deeply.

How strange it was, he thought. If he asked her to be his wife and they married, he would at once become a wealthy man and inherit all his father's possessions. True, she was very sweet and possessed more than the ordinary *chic* and good taste in dress. Yet he felt that he could never fulfil his dead father's curious desire.

He could never marry her—*never*!

XVIII

The Man with the Black Glove

On his way out of London, Hugh had made excuse and stopped the car at a post office in Putney, whence he sent an express note to Dorise, telling her his change of address. He though it wiser not to post it.

Hence it was on the morning following Louise's arrival at Shapley, he received a letter from Dorise, enclosing one she had received under cover for him. He had told Dorise to address him as "Mr. Carlton Symes."

It was on dark-blue paper, such as is usually associated with the law or officialdom. Written in a neat, educated hand, it read:

> Dear Mr. Henfrey,
>
> I hear that you have left Abingdon Road, and am greatly interested to know the reason. You will, no doubt, recognize me as the friend who sent a car for you at Monte Carlo. Please call at the above address at the earliest possible moment. Be careful that you are not watched. Say nothing to anybody, wherever you may be. Better call about ten-thirty p.m., and ask for me. Have no fear. I am still your friend,
>
> George Peters

The address given was 14, Ellerston Street, Mayfair.

Hugh knew the street, which turned off Curzon Street, a short thoroughfare, but very exclusive. Some smart society folk lived there.

But who was George Peters? Was it not The Sparrow who had sent him the car with the facetious chauffeur to that spot in Monte Carlo? Perhaps the writer was the White Cavalier!

During the morning Hugh strolled down the hill and through the woods with Louise. The latter was dressed in a neat country kit, a tweed suit, a suede tam-o'-shanter, and carried a stout ash-plant as a walking-stick. They were out together until luncheon time.

Meanwhile, Benton sat with his hostess, and had a long confidential chat.

"You see, Molly," he said, as he smoked lazily, "I thought it an excellent plan to bring them together, and to let them have an opportunity of really knowing each other. It's no doubt true that he's over head and ears in love with the Ranscomb girl, but Lady Ranscomb has set her mind on having Sherrard as her son-in-law. She's a clever woman, Lady Ranscomb, and of course, in her eyes, Hugh is for ever beneath a cloud. That he went to the woman's house at night is quite sufficient."

"Well, if I know anything of young men, Charles, I don't think you'll ever induce that boy to marry Louise," remarked the handsome adventuress whom nobody suspected.

"Then if he doesn't, we'll just turn him over to Scotland Yard. We haven't any further use for him," said Benton savagely. "It's the money we want."

"And I fear we shall go on wanting it, my dear Charles," declared the woman, who was so well versed in the ways of men. "Louise likes him. She has told me so. But he only tolerates her—that's all! He's obsessed by the mystery of old Henfrey's death."

"I wonder if that was the reason he went that night to see Yvonne?" exclaimed Benton in a changed voice, as the idea suddenly occurred to him. "I wonder if—if he suspected something, and went boldly and asked her?"

"Ah! I wonder!" echoed the woman. "But Yvonne would surely tell him nothing. It would implicate her far too deeply if she did. Yvonne is a very shrewd person. She isn't likely to have told the old man's son very much."

"No, you're right, Molly," replied the man. "You're quite right! I don't think we have much to fear on that score. We've got Hugh with us, and if he again turns antagonistic the end is quite easy—just an anonymous line to the police."

"We don't want to do that if there is any other way," the woman said.

"I don't see any other way," replied the adventurer. "If he won't marry Louise, then the money passes out of our reach."

"I don't like The Sparrow taking such a deep interest in his welfare," growled the woman beneath her breath.

"And I don't like the fact that Yvonne is still alive. If she were dead—then we should have nothing to fear—nothing!" Benton said grimly.

"But who fired the shot if Hugh didn't?" asked Mrs. Bond.

"Personally, I think he did. He discovered something—something we don't yet know—and he went to the Villa Amette and shot her in revenge for the old man's death. That's my firm belief."

"Then why has The Sparrow taken all these elaborate precautions?"

"Because he's afraid himself of the truth coming out," said Benton. "He certainly has looked after Hugh very well. I had some trouble to persuade the lad to come down here, for he evidently believes that The Sparrow is his best friend."

"He may find him his enemy one day," laughed the woman. And then they rose and strolled out into the grounds, across the lawn down to the great pond.

When at half-past seven they sat down to dinner, Hugh suddenly remarked that he found it imperative to go to London that evening, and asked Mrs. Bond if he might have the car.

Benton looked up at him quickly, but said nothing before Louise.

"Certainly; Mead shall take you," was the woman's reply, though she was greatly surprised at the sudden request. Both she and Benton instantly foresaw that his intention was to visit Dorise in secret. For what other reason could he wish to run the risk of returning to London?

"When do you wish to start?" asked his hostess.

"Oh! about nine—if I may," was the young man's reply.

"Will you be back to-night?" asked the girl who, in a pretty pink dinner frock, sat opposite him.

"Yes. But it won't be till late, I expect," he replied.

"Remember, to-morrow we are going for a run to Bournemouth and back," said the girl. "Mrs. Bond has kindly arranged it, and I daresay she will come, too."

"I don't know yet, dear," replied Mrs. Bond. The truth was that she intended that the young couple should spend the day alone together.

Benton was filled with curiosity.

As soon as the meal was over, and the two ladies had left the room, he poured out a glass of port and turning to the young fellow, remarked:

"Don't you think it's a bit dangerous to go to town, Hugh?"

"It may be, but I must take the risk," was the other's reply.

"What are you going up for?" asked Benton bluntly.

"To see somebody—important," was his vague answer. And though the elder man tried time after time to get something more definite from him, he remained silent. Had not his unknown friend urged him to say nothing to anybody wherever he might be?

So at nine Mead drove up the car to the door, and Hugh, slipping on his light overcoat, bade his hostess good-night, thanked her for allowing him the use of the limousine, and promised to be back soon after midnight.

"Good-night, Hugh!" cried Louise from the other end of the fine old hall. And a moment later the car drove away in the darkness.

Along the Hog's Back they went, and down into Guildford. Then up the long steep High Street, past the ancient, overhanging clock at the Guildhall, and out again on the long straight road to Ripley and London.

As soon as they were beyond Guildford, he knocked at the window, and afterwards mounted beside Mead. He hated to be in a car alone, for he himself was a good driver and used always to drive his father's old "bus."

"I'll go to the Berkeley Hotel," he said to the man. "Drop me there, and pick me up outside there at twelve, will you?"

The man promised to do so, and then they chatted as they continued on their way to London. Mead, a Guildfordian, knew every inch of the road. Before entering Mrs. Bond's service he had, for a month, driven a lorry for a local firm of builders, and went constantly to and from London.

They arrived at the corner of St. James's Street at half-past ten. Hugh gave Mead five shillings to get his evening meal, and said:

"Be back here at midnight, Mead. I expect I'll be through my business long before that. But it's a clear night, and we shall have a splendid run home."

"Very well, sir. Thank you," replied his hostess's chauffeur.

Hugh Henfrey, instead of entering the smart Society hotel, turned up the street, and, walking quickly, found himself ten minutes later in Ellerston Street before a spacious house, upon the pale-green door of which was marked in Roman numerals the number fourteen.

By the light of the street lamp he saw it was an old Georgian town house. In the ironwork were two-foot-scrapers, relics of a time long before macadam or wood paving.

The house, high and inartistic, was a relic of the days of the dandies, when country squires had their town houses, and before labour found itself in London drawing-rooms. Consumed by curiosity, Hugh pressed the electric button marked "visitors," and a few moments later a smart young footman opened the door.

"Mr. George Peters?" inquired Hugh. "I have an appointment."

"What name, sir?" the young, narrow-eyed man asked.

"Henfrey."

"Oh, yes, sir! Mr. Peters is expecting you," he said. And at once he conducted him along the narrow hall to a room beyond.

The house was beautifully appointed. Everywhere was taste and luxury. Even in the hall there were portraits by old Spanish masters and many rare English sporting prints.

The room into which he was shown was a long apartment furnished in the style of the Georgian era. The genuine Adams ceiling, mantelpiece, and dead white walls, with the faintly faded carpet of old rose and light-blue, were all in keeping. The lights, too, were shaded, and over all was an old-world atmosphere of quiet and dignified repose.

The room was empty, and Hugh crossed to examine a beautiful little marble statuette of a girl bather, with her arms raised and about to dive. It was, no doubt, a gem of the art of sculpture, mounted upon a pedestal of dark-green marble which revolved.

The whole conception was delightful, and the girl's laughing face was most perfect in its portraiture.

Of a sudden the door reopened, and he was met by a stout, rather wizened old gentleman with white bristly hair and closely cropped moustache, a man whose ruddy face showed good living, and who moved with the brisk alertness of a man twenty years his junior.

"Ah! here you are, Mr. Henfrey!" he exclaimed warmly, as he offered his visitor his hand. Upon the latter was a well-worn black glove—evidently to hide either some disease or deformity. "I was wondering if you received my letter safely?"

"Yes," replied Hugh, glancing at the shrewd little man whose gloved right hand attracted him.

"Sit down," the other said, as he closed the door. "I'm very anxious to have a little chat with you."

Hugh took the arm-chair which Mr. Peters indicated. Somehow he viewed the man with suspicion. His eyes were small and piercing, and his face with its broad brow and narrow chin was almost triangular. He was a man of considerable personality, without a doubt. His voice was high pitched and rather petulant.

"Now," he said. "I was surprised to learn that you had left your safe asylum in Kensington. Not only was I surprised—but I confess, I was alarmed."

"I take it that I have to thank you for making those arrangements for my escape from Monte Carlo?" remarked Hugh, looking him straight in the face.

"No thanks are needed, my dear Mr. Henfrey," replied the elder man. "So long as you are free, what matters? But I do not wish you to deliberately run risks which are so easily avoided. Why did you leave Abingdon Road?"

"I was advised to do so by a friend."

"Not by Miss Ranscomb, I am sure."

"No, by a Mr. Benton, whom I know."

The old man's eyebrows narrowed for a second.

"Benton?" he echoed. "Charles Benton—is he?"

"Yes. As he was a friend of my late father I naturally trust him."

Mr. Peters paused.

"Oh, naturally," he said a second later. "But where are you living now?"

Hugh told him that he was the guest of Mrs. Bond of Shapley Manor, whereupon Mr. Peters sniffed sharply, and rising, obtained a box of good cigars from a cupboard near the fireplace.

"You went there at Benton's suggestion?"

"Yes, I did."

Mr. Peters gave a grunt of undisguised dissatisfaction, as he curled himself in his chair and examined carefully the young man before him.

"Now, Mr. Henfrey," he said at last. "I am very sorry for you. I happen to know something of your present position, and the great difficulty in which you are to-day placed by the clever roguery of others. Will you please describe to me accurately exactly what occurred on that fateful night at the Villa Amette? If I am to assist you further it is necessary for you to tell me everything—remember, *everything*!"

Hugh paused and looked the stranger straight in the face.

"I thought you knew all about it," he said.

"I know a little—not all. I want to know everything. Why did you venture there at all? You did not know the lady. It was surely a very unusual hour to pay a call?" said the little man, his shrewd eyes fixed upon his visitor.

"Well, Mr. Peters, the fact is that my father died in very suspicious circumstances, and I was led to believe the Mademoiselle was cognizant of the truth."

The other man frowned slightly.

"And so you went there with the purpose of getting the truth from her?" he remarked, with a grunt.

Hugh nodded in the affirmative.

"What did she tell you?"

"Nothing. She was about to tell me something when the shot was fired by someone on the veranda outside."

"H'm! Then the natural surmise would be that you, suspecting that woman of causing your father's death, shot her because she refused to tell you anything?"

"I repeat she was about to disclose the circumstances—to divulge her secret, when she was struck down."

"You have no suspicion of anyone? You don't think that her manservant—I forget the fellow's name—fired the shot? Remember, he was not in the room at the time!"

"I feel confident that he did not. He was far too distressed at the terrible affair," said Hugh. "The outrage must have been committed by someone to whom the preservation of the secret of my father's end was of most vital importance."

"Agreed," replied the man with the black glove. "The problem we have to solve is who was responsible for your father's death."

"Yes," said Hugh. "If that shot had not been fired I should have known the truth."

"You think, then, that Mademoiselle of Monte Carlo would have told you the truth?" asked the bristly-haired man with a mysterious smile.

"Yes. She would."

"Well, Mr. Henfrey, I think I am not of your opinion."

"You think possibly she would have implicated herself if she had told me the truth?"

"I do. But the chief reason I asked you to call and see me to-night is to learn for what reason you have been induced to go on a visit to this Mrs. Bond."

"Because Benton suggested it. He told me that Scotland Yard knew of my presence in Kensington, making further residence there dangerous."

"H'm!" And the man with the black glove paused again.

"You don't like Benton, do you?"

"I have no real reason to dislike him. He has always been very friendly towards me—as he was to my late father. The only thing which causes me to hold aloof from him as much as I can is the strange clause in my father's will."

"Strange clause?" echoed the old man. "What clause?"

"My father, in his will, cut me off every benefit he could unless I married Benton's adopted daughter, Louise. If I marry her, then I obtain a quarter of a million. I at first thought of disputing the will, but

Mr. Charman, our family solicitor, says that it is perfectly in order. The will was made in Paris two years before his death. He went over there on some financial business."

"Was Benton with him?" asked Mr. Peters.

"No. Benton went to New York about two months before."

"H'm! And how soon after your father's return did he come home?"

"I think it was about three months. He was in America five months altogether, I believe."

The old man, still curled in his chair, smoked his cigar in silence. Apparently he was thinking deeply.

"So Benton has induced you to go down to Shapley in order that you may be near his adopted daughter, in the hope that you will marry her! In the meantime you are deeply in love with Lady Ranscomb's daughter. I know her—a truly charming girl. I congratulate you," he added, as though speaking to himself. "But the situation is indeed a very complicated one."

"For me it is terrible. I am living under a cloud, and in constant fear of arrest. What can be done?"

"I fear nothing much can be done at present," said the old man, shaking his head gravely. "I quite realize that you are victim of certain enemies who intend to get hold of your father's fortune. It is for us to combat them—if we can."

"Then you will continue to help me?" asked Hugh eagerly, looking into the mysterious face of the old fellow who wore the black glove.

"I promise you my aid," he replied, putting out his gloved hand as pledge.

Then, as Hugh took it, he looked straight into those keen eyes, and asked:

"You have asked me many questions, sir, and I have replied to them all. May I ask one of you—my friend?"

"Certainly," replied the older man.

"Then am I correct in assuming that you are actually the person of whom I have heard so much up and down Europe—the man of whom certain men and women speak with admiration, and with bated breath—the man known in certain circles as—as *Il Passero*?"

The countenance of the little man with the bristly white hair and the black glove relaxed into a smile, as, still holding Hugh's hand in friendship, he replied:

"Yes. It is true. Some know me as 'The Sparrow!'"

XIX

The Sparrow

H ugh Henfrey was at last face to face with the most notorious criminal in Europe!

The black-gloved hand of the wizened, bristly-haired old man was the hand that controlled a great organization spread all over Europe—an organization which only knew Il Passero by repute, but had never seen him in the flesh.

Yet there he was, a discreet, rather petulant old gentleman, who lived at ease in an exclusive West End street, and was entirely unsuspected!

When "Mr. Peters" admitted his identity, Hugh drew a long breath. He was staggered. He was profuse in his thanks, but "The Sparrow" merely smiled, saying:

"It is true that I and certain of my friends make war upon Society—and more especially upon those who have profiteered upon those brave fellows who laid down their lives for us in the war. Whatever you have heard concerning me I hope you will forgive, Mr. Henfrey. At least I am the friend of those who are in distress, or who are wrongly judged—as you are to-day."

"I have heard many strange things concerning you from those who have never met you," Hugh said frankly. "But nothing to your detriment. Everyone speaks of you, sir, as a gallant sportsman, possessed of an almost uncanny cleverness in outwitting the authorities."

"Oh, well!" laughed the shrewd old man. "By the exercise of a little wit, and the possession of a little knowledge of the *personnel* of the police, one can usually outwit them. Curious as you may think it, a very high official at Scotland Yard dined with me here only last night. As I am known as a student of criminology, and reputed to be the author of a book upon that subject, he discussed with me the latest crime problem with which he had been called upon to deal—the mysterious murder of a young girl upon the beach on the north-east coast. His frankness rather amused me. It was, indeed, a quaint situation," he laughed.

"But does he not recognize you, or suspect?" asked Hugh.

"Why should he? I have never been through the hands of the police in my life. Hence I have never been photographed, nor have my finger prints been taken. I merely organize—that is all."

"Your organization is most wonderful, Mr.—er—Mr. Peters," declared the young man. "Since my flight I have had opportunity of learning something concerning it. And frankly, I am utterly astounded."

The old man's face again relaxed into a sphinx-like smile.

"When I order, I am obeyed," he said in a curious tone. "I ordered your rescue from that ugly situation in Monte Carlo. You and Miss Ranscomb no doubt believed the tall man who went to the ball at Nice as a cavalier to be myself. He did not tell you anything to the contrary, because I only reveal my identity to persons whom I can trust, and then only in cases of extreme necessity."

"Then I take it, sir, that you trust me, and that my case is one of extreme necessity?"

"It is," was The Sparrow's reply. "At present I can see no solution of the problem. It will be best, perhaps, for you to remain where you are for the present," he added. He did not tell the young man of his knowledge of Benton and his hostess.

"But I am very desirous of seeing Miss Ranscomb," Hugh said. "Is there any way possible by which I can meet her without running too great a risk?"

The Sparrow reflected in silence for some moments.

"To-day is Wednesday," he remarked slowly at last. "Miss Ranscomb is in London. That I happen to know. Well, go to the Bush Hotel, in Farnham, on Friday afternoon and have tea. She will probably motor there and take tea with you."

"Will she?" cried Hugh eagerly. "Will you arrange it? You are, indeed, a good Samaritan!"

The little old man smiled.

"I quite understand that this enforced parting under such circumstances is most unfortunate for you both," he said. "But I have done, and will continue to do, all I can in your interest."

"I can't quite make you out, Mr. Peters," said the young man. "Why should you evince such a paternal interest in me?"

The Sparrow did not at once reply. A strange expression played about his lips.

"Have I not already answered that question twice?" he asked. "Rest assured, Mr. Henfrey, that I have your interests very much at heart."

"You have some reason for that, I'm sure."

"Well—yes, I have a reason—a reason which is my own affair." And he rose to wish his visitor "good-night."

"I'll not forget to let Miss Ranscomb know that you will be at Farnham. She will, no doubt, manage to get her mother's car for the afternoon," he said. "Good-night!" and with his gloved fingers he took the young man's outstretched hand.

The instant he heard the front door close he crossed to the telephone, and asking for a number, told the person who answered it to come round and see him without a moment's delay.

Thus, while Hugh Henfrey was seated beside Mead as Mrs. Bond's car went swiftly towards Kensington, a thin, rather wiry-looking man of middle age entered The Sparrow's room.

The latter sprang to his feet quickly at sight of his visitor.

"Ah! Howell! I'm glad you've come. Benton and Molly Maxwell are deceiving us. They mean mischief!"

The man he addressed as Howell looked aghast.

"Mischief?" he echoed. "In what way?"

"I've not yet arrived at a full conclusion. But we must be on the alert and ready to act whenever the time is ripe. You know what they did over that little affair in Marseilles not so very long ago? They'll repeat, if we're not very careful. That girl of Benton's they are using as a decoy— and she's a dangerous one."

"For whom?"

"For old Henfrey's son."

The Sparrow's visitor gave vent to a low whistle.

"They intend to get old Henfrey's money?"

"Yes—and they will if we are not very wary," declared the little, bristly-haired old gentleman known as The Sparrow. "The boy has been entirely entrapped. They made one *faux pas*, and it is upon that we may—if we are careful—get the better of them. I don't like the situation at all. They have a distinctly evil design against the boy."

"Benton and Molly are a combination pretty hard to beat," remarked Mr. Howell. "But I thought they were friends of ours."

"True. They were. But after the little affair in Marseilles I don't trust them," replied The Sparrow. "When anyone makes a slip, either by design or sheer carelessness, or perhaps by reason of inordinate avarice, then I always have to safeguard myself. I suspect—and my suspicion usually proves correct."

His midnight visitor drew a long breath.

"What we all say of you is that The Sparrow is gifted with an extra sense," he said.

The little old man with the gloved hand smiled contentedly.

"I really don't know why," he said. "But I scent danger long before others have any suspicion of it. If I did not, you would, many of you who are my friends, have been in prison long ago."

"But you have such a marvellous memory."

"Memory!" he echoed. "Quite wrong. I keep everything filed. I work yonder at my desk all day. See this old wardrobe," and he crossed to a long, genuine Jacobean wardrobe which stood in a corner and, unlocking it, opened the carved doors. "There you see all my plans arranged and docketed. I can tell you what has been attempted to-night. Whether the coup is successful I do not yet know."

Within were shelves containing many bundles of papers, each tied with pink tape in legal fashion. He took out a small, black-covered index book and, after consulting it, drew out a file of papers from the second shelf.

These he brought to his table, and opened.

"Ah, yes!" he said, knitting his brows as he read a document beneath the green-shaded electric lamp. "You know Franklyn, don't you?"

"Harold Franklyn?"

"Yes. Well, he's in the Tatra, in Hungary. He and Matthews are with three Austrian friends of ours, and to-night they are at the Castle of Szombat, belonging to Count Zsolcza, the millionaire banker of Vienna. The Countess has some very valuable jewels, which were indicated to me several months ago by her discharged lady's maid— through another channel, of course. I hope that before dawn the jewels will be no longer at Szombat, for the Count is an old scoundrel who cornered the people's food in Austria just before the Armistice and is directly responsible for an enormous amount of suffering. The Countess was a cafe singer in Budapest. Her name was Anna Torna."

Mr. Howell sat open-mouthed. He was a crook and the bosom friend of the great Passero. Like all others who knew him, he held the master criminal in awe and admiration. The Sparrow, whatever he was, never did a mean action and never took advantage of youth or inexperience. To his finger-tips he was a sportsman, whose chief delight in life was to outwit and puzzle the police of Europe. In the underworld he was believed to be fabulously wealthy, as no doubt he was. To the outside world he was a very rich old gentleman, who contributed generously to charities, kept two fine cars, and, as well as his town house, had a pretty place down in Gloucestershire, and usually rented a grouse moor in Scotland, where he entertained Mr. Howell and several other of his intimate friends who were in the same profitable profession as himself, and in whose "business" he held a controlling interest.

In Paris, Rome, Madrid, or Brussels, he was well known as an idler who stayed at the best hotels and patronized the most expensive restaurants, while his villa on the Riviera he had purchased from a Roumanian prince who had ruined himself by gambling. His gloved hand—gloved because of a natural deformity—was the hand which controlled most of the greater robberies, for his war upon society was constantly far-reaching.

"Is Franklyn coming straight back?" asked Howell.

"That is the plan. He should leave Vienna to-morrow night," said The Sparrow, again consulting the papers. "And he comes home with all speed. But first he travels to Brussels, and afterwards to The Hague, where he will hand over Anna Torna's jewels to old Van Ort, and they'll be cut out of all recognition by the following day. Franklyn will then cross from the Hook to Harwich. He will wire me his departure from Vienna. He's bought a car for the job, and will have to abandon it somewhere outside of Vienna, for, as in most of our games, time is the essence of the contract," and the old fellow laughed oddly.

"I thought Franklyn worked with Molly," said Mr. Howell.

"So he does. I want him back, for I've a delicate mission for him," replied the sphinx-like man known as The Sparrow.

Mr. Howell, at the invitation of the arch-criminal, helped himself to a drink. Then The Sparrow said:

"You are due to leave London the day after to-morrow on that little business in Madrid. You must remain in town. I may want you."

"Very well. But Tresham is already there. I had a letter from him from the Palace Hotel yesterday."

"I will recall him by wire to-morrow. Our plans are complete. The Marquis's picture will still hang in his house until we are ready for it. It is the best specimen of Antonio del Rincon, and will fetch a big price in New York—when we have time to go and get it," he laughed.

"Is Franklyn to help the Maxwell woman again?" asked Mr. Howell, who was known as an expert valuer of antiques and articles of worth, and who had an office in St. James's. He only dealt in collectors' pieces, and in the trade bore an unblemished reputation, on account of his expert knowledge and his sound financial condition. He bought old masters and pieces of antique silver now and then, but none suspected that the genuine purchases at big prices were only made in order to blind his friends as to the actual nature of his business.

Indeed, to his office came many an art gem stolen from its owner on the Continent and smuggled over by devious ways known only to The Sparrow and his associates. And just as ingeniously the stolen property was sent across to America, so well camouflaged that the United States Customs officers were deceived. With pictures it was their usual method to coat the genuine picture with a certain varnish, over which one of the organization, an old artist living in Chelsea, would paint a modern and quite passable picture and add a new canvas back.

Then, on its arrival in America, the new picture was easily cleaned off, the back removed, and lo! it was an old master once more ready for purchase at a high price by American collectors.

Truly, the gloved hand of The Sparrow was a master hand. He had brought well-financed and well-organized theft to a fine art. His "indicators," both male and female, were everywhere, and cosmopolitan as he was himself, and a wealthy man, he was able to direct—and finance—all sorts of coups, from a barefaced jewel theft to the forgery of American banknotes.

And yet, so strange and mysterious a personality was he that not twenty persons in the whole criminal world had ever met him in the flesh. The tall, good-looking man whom Dorise knew as the White Cavalier was one of four other men who posed in his stead when occasion arose.

Scotland Yard, the Surete in Paris, the Pubblica Sicurezza in Rome, and the Detective Department of the New York police knew, quite naturally, of the existence of the elusive Sparrow, but none of them had been able to trace him.

Why? Because he was only the brains of the great, widespread criminal organization. He remained in smug respectability, while others beneath his hand carried out his orders—they were the servants, well-paid too, and he was the master.

No more widespread nor more wonderful criminal combine had ever been organized than that headed by The Sparrow, the little old man whom Londoners believed to be Cockney, yet Italians believed to be pure-bred Tuscan, while in Paris he was a true Parisian who could speak the argot of the Montmartre without a trace of English accent.

As a politician, as a City man, as a professional man, The Sparrow, whose real name was as obscure as his personality, would have made his mark. If a lawyer, he would have secured the honour of a knighthood— or of a baronetcy, and more than probable he would have entered Parliament.

The Sparrow was a philosopher, and a thorough-going Englishman to boot. Though none knew it, he was able by his unique knowledge of the underworld of Europe to give information—as he did anonymously to the War Office—of certain trusted persons who were, at the moment of the outbreak of war, betraying Britain's secrets.

The Department of Military Operations was, by means of the anonymous information, able to quash a gigantic German plot against us; but they had been unable to discover either the true source of their information or the identity of their informant.

"I'd better be off. It's late!" said Mr. Howell, after they had been in close conversation for nearly half an hour.

"Yes; I suppose you must go," The Sparrow remarked, rising. "I must get Franklyn back. He must get to the bottom of this curious affair. I fell that I am being bamboozled by Benton and Molly Maxwell. The boy is innocent—he is their victim," he added; "but if I can save him, by gad! I will! Yet it will be difficult. There is much trouble ahead, I anticipate, and it is up to us, Howell, to combat it!"

"Perhaps Franklyn can assist us?"

"Perhaps. I shall not, however, know before he gets back here from his adventures in Hungary. But I tell you, Howell, I am greatly concerned about the lad. He has fallen into the hands of a bad crowd—a very bad crowd indeed."

XX

The Man Who Knew

L ate on Thursday night Dorise and her mother were driving home from Lady Strathbayne's, in Grosvenor Square, where they had been dining. It was a bright starlight night, and the myriad lamps of the London traffic flashed past the windows as Dorise sat back in silence.

She was tired. The dinner had been followed by a small dance, and she had greatly enjoyed it. For once, George Sherrard, her mother's friend, had not accompanied them. As a matter of fact, Lady Strathbayne disliked the man, hence he had not been invited.

Suddenly Lady Ranscomb exclaimed:

"I heard about Hugh Henfrey this evening."

"From whom?" asked her daughter, instantly aroused.

"From that man who took me in to dinner. I think his name was Bowden."

"Oh! That stout, red-faced man. I don't know him."

"Neither do I. He was, however, very pleasant, and seems to have travelled a lot," replied her mother. "He told me that your precious friend, Henfrey, is back, and is staying down in Surrey as guest of some woman named Bond."

Dorise sat staggered. Then her lover's secret was out! If his whereabouts were known in Society, then the police would quickly get upon his track! She felt she must warn him instantly of his peril.

"How did he know, I wonder?" she asked anxiously.

"Oh! I suppose he's heard. He seemed to know all about the fellow. It appears that at last he's become engaged."

"Engaged? Hugh engaged?"

"Yes, to a girl named Louise Lambert. She's the adopted daughter of a man named Benton, who was, by the way, a great friend of old Mr. Henfrey."

Hugh engaged to Louise Lambert! Dorise sat bewildered.

"I—I don't believe it!" she blurted forth at last.

"Ah, my dear. You mean you don't want to believe it—because you are in love with him!" said her mother as the car rushed homeward. "Now put all this silly girlish nonsense aside. The fellow is under a cloud, and no good. I tell you frankly I will never have him as my son-in-law. How he has escaped the police is a marvel; but if the man Bowden knows where he is, Scotland Yard will, no doubt, soon hear."

The girl remained silent. Could it be possible that, after all, Hugh had asked Louise Lambert to be his wife? She had known of her, and had met her with Hugh, but he had always assured her that they were merely friends. Yet it appeared that he was now living in concealment under the same roof as she!

Lady Ranscomb, clever woman of the world as she was, watched her daughter's face in the fleeting lights as they sped homeward, and saw what a crushing blow the announcement had dealt her.

"I don't believe it," the girl cried.

She had received word in secret—presumably from the White Cavalier—to meet Hugh at the Bush Hotel at Farnham on the following afternoon, but this secret news held her in doubt and despair.

Lady Ranscomb dropped the subject, and began to speak of other things—of a visit to the flying-ground at Hendon on the following day, and of an invitation they had received to spend the following week with a friend at Cowes.

On arrival home Dorise went at once to her room, where her maid awaited her.

After the distracted girl had thrown off her cloak, her maid unhooked her dress, whereupon Dorise dismissed her to bed.

"I want to read, so go to bed," she said in a petulant voice which rather surprised the neat muslin-aproned maid.

"Very well, miss. Good-night," the latter replied meekly.

But as soon as the door was closed Dorise flung herself upon the chintz-covered couch and wept bitterly as though her heart would break.

She had met Louise Lambert—it was Hugh who had introduced them. George Sherrard had several times told her of the friendship between the pair, and one night at the Haymarket Theatre she had seen them together in a box. On another occasion she had met them at Ciro's, and they had been together at the Embassy, at Ranelagh, and yet again she had seen them lunching together one Sunday at the Metropole at Brighton.

All this had aroused suspicion and jealousy in her mind. It was all very well for Hugh to disclaim anything further than pure friendship, but now that Gossip was casting her hydra-headed venom upon their affairs, it was surely time to act.

Hugh would be awaiting her at Farnham next afternoon.

She crossed to the window and looked at the bright stars. In war time she used to see the long beams of searchlights playing to and fro. But now all was peace in London, and the world-war half forgotten.

Within herself arose a great struggle. Hugh was accused of a crime—an accusation of which he could not clear himself. He had been hunted across Europe by the police and had, up to the present, been successful in slipping through their fingers.

But why did he visit that notorious woman at that hour of the night? What could have been the secret bond between them?

The woman had narrowly escaped death presumably on account of his murderous attack upon her, while he had cleverly evaded arrest, until, at the present moment, his whereabouts was known only to a dinner-table gossip, and he was staying in the same house as the girl, love for whom he had always so vehemently disclaimed.

Poor Dorise spent a sleepless night. She lay awake thinking—and yet thinking!

At breakfast her mother looked at her and, with satisfaction, saw that she had gained a point nearer her object.

Dorise went into Bond Street shopping at eleven o'clock, still undecided whether to face Hugh or not. The shopping was a fiasco. She bought only a bunch of flowers.

But in her walk she made a resolve not to make further excuse. She would not ask her mother for the car, and Hugh, by waiting alone, should be left guessing.

On returning home, her mother told her of George's acceptance of an invitation to lunch.

"There's a matinee at the Lyric, and he's taking us there," she added. "But, dear," she went on, "you look ever so pale! What is worrying you? I hope you are not fretting over that good-for-nothing waster, Henfrey! Personally, I'm glad to be rid of a fellow who is wanted by the police for a very serious crime. Do brighten up, dear. This is not like you!"

"I—well, mother, I—I don't know what to do," the girl confessed.

"Do! Take my advice, darling. Think no more of the fellow. He's no use to you—or to me."

"But, mother dear—"

"No, Dorise, no more need be said!" interrupted Lady Ranscomb severely. "You surely would not be so idiotic as to throw in your lot with a man who is certainly a criminal."

"A criminal! Why do you denounce him, mother?"

"Well, he stands self-condemned. He has been in hiding ever since that night at Monte Carlo. If he were innocent, he would surely, for your sake, come forward and clear himself. Are you mad, Dorise—or are you blind?"

The girl remained silent. Her mother's argument was certainly a very sound one. Had Hugh deceived her?

Her lover's attitude was certainly that of a guilty man. She could not disguise from herself the fact that he was fleeing from justice, and that he was unable to give an explanation why he went to the house of Mademoiselle at all.

Yvonne Ferad, the only person who could tell the truth, was a hopeless idiot because of the murderous attack. Hence, the onus of clearing himself rested upon Hugh.

She loved him, but could she really trust him in face of the fact that he was concealed comfortably beneath the same roof as Louise Lambert?

She recalled that once, when they had met at Newquay in Cornwall over a tete-a-tete lunch, he had said, in reply to her banter, that Louise was a darling! That he was awfully fond of her, that she had the most wonderful eyes, and that she was always alert and full of a keen sense of humour.

Such a compliment Hugh had never paid to her. The recollection of it stung her.

She wondered what sort of woman was the person named Bond. Then she decided that she had acted wisely in not going to Farnham. Why should she? If Hugh was with the girl he admired, then he might return with her.

Her only fear was lest he should be arrested. If his place of concealment were spoken of over a West End dinner-table, then it could not be long before detectives arrested him for the affair at the Villa Amette.

On that afternoon Hugh had borrowed Mrs. Bond's car upon a rather lame pretext, and had pulled up in the square, inartistic yard before the Bush—the old coaching house, popular before the new road over the Hog's Back was made, and when the coaches had to ascend that steep hill out of Guildford, now known as The Mount. For miles the old road is now grass-grown and forms a most delightful walk, with magnificent views from the Thames Valley to the South Downs. The days of the coaches have, alas! passed, and the new road, with its tangle of telegraph wires, is beloved by every motorist and motor-cyclist who spins westward in Surrey.

Hugh waited anxiously in the little lounge which overlooks the courtyard. He went into the garden, and afterwards stood in impatience beneath the archway from which the street is approached. Later, he strolled along the road over which he knew Dorise must come. But all to no avail.

There was no sign of her.

Until six o'clock he waited, when, in blank despair, he mounted beside Mead again and drove back to Shapley Manor. It was curious that Dorise had not come to meet him, but he attributed it to The Sparrow's inability to convey a message to her. She might have gone out of town with her mother, he thought. Or, perhaps, at the last moment, she had been unable to get away.

On his return to Shapley he found Louise and Mrs. Bond sitting together in the charming, old-world drawing-room. A log fire was burning brightly.

"Did you have a nice run, Hugh?" asked the girl, clasping her hands behind her head and looking up at him as he stood upon the pale-blue hearthrug.

"Quite," he replied. "I went around Hindhead down to Frensham Ponds and back through Farnham—quite a pleasant run."

"Mr. Benton has had to go to town," said his hostess. "Almost as soon as you had gone he was rung up, and he had to get a taxi out from Guildford. He'll be back to-morrow."

"Oh, yes—and, by the way, Hugh," exclaimed Louise, "there was a call for you about a quarter of an hour afterwards. I thought nobody knew you were down here."

"For me!" gasped Henfrey, instantly alarmed.

"Yes, I answered the 'phone. It was a girl's voice!"

"A girl! Who?"

"I don't know who she was. She wouldn't give her name," Louise replied. "She asked if we were Shapley, and I replied. Then she asked for you. I told her that you were out in the car and asked her name. But she said it didn't matter at all, and rang off."

"I wonder who she was?" remarked Hugh, much puzzled and, at the same time, greatly alarmed. He scented danger. The fact in itself showed that somebody knew the secret of his hiding-place, and, if they did, then the police were bound to discover him sooner or later.

Half an hour afterwards he took Mrs. Bond aside, and pointed out the peril in which he was placed. His hostess, on her part, grew alarmed, for though Hugh was unaware of it, she had no desire to meet the police. That little affair in Paris was by no means forgotten.

"It is certainly rather curious," the woman admitted. "Evidently it is known by somebody that you are staying with me. Don't you think it would be wiser to leave?"

Hugh hesitated. He wished to take Benton's advice, and told his hostess so. With this she agreed, yet she was inwardly highly nervous at the situation. Any police inquiry at Shapley would certainly be most unwelcome to her, and she blamed herself for agreeing to Benton's proposal that Hugh should stay there.

"Benton will be back to-morrow," Hugh said. "Do you think it safe for me to remain here till then?" he added anxiously.

"I hardly know what to think," replied the woman. She herself had a haunting dread of recognition as Molly Maxwell. She had crossed and recrossed the Atlantic, carefully covering her tracks, and she did not intend to be cornered at last.

After dinner, Hugh, still greatly perturbed at the mysterious telephone call, played billiards with Louise. About a quarter to eleven, however, Mrs. Bond was called to the telephone and, closing the door, listened to an urgent message.

It was from Benton, who spoke from London—a few quick, cryptic, but reassuring words—and when the woman left the room three minutes later all her anxiety as to the police had apparently passed.

She joined the young couple and watched their game. Louise handled her cue well, and very nearly beat her opponent. Afterwards, when Louise went out, Mrs. Bond closed the door swiftly, and said:

"I've been thinking over that little matter, Mr. Henfrey. I really don't think there is much cause for alarm. Charles will be back to-morrow, and we can consult him."

Hugh shrugged his shoulders. He was much puzzled.

"The fact is, Mrs. Bond, I'm tired of being hunted like this!" he said. "This eternal fear of arrest has got upon my nerves to such an extent that I feel if they want to bring me for trial—well, they can. I'm innocent—therefore, how can they prove me guilty?"

"Oh! you mustn't let it obsess you," the woman urged. "Mr. Benton has told me all about the unfortunate affair, and I greatly sympathize with you. Of course, to court the publicity of a trial would be fatal. What would your poor father think, I wonder, if he were still alive?"

"He's dead," said the young man in a low, hoarse voice; "but Mademoiselle Ferad knows the secret of his death."

"He died suddenly—did he not?"

"Yes. He was murdered, Mrs. Bond. I'm certain of it. My father was murdered!"

"Murdered?" she echoed. "What did the doctors say?"

"They arrived at no definite conclusion," was Hugh's response. "He left home and went up to London on some secret and mysterious errand. Later, he was found lying upon the pavement in a dying condition. He never recovered consciousness, but sank a few hours afterwards. His death is one of the many unsolved mysteries of London."

"The police believe that you went to the Villa Amette and murdered Mademoiselle out of revenge."

"Let them prove it!" said the young fellow defiantly. "Let them prove it!"

"Prove what?" asked Louise, as she suddenly reopened the door, greatly to the woman's consternation.

"Oh! Only somebody—that Spicer woman over at Godalming—has been saying some wicked and nasty things about Mr. Henfrey," replied Mrs. Bond. "Personally, I should be annoyed. Really those gossiping people are simply intolerable."

"What have they been saying, Hugh?" asked the girl.

"Oh, it's really nothing," laughed Henfrey. "I apologize. I was put out a moment ago, but I now see the absurdity of it. Forgive me, Louise."

The girl looked from Mrs. Bond to her guest in amazement.

"What is there to forgive?" she asked.

"The fact that I was in the very act of losing my temper. That's all."

Presently, when Louise was ascending the stairs with Mrs. Bond, the girl asked:

"Why was Hugh so put out? What has Mrs. Spicer been saying about him?"

"Only that he was a shirker during the war. And, naturally, he is highly indignant."

"He has a right to be. He did splendidly. His record shows that," declared the girl.

"I urged him to take no notice of the insults. The Spicer woman has a very venomous tongue, my dear! She is a vicar's widow!"

And then they separated to their respective rooms.

Half an hour later Hugh Henfrey retired, but he found sleep impossible; so he got up and sat at the open window, gazing across to the dim outlines of the Surrey hills, picturesque and undulating beneath the stars.

Who could have called him on the telephone? It was a woman, but the voice might have been that of a female telephone operator. Or yet— it might have been that of Dorise! She knew that he was at Shapley and looked it up in the telephone directory. If that were the explanation, then she certainly would not give away the secret of his hiding-place.

Still he was haunted by a great dread the whole of that night. The Sparrow had told him he had acted foolishly in leaving his place of concealment in Kensington. The Sparrow was his firm friend, and in future he intended to obey the little old man's orders implicitly—as so many others did.

Next morning he came down to breakfast before the ladies, and beside his plate he found a letter—addressed to him openly. He had not received one addressed in his real name for many months. Sight of it caused his heart to bound in anxiety, but when he read it he stood rooted to the spot.

Those lines which he read staggered him; the room seemed to revolve, and he re-read them, scarce believing his own eyes.

He realized in that instant that a great blow had fallen upon him, and that all was now hopeless. The sunshine of his life, had in that single instant, been blotted out!

XXI

The Man with Many Names

At the moment he had read the letter Mrs. Bond entered the room. "Hallo! You're down early," she remarked. "And already had your letters, I see! They don't generally come so early. The postman has to walk over from Puttenham."

Then she took up her own and carelessly placed them aside. They consisted mostly of circulars and the accounts of Guildford tradesmen.

"Yes," he said, "I was down early. Lately I've acquired the habit of early rising."

"An excellent habit in a young man," she laughed. "All men who achieve success are early risers—so a Cabinet Minister said the other day. And really, I believe it."

"An hour in the early morning is worth three after dinner. That is why Cabinet Ministers entertain people at breakfast nowadays instead of at dinner. In the morning the brain is fresh and active—a fact recently discovered in our post-war days," Hugh said.

Then, as his hostess turned to the hot-plate upon the sideboard, lifting the covers to see what her cook had provided, he re-scanned the letter which had been openly addressed to him. It was from Dorise:

> I refuse to be deceived any longer, I have discovered that you
> are now a fellow-guest with the girl Louise, to whom you
> introduced me. And yet you arranged to meet me at Farnham,
> believing that I was not aware of your close friendship with
> her! I have believed in you up to the present, but the scales
> have now fallen from my eyes. I thought you loved me too
> well to deceive me—as you are doing. Hard things are being
> said about you—but you can rest content that I shall reveal
> nothing that I happen to know. What I do know, however,
> has changed my thoughts concerning you. I believed you
> to be the victim of circumstance. Now I know you have
> deceived me, and that I, myself, am the victim. I need only
> add that someone else—whom I know not—knows of your

hiding-place, for, by a roundabout way, I heard of it, and hence, I address this letter to you.

Dorise

Hugh Henfrey stood staggered. There was no mistaking the meaning of that letter now that he had read it a second time.

Dorise doubted him! And what answer could he give her? Any explanation must, to her, be but a lame excuse.

Hugh ate his breakfast sullenly. To Louise, who put in a late appearance, and helped herself off the hot-plate, he said cheerfully:

"How lazy you are!"

"It's not laziness, Hugh," replied the girl. "The maid was so late with my tea—and—well, to tell the truth, I upset a whole new box of powder on my dressing-table and had to clean up the mess."

"More haste—less speed," laughed Hugh. "It is always the same in the morning—eh?"

When the girl sat down at the table Hugh had brightened up. Still the load upon his shoulders was a heavy one. He was ever obsessed by the mystery of his father's death, combined with that extraordinary will by which it was decreed that if he married Louise he would acquire his father's fortune.

Louise was certainly very good-looking, and quite charming. He admitted that as he gazed across at her fresh figure on the opposite side of the table. He, of course, was in ignorance of the fact that Benton, who had adopted her, was a clever and unscrupulous adventurer, whose accomplice was the handsome woman who was his hostess.

Naturally, he never dreamed that that quiet and respectable house, high on the beautiful Surrey hills, was the abode of a woman for whom the police of Europe were everywhere searching.

His thoughts all through breakfast were of The Sparrow—the great criminal, who was his friend. Hence, after they rose, he strolled into the morning-room with his hostess, and said:

"I'll have to go to town again this morning. I have an urgent letter. Can Mead take me?"

"Certainly," was the woman's reply. "I have to make a call at Worplesdon this afternoon, and Louise is going with me. But Mead can be back before then to take us."

So half an hour later Hugh was driving up the steep High Street of Guildford on his way to London.

He alighted in Piccadilly, at the end of Half Moon Street, soon after eleven, and, dismissing Mead, made his way to Ellerston Street to the house of Mr. George Peters.

He rang the bell at the old-fashioned mansion, and a few moments later the door was opened by the manservant he had previously seen.

In an instant the servant recognized the visitor.

"Mr. Peters will not be in for a quarter of an hour," he said. "Would you care to wait, sir?"

"Yes," Hugh replied. "I want to see him very urgently."

"Will you come in? Mr. Peters has left instructions that you might probably call; Mr. Henfrey, is it not?"

"Yes," replied Hugh. The man seemed to possess a memory like that of a club hall-porter.

Young Henfrey was ushered into a small but cosy little room, which, in the light of day, he saw was well-furnished and upholstered. The door closed, and he waited.

A few moments after he distinctly heard a man's voice, which he at once recognized as that of The Sparrow.

The servant had told him that Mr. Peters was absent, yet he recognized his voice—a rather high-pitched, musical one.

"Mr. Henfrey is waiting," he heard the servant say.

"Right! I hope you told him I was out," The Sparrow replied.

Then there was silence.

Hugh stood there very much puzzled. The room was cosy and well-furnished, but the light was somewhat dim, while the atmosphere was decidedly murky, as it is in any house in Mayfair. One cannot obtain brightness and light in a West End house, where one's vista is bounded by bricks and mortar. The dukes in their great town mansions are no better off for light and air than the hard-working and worthy wage-earners of Walworth, Deptford, or Peckham. The air in the working-class districts of London is not one whit worse than it is in Mayfair or in Belgravia.

Hugh stood before an old coloured print representing the hobby-horse school—the days of the "bone-shakers"—and studied it. He awaited Il Passero and the advice which he had promised to give.

His ears were strained. That house was curiously quiet and forbidding. The White Cavalier, whom he had believed to be the notorious Sparrow, had been proved to be one of his assistants. He had now met the real, elusive adventurer, who controlled half the criminal adventurers in Europe, and had found in him a most genial friend. He was there to seek his advice and to act upon it.

As he reflected, he realized that without the aid of The Sparrow he would have long ago been in the hands of the police. So widespread was the organization which The Sparrow controlled that it mattered not in what capital he might be, the paternal hand of protection was placed upon him—in Genoa, in Brussels, in London—anywhere.

It seemed that when The Sparrow protected any criminal the fugitive was safe. He had been sent to Mrs. Mason in Kensington, and he had left her room against The Sparrow's will.

Hence his peril of arrest. It was that point which he wished to discuss with the great arch-criminal of Europe.

That house was one of mystery. The servant had told him that he was expected. Why? What did The Sparrow suspect?

The whole atmosphere of that old-fashioned place was mysterious and apprehensive. And yet its owner had succeeded in extricating him from that very perilous position at Monte Carlo!

Suddenly, as he stood there, he heard voices again. They were raised in discussion.

One voice he recognized as that of The Sparrow.

"Well, I tell you my view is still the same," he exclaimed. "What you have told me does not alter it, however much you may ridicule me!"

"Then you know the truth—eh?"

"I really didn't say so, my dear Howell. But I have my suspicions—strong suspicions."

"Which you will, in due course, impart to young Henfrey, I suppose?"

"I shall do nothing of the sort," was The Sparrow's reply. "The lad is in serious peril. I happen to know that."

"Then why don't you warn him at once?"

"That's my affair!" snapped the gentleman known in Mayfair as Mr. Peters.

"If Henfrey is here, then I'd like to meet him," Howell said.

It seemed as though the pair were in a room on the opposite side of the passage, and yet, though Hugh stood at some distance away, he could hear the words quite distinctly. At this he was much surprised. He did not, however, know that in that house in Ellerston Street there had been constructed a curious system of ventilation of the rooms by which a conversation taking place in a distant apartment could be heard in certain other rooms.

WILLIAM LE QUEUX

The fact was that The Sparrow received a good many queer visitors, and some of their whispered conversations while they awaited him were often full of interest.

The house was, in more than one way, a curiosity. It had a secret exit through a mews at the rear—now converted into a garage—and several other mysterious contrivances which were unsuspected by visitors.

"It would hardly do for him to know what we know, Mr. Peters—eh?" Hugh heard Howell say a moment later. It was the habit of The Sparrow's accomplices to address their great director—the brain of criminal Europe—by the name under which they inquired for him. The Sparrow had twenty names—one for every city in which he had a cosy *pied-a-terre*. In Paris, Lisbon, Madrid, Marseilles, Vienna, Hamburg, Budapest, Stockholm and on the Riviera, he was, in all the cities, known by a different name. Yet each was so distinct, and each individuality so well kept up, that he snapped his fingers at the police and pitied them their red tape, ignorance, and lack of initiative.

Truly, Il Passero, the cosmopolitan of many names and half a dozen nationalities, had brought criminality to a fine art.

Hugh, standing there breathless, listened to every word. Who was this man Howell?

"Hush!" cried The Sparrow suddenly. "What a fool I am! I quite forgot to close the ventilator in the room to which the young fellow has been shown! I hope he hasn't overheard! I had Evans and Janson in there an hour ago, and they were discussing me, as I expected they would! It was a good job that I took the precaution of opening the ventilator, because I learned a good deal that I had never suspected. It has placed me on my guard. I'll go and get young Henfrey. But," he added, "be extremely careful. Disclose nothing you know concerning the affair."

"I shall be discreet, never fear," replied his visitor.

A moment later The Sparrow entered the room where Henfrey was, and greeted him warmly. Then he ushered him down the passage to the room wherein stood his mysterious visitor.

The room was such a distance away that Hugh was surprised that he could have heard so distinctly. But, after all, it was an uncanny experience to be associated with that man of mystery, whose very name was uttered by his accomplices with bated breath.

"My friend, Mr. George Howell," said The Sparrow, introducing the slim, wiry-looking, middle-aged man, who was alert and clean-shaven, and plainly but well dressed—a man whom the casual acquaintance would take to be a solicitor of a fair practice. He bore the stamp of suburbia all over him, and his accent was peculiarly that of London.

His bearing was that of high respectability. The diamond scarf-pin was his only ornament—a fine one, which sparkled even in that dull London light. He was a square-shouldered man, with peculiarly shrewd, rather narrow eyes, and dark, bushy eyebrows.

"Glad to meet you, Mr. Henfrey," he replied, with a gay, rather nonchalant air. "My friend Mr. Peters has been speaking about you. Had a rather anxious time, I hear."

Henfrey looked at the stranger inquisitively, and then glanced at The Sparrow.

"Mr. Howell is quite safe," declared the man with the gloved hand. "He is one of Us. So you may speak without fear."

"Well," replied the young man, "the fact is, I've had a very apprehensive time. I'm here to seek Mr. Peters' kind advice, for without him I'm sure I'd have been arrested and perhaps convicted long ago."

"Oh! A bit of bad luck—eh? Nearly found out, have you been? Ah! All of us have our narrow escapes. I've had many in my time," and he grinned.

"So have all of us," laughed the bristly-haired man. "But tell me, Henfrey, why have you come to see me so quickly?"

"Because they know where I'm in hiding!"

"They know? Who knows?"

"Miss Ranscomb knows my whereabouts and has written to me in my real name and addressed the letter to Shapley."

"Well, what of that?" he asked. "I told her."

"She tells me that my present hiding-place is known!"

"Not known to the police? *Impossible*!" gasped the black-gloved man.

"I take it that such is a fact."

"Why, Molly is there!" cried the man Howell. "If the police suspect that Henfrey is at Shapley, then they'll visit the place and have a decided haul."

"Why?" asked Hugh in ignorance.

"Nothing. I never discuss other people's private affairs, Mr. Henfrey," Howell answered very quietly.

Hugh was surprised at the familiar mention of "Molly," and the declaration that if the Manor were searched the police would have "a decided haul."

"This is very interesting," declared The Sparrow. "What did Miss Ranscomb say in her letter?"

For a second Hugh hesitated; then, drawing it from his pocket, he gave it to the gloved man to read.

Hugh knew that The Sparrow was withholding certain truths from him, yet had he not already proved himself his best and only friend? Brock was a good friend, but unable to assist him.

The Sparrow's strongly marked face changed as he read Dorise's angry letter.

"H'm!" he grunted. "I will see her. We must discover why she has sent you this warning. Come back again this evening. But be very careful where you go in the meantime."

Thus dismissed, Hugh walked along Ellerston Street into Curzon Street towards Piccadilly, not knowing where to go to spend the intervening hours.

The instant he had gone, however, The Sparrow turned to his companion, who said:

"I wonder if Lisette has revealed anything?"

"By Jove!" remarked The Sparrow, for once suddenly perturbed. *"I never thought of that!"*

XXII

CLOSING THE NET

W ell—recollect how much the girl knows!" Howell remarked as he stood before The Sparrow in the latter's room.

"I have not forgotten," said the other. "The whole circumstances of old Henfrey's death are not known to me. That it was an unfortunate affair has long ago been proved."

"Yvonne was the culprit, of course," said Howell. "That was apparent from the first."

"I suppose she was," remarked The Sparrow reflectively. "But that attempt upon her life puzzles me."

"Who could have greater motive in killing her out of revenge than the dead man's son?"

"Agreed. But I am convinced that the lad is innocent. Therefore I gave him our protection."

"I was travelling abroad at the time, you recollect. When I learnt of the affair through Franklyn about a week afterwards I was amazed. The loss of Yvonne to us is a serious one."

"Very—I agree. She had done some excellent work—the affair in the Rue Royale, for instance."

"And the clever ruse by which she got those emeralds of the Roumanian princess. The Vienna police are still searching for her—after three years," laughed the companion of the chief of the international organization, whose word was law in the criminal underworld of Europe.

"Knowing what you did regarding the knowledge of old Mr. Henfrey's death possessed by Lisette, I have been surprised that you placed her beneath your protection."

"If she had been arrested she might have told some very unpleasant truths, in order to save herself," The Sparrow remarked, "so I chose the latter evil."

"Young Henfrey met her. I wonder whether she told him anything?"

"No. I questioned her. She was discreet, it seems. Or at least, she declares that she was."

"That's a good feature. But, speaking frankly, have you any idea of the identity of the person—man or woman—who attempted to kill Yvonne?" asked Howell.

"I have a suspicion—a pretty shrewd suspicion," replied the little bristly-haired man.

His companion was silent.

"And you don't offer to confide in me your suspicions—eh?"

"It is wiser to obtain proof before making any allegations," answered The Sparrow, smiling.

"You will still protect Lisette?" Howell asked. "I agree that, like Yvonne, she has been of great use to us in many ways. Beauty and wit are always assets in our rather ticklish branch of commerce. Where is Lisette now?"

"At the moment, she's in Madrid," The Sparrow replied. "There is a little affair there—the jewels of a Belgian's wife—a fellow who, successfully posing as a German during the occupation of Brussels, made a big fortune by profiteering in leather. They are in Madrid for six months, in order to escape unwelcome inquiries by the Government in Brussels. They have a villa just outside the city, and I have sent Lisette there with certain instructions."

"Who is with her?"

"Nobody yet. Franklyn will go in due course."

Howell's thin lips relaxed into a curious smile.

"Franklyn is in love with Lisette," he remarked.

"That is why I am sending them together to execute the little mission," The Sparrow said. "Lisette was here a fortnight ago, and I mapped out for her a plan. I went myself to Madrid not long ago, in order to survey the situation."

"The game is worth the candle, I suppose—eh?"

"Yes. If we get the lot Van Groot, in Amsterdam, will give at least fifteen thousand for them. Moulaert bought most of them from old Leplae in the Rue de la Paix. There are some beautiful rubies among them. I saw Madame wearing some of the jewels at the Palace Hotel, in Madrid, while they were staying there before their villa was ready. Moulaert, with his wife and two friends from the Belgian Legation, dined at a table next to mine, little dreaming with what purpose I ate my meal alone."

Truly, the intuition and cleverness of The Sparrow were wonderful. He never moved without fully considering every phase of the consequences. Unlike most adventurers, he drank hardly anything. Half a glass of dry sherry at eleven in the morning, the same at luncheon, and one glass of claret for his dinner.

Yet often at restaurants he would order champagne, choice vintage clarets, and liqueurs—when occasion demanded. He would offer them to his friends, but just sip them himself, having previously arranged with the waiter to miss filling his glass.

Of the peril of drink "Mr. Peters" was constantly lecturing the great circle of his friends.

Each year—on the 26th of February to be exact—there was held a dinner at a well-known restaurant in the West End—the annual dinner of a club known as "The Wonder Wizards." It was supposed to be a circle of professional conjurers.

This dinner was usually attended by fifty guests of both sexes, all well-dressed and prosperous, and of several nationalities. It was presided over by a Mr. Charles Williams.

Now, to tell the truth, the guests believed him to be The Sparrow; but in reality Mr. Williams was the tall White Cavalier whom Hugh had believed to be the great leader, until he had gone to Mayfair and met the impelling personality whom the police had for so long failed to arrest.

The situation was indeed humorous. It was The Sparrow's fancy to hold the reunion at a public restaurant instead of at a private house. Under the very nose of Scotland Yard the deputy of the notorious Sparrow entertained the chiefs of the great criminal octopus. There were speeches, but from them the waiters learned nothing. It was simply a club of conjurers. None suspected that the guests were those who conjured fortunes out of the pockets of the unsuspecting. And while the chairman—believed by those who attended to be The Sparrow himself—sat there, the bristly-haired, rather insignificant-looking little man occupied a seat in a far-off corner, from where he scrutinized his guests very closely, and smiled at the excellent manner in which his deputy performed the duties of chairman.

Because it was a club of conjurers, and because the conjurers displayed their new tricks and illusions, after an excellent dinner the waiters were excluded and the doors locked after the coffee.

It was then that the bogus Sparrow addressed those present, and gave certain instructions which were later on carried into every corner of Europe. Each member had his speciality, and each group its district and its sanctuary, in case of a hue-and-cry. Every crime that could be committed was committed by them—everything save murder.

WILLIAM LE QUEUX

The tall, thin man whom everyone believed to be The Sparrow never failed to impress upon his hearers, after the doors were carefully locked, that however they might attack and rob the rich, human life was sacred.

It was the real Sparrow's order. He abominated the thought of taking human life, hence when old Mr. Henfrey had been foully done to death in the West End he had at once set to work to discover the actual criminal. This he had failed to do. And afterwards there had followed the attempted assassination of Yvonne Ferad, known as Mademoiselle of Monte Carlo.

The two men stood discussing the young French girl, Lisette, whom Hugh had met when in hiding in the Via della Maddalena in Genoa.

"I only hope; that she has not told young Henfrey anything," Howell said, with distinct apprehension.

"No," laughed The Sparrow. "She came to me and told me how she had met him in Genoa and discovered to her amazement that he was old Henfrey's son."

"How curious that the pair should meet by accident," remarked Howell. "I tell you that Benton is not playing a straight game. That iniquitous will which the old man left he surely must have signed under some misapprehension. Perhaps he thought he was applying for a life policy—or something of that short. Signatures to wills have been procured under many pretexts by scoundrelly relatives and unscrupulous lawyers."

"I know. And the witnesses have placed their signatures afterward," remarked The Sparrow thoughtfully. "But in this case all seems above board—at least so far as the will is concerned. Benton was old Henfrey's bosom friend. Henfrey was very taken with Louise, and I know that he was desirous Hugh should marry her."

"And if he did, Hugh would acquire the old man's fortune, and Benton would step in and seize it—as is his intention."

"Undoubtedly. All we can do is to keep Hugh and Louise apart. The latter is in entire ignorance of the true profession of her adopted father, and she'd be horrified if she knew that Molly was simply a clever adventuress, who is very much wanted in Paris and in Brussels," said the gloved man.

"A good job that she knows nothing," said Howell. "But it would be a revelation to her if the police descended upon Shapley Manor—wouldn't it?"

"Yes. That is why I must see Dorise Ranscomb and ascertain from her exactly what she has heard. I know the police tracked Hugh to London, and for that reason he went with Benton down into Surrey—out of the frying-pan into the fire."

"Well, before we can go farther, it seems that we should ascertain who shot Yvonne," Howell suggested. "It was a most dastardly thing, and whoever did it ought to be punished."

"He ought. But I'm as much in the dark as you are, Howell; but, as I have already said, I entertain strong suspicions."

"I'll suggest one name—Benton?"

The Sparrow shook his head.

"The manservant, Giulio Cataldi?" Howell ventured. "I never liked that sly old Italian."

"What motive could the old fellow have had?"

"Robbery, probably. We have no idea what were Yvonne's winnings that night—or of the money she had in her bag."

"Yes, we do know," was The Sparrow's reply. "According to the police report, Yvonne, on her return home, went to her room, carrying her bag, which she placed upon her dressing-table. Then, after removing her cloak and hat, she went downstairs again and out on to the veranda. A few minutes later the young man was announced. High words were heard by old Cataldi, and then a shot."

"And Yvonne's bag?"

"It was found where she had left it. In it were three thousand eight hundred francs, all in notes."

"Yet Franklyn told me that he had heard how Yvonne won quite a large sum that night."

"She might have done so—and have lost the greater part of it," The Sparrow replied.

"On the other hand, what more feasible than that the old manservant, watching her place it there, abstracted the bulk of the money—a large sum, no doubt—and afterwards, in order to conceal his crime, shot his mistress in such circumstances as to place the onus of the crime upon her midnight visitor?"

"That the affair was very cleverly planned there is no doubt," said The Sparrow. "There is a distinct intention to fasten the guilt upon young Henfrey, because he alone would have a motive for revenge for the death of his father. Of that fact the man or woman who fired the shot was most certainly aware. How could Cataldi have known of it?"

"I certainly believe the Italian robbed his mistress and afterwards attempted to murder her," Howell insisted.

"He might rob his mistress, certainly. He might even have robbed her of considerable sums systematically," The Sparrow assented. "The maids told the police that Mademoiselle's habit was to leave her bag with her winnings upon the dressing-table while she went downstairs and took a glass of wine."

"Exactly. She did so every evening. Her habits were regular. Yet she never knew the extent of her winnings at the tables before she counted them. And she never did so until the following morning. That is what Franklyn told me in Venice when we met a month afterwards."

"He learnt that from me," The Sparrow said with a smile. "No," he went on; "though old Cataldi could well have robbed his mistress, just as the maids could have done, and Yvonne would have been none the wiser, yet I do not think he would attempt to conceal his crime by shooting her, because by so doing he cut off all future supplies. If he were a thief he would not be such a fool. Therefore you may rest assured, Howell, that the hand that fired the shot was that of some person who desired to close Yvonne's mouth."

"She might have held some secret concerning old Cataldi. Or, on his part, he might have cherished some grievance against her. Italians are usually very vindictive," replied the visitor. "On the other hand, it would be to Benton's advantage that the truth concerning old Henfrey's death was suppressed. Yvonne was about to tell the young man something—perhaps confess the truth, who knows?—when the shot was fired."

"Well, my dear Howell, you have your opinion and I have mine," laughed The Sparrow. "The latter I shall keep to myself—until my theory is disproved."

Thereupon Howell took a cigar that his host offered him, and while he slowly lit it, The Sparrow crossed to the telephone.

He quickly found Lady Ranscomb's number in the directory, and a few moments later was talking to the butler, of whom he inquired for Miss Dorise.

"Tell her," he added, "that a friend of Mr. Henfrey's wishes to speak to her."

In a few moments The Sparrow heard the girl's voice.

"Yes?" she inquired. "Who is speaking?"

"A friend of Mr. Henfrey," was the reply of the man with the gloved hand. "You will probably guess who it is."

He heard a little nervous laugh, and then:

"Oh, yes. I—I have an idea, but I can't talk to you over the 'phone. I've got somebody who's just called. Mother is out—and—" Then she lowered her voice, evidently not desirous of being heard in the adjoining room. "Well, I don't know what to do."

"What do you mean? Does it concern Mr. Henfrey?"

"Yes. It does. There's a man here to see me from Scotland Yard! What shall I do?"

The Sparrow gasped at the girl's announcement.

Next second he recovered himself.

"A man from Scotland Yard!" he echoed. "Why has he called?"

"He knows that Mr. Henfrey is living at Shapley, in Surrey. And he has been asking whether I am acquainted with you."

XXIII

What Lisette Knew

A fortnight had gone by.

Ten o'clock in the morning in the Puerta del Sol, that great plaza in Madrid—the fine square which, like the similarly-named gates at Toledo and Segovia, commands a view of the rising sun, as does the ancient Temple of Abu Simbel on the Nile.

Hugh Henfrey—a smart, lithe figure in blue serge—had been lounging for ten minutes before the long facade of the Ministerio de la Gobernacion (or Ministry of the Interior) smoking a cigarette and looking eagerly across the great square. The two soldiers on sentry at the door, suspicious of all foreigners in the days of Bolshevism and revolution, had eyed him narrowly. But he appeared to be inoffensive, so they had passed him by as a harmless lounger.

Five minutes later a smartly-dressed girl, with short skirt, silk stockings, and a pretty hat, came along the pavement, and Hugh sprang forward to greet her.

It was Lisette, the girl whom he had met when in hiding in that back street in Genoa.

"Well?" he exclaimed. "So here we are! The Sparrow sent me to you."

"Yes. I had a telegram from him four days ago ordering me to meet you. Strange things are happening—it seems!"

"How?" asked the young Englishman, in ignorance of the great conspiracy or of what was taking place. "Since I saw you last, mademoiselle, I have been moving about rapidly, and always in danger of arrest."

"So have I. But I am here at The Sparrow's orders—on a little business which I hope to bring off successfully on any evening. I have an English friend with me—a Mr. Franklyn."

"I left London suddenly. I saw The Sparrow in the evening, and next morning, at eleven o'clock, without even a bag, I left London for Madrid with a very useful passport."

"You are here because Madrid is safer for you than London, I suppose?" said the girl in broken English.

"That is so. A certain Mr. Howell, a friend of The Sparrow's suggested that I should come here," Hugh explained. "Ever since we met in Italy I have been in close hiding until, by some means, my whereabouts became known, and I had to fly."

The smartly-dressed girl walked slowly at his side and, for some moments, remained silent.

"Ah! So you have met Hamilton Shaw—alias Howell?" she remarked at last in a changed voice. "He certainly is not your friend."

"Not my friend! Why? I've only met him lately."

"You say that the police knew of your hiding-place," said mademoiselle, speaking in French, as it was easier for her. "Would you be surprised if Howell had revealed your secret?"

"Howell!" gasped Hugh. "Yes, I certainly would. He is a close friend of The Sparrow!"

"That may be. But that does not prove that he is any friend of yours. If you came here at Howell's suggestion—then, Mr. Henfrey, I should advise you to leave Madrid at once. I say this because I have a suspicion that he intends both of us to fall into a trap!"

"But why? I don't understand."

"I can give you no explanation," said the girl. "Now I know that Hamilton Shaw sent you here, I can, I think, discern his motive. I myself will see Mr. Franklyn at once, and shall leave Madrid as soon as possible. And I advise you, Mr. Henfrey, to do the same."

"Surely you don't suspect that it was this Mr. Howell who gave me away to Scotland Yard!" exclaimed Hugh, surprised, but at the same time recollecting that The Sparrow had been alarmed at the detective's visit to Dorise. He knew that Benton and Mrs. Bond had suddenly disappeared from Shapley, but the reason he could only guess. He had, of course, no proof that Benton and Molly were members of the great criminal organization. He only knew that Benton had been his late father's closest friend.

He discussed the situation with the girl jewel-thief as they walked along the busy Carrera de San Jeronimo wherein are the best shops in Madrid, to the great Plaza de Canovas in the leafy Prado.

Again he tried to extract from her what she knew concerning his father's death. But she would tell him nothing.

"I am not permitted to say anything, Mr. Henfrey. I can only regret it," she said quietly. "Mr. Franklyn is at the Ritz opposite. I should like you to meet him."

And she took him across to the elegant hotel opposite the Neptune fountain, where, in a private sitting-room on the second floor, she introduced him to a rather elderly, aristocratic-looking Englishman, whom none would take to be one of the most expert jewel-thieves in Europe.

When the door was closed and they were alone, mademoiselle suddenly revealed to her friend what Hugh had said concerning Howell's suggestion that he should travel to Madrid.

Franklyn's face changed. He was instantly apprehensive.

"Then we certainly are not safe here any longer. Howell probably intends to play us false! We shall know from The Sparrow the reason we are here, and, for aught we know, the police are watching and will arrest us red-handed. No," he added, "we must leave this place—all three of us—as soon as possible. You, Lisette, had better go to Paris and explain matters to The Sparrow, while I shall fade away to Switzerland. And you, Mr. Henfrey? Where will you go?"

"To France," was Hugh's reply, on the spur of the moment. "I can get to Marseilles."

"Yes. Go by way of Barcelona. It is quickest," said the Englishman. "The express leaves just after three o'clock."

Then, after he had thanked Hugh for his timely warning, the latter walked out more than ever mystified at the attitude of The Sparrow's accomplices.

It did not seem possible that Howell should have told Scotland Yard that he was hiding at Shapley; yet it was quite evident that both mademoiselle and her companion were equally in fear of the man Howell, whose real name was Hamilton Shaw. The theory seemed to him a thin one, for Howell was The Sparrow's intimate friend.

Yet, mademoiselle, while they had been discussing the situation, had denounced him as their enemy, declaring that The Sparrow himself should be warned of him.

That afternoon Hugh, having only been in Madrid twelve hours, left again on the long, dusty railway journey across Spain to Zaragoza and down the valley of the Ebro to the Mediterranean. After crossing the French frontier, he broke the journey at the old-world town of Nimes for a couple of days, and then went on to Marseilles, where he took up his quarters in the big Louvre et Paix Hotel, still utterly mystified, and still not daring to write to Dorise.

It was as well that he left Madrid, for, just as Lisette and Franklyn had suspected, the police called at his hotel—an obscure one near the station—only two hours after his departure. Then, finding him gone, they sought both mademoiselle and Franklyn, only to find that they also had fled.

Someone had given away their secret!

On arrival at Marseilles in the evening Hugh ate his dinner alone in the hotel, and then strolled up the well-lit Cannebiere, with its many smart shops and gay cafes—that street which, to many thousands on their way to the Near or Far East, is their last glimpse of European life. He was entirely at a loose end.

Unnoticed behind him there walked an undersized little Frenchman, an alert, business-like man of about forty-five, who had awaited him outside his hotel, and who leisurely followed him up the broad, main street of that busy city.

He was well-dressed, possessing a pair of shrewd, searching eyes, and a moustache carefully trimmed. His appearance was that of a prosperous French tradesman—one of thousands one meets in the city of Marseilles.

As Hugh idled along, gazing into some of the shop windows as he lazily smoked his cigarette, the under-sized stranger kept very careful watch upon his movements. He evidently intended that he should not escape observation. Hugh paused at a tobacconist's and bought some stamps, but as he came out of the shop, the watcher drew back suddenly and in such a manner as to reveal to anyone who might have observed him that he was no tyro in the art of surveillance.

Walking a little farther along, Hugh came to the corner of the broad Rue de Rome, where he entered a crowded cafe in which an orchestra was playing.

He had taken a corner seat in the window, had ordered his coffee, and was glancing at the *Petit Parisien*, which he had taken from his pocket, when another man entered, gazed around in search of a seat and, noticing one at Hugh's table, crossed, lifted his hat, and took the vacant chair.

He was the stranger who had followed him from the Louvre et Paix.

The young Englishman, all unsuspecting, glanced at the newcomer, and then resumed his paper, while the keen-eyed little man took a long, thin cigar which the waiter brought, lit it carefully, and sipped his coffee, his interest apparently centred in the music.

Suddenly a tall, dark-haired woman, who had been sitting near by with a man who seemed to be her husband, rose and left. A moment

WILLIAM LE QUEUX

before she had exchanged glances with the watcher, who, apparently at her bidding, rose and followed her.

All this seemed quite unnoticed by Hugh, immersed as he was in his newspaper.

Outside the man and woman met. They held hurried consultation. The woman told him something which evidently caused him sudden surprise.

"I will call on you at eleven to-morrow morning, madame," he said.

"No. I will meet you at the Reserve. I will lunch there at twelve. You will lunch with me?"

"Very well," he answered. "*Au revoir*," and he returned to his seat in the cafe, while she disappeared without returning to her companion.

The mysterious watcher resumed his coffee, for he had only been absent for a few moments, and the waiter had not cleared it away.

Hugh took out his cigarette-case and, suddenly finding himself without a match, made the opportunity for which the mysterious stranger had been waiting.

He struck one and handed it to his *vis-a-vis*, bowing with his foreign grace.

Then they naturally dropped into conversation.

"Ah! m'sieur is English!" exclaimed the shrewd-eyed little man. "Here, in Marseilles, we have many English who pass to and fro from the boats. I suppose, m'sieur is going East?" he suggested affably.

"No," replied Hugh, speaking in French, "I have some business here—that is all." He was highly suspicious of all strangers, and the more so of anyone who endeavoured to get into conversation with him.

"You know Marseilles—of course?" asked the stranger, sharply scrutinizing him.

"I have been here several times before. I find the city always gay and bright."

"Not so bright as before the war," declared the little man, smoking at his ease. "There have been many changes lately."

Hugh Henfrey could not make the fellow out. Yet many times before he had been addressed by strangers who seemed to question him out of curiosity, and for no apparent reason. This man was one of them, no doubt.

The man, who had accompanied the woman whom the stranger had followed out, rose, exchanged a significant glance with the little man, and walked out. That the three were in accord seemed quite apparent, though Hugh was still unsuspicious.

He chatted merrily with the stranger for nearly half an hour, and then rose and left the cafe. When quite close to the hotel the stranger overtook him, and halting, asked in a low voice, in very good English:

"I believe you are Mr. Henfrey—are you not?"

"Why do you ask that?" inquired Hugh, much surprised. "My name is Jordan—William Jordan."

"Yes," laughed the man. "That is, I know, the name you have given at the hotel. But your real name is Henfrey."

Hugh started. The stranger, noticing his alarm, hastened to reassure him.

XXIV

Friend or Enemy?

"You need not worry," said the stranger to Hugh. "I am not your enemy, but a friend. I warn you that Marseilles is unsafe for you. Get away as soon as possible. The Spanish police have learnt that you have come here," he went on as he strolled at his side.

Hugh was amazed.

"How did you know my identity?" he asked eagerly.

"I was instructed to watch for your arrival—and to warn you."

"Who instructed you?"

"A friend of yours—and mine—The Sparrow."

"Has he been here?"

"No. He spoke to me on the telephone from Paris."

"What were his instructions?"

"That you were to go at once—to-night—by car to the Hotel de Paris, at Cette. A car and driver awaits you at the Garage Beauvau, in the Rue Beauvau. I have arranged everything at The Sparrow's orders. You are one of Us, I understand," and the man laughed lightly.

"But my bag?" exclaimed Hugh.

"Go to the hotel, pay your bill, and take your bag to the station cloak-room. Then go and get the car, pick up your bag, and get out on the road to Cette as soon as ever you can. Your driver will ask no questions, and will remain silent. He has his orders from The Sparrow."

"Does The Sparrow ever come to Marseilles?" Hugh asked.

"Yes, sometimes—when anything really big brings him here. I have, however, only seen him once, five years ago. He was at your hotel, and the police were so hot upon his track that only by dint of great promptitude and courage he escaped by getting out of the window of his room and descending by means of the rain-water pipe. It was one of the narrowest escapes he has ever had."

As the words left the man's mouth, they were passing a well-lit brasserie. A tall, cadaverous man passed them and Hugh had a suspicion that they exchanged glances of recognition.

Was his pretended friend an agent of the police?

For a few seconds he debated within himself how he should act. To refuse to do as he was bid might be to bring instant arrest upon himself. If the stranger were actually a detective—which he certainly did not appear to be—then the ruse was to get him on the road to Cette because the legal formalities were not yet complete for his arrest as a British subject.

Yet he knew all about The Sparrow, and his attitude was not in the least hostile.

Hugh could not make up his mind whether the stranger was an associate of the famous Sparrow, or whether he was very cleverly inveigling him into the net.

It was only that exchange of glances with the passer-by which had aroused Hugh's suspicions.

But that significant look caused him to hesitate to accept the mysterious stranger as his friend.

True, he had accepted as friends numbers of other unknown persons since that fateful night at Monte Carlo. Yet in this case, he felt, by intuition, that all was not plain sailing.

"Very well," he said, at last. "I esteem it a very great favour that you should have interested yourself on behalf of one who is an entire stranger to you, and I heartily thank you for warning me of my danger. When I see The Sparrow I shall tell him how cleverly you approached me, and how perfect were your arrangements for my escape."

"I require no thanks or reward, Mr. Henfrey," replied the man politely. "My one desire is to get you safely out of Marseilles."

And with that the stranger lifted his hat and left him.

Hugh went about fifty yards farther along the broad, well-lit street full of life and movement, for the main streets of Marseilles are alive both day and night.

By some intuition—why, he knew not—he suspected that affable little man who had posed as his friend. Was it possible that, believing the notorious Sparrow to be his friend, he had at haphazard invented the story, and posed as one of The Sparrow's gang?

If so, it was certainly a very clever and ingenious subterfuge.

He was undecided how to act. He did not wish to give offence to his friend, the king of the underworld, and yet he felt a distinct suspicion of the man who had so cleverly approached him, and who had openly declared himself to be a crook.

That strange glance he had exchanged with the passer-by beneath the rays of the street-lamp had been mysterious and significant. If the passer-by had been a crook, like himself, the sign of recognition would be one of salutation. But the expression upon his alleged friend's face was one of triumph. That made all the difference, and to Hugh, with his observation quickened as it had been in those months of living with daily dread of arrest, it had caused him to be seized with strong and distinct suspicions.

He felt in his hip pocket and found that his revolver, an American Smith-Wesson, was there. He had a dislike of automatic pistols, as he had once had a very narrow escape. He had been teaching a girl to shoot with a revolver, when, believing that she had discharged the whole magazine, he was examining the weapon and pulled the trigger, narrowly escaping shooting her dead.

For a few seconds he stood upon the broad pavement. Then he drew out his cigarette-case. In it were four cigarettes, two of which The Sparrow had given him when in London.

"Yes," he muttered to himself. "Somebody must have given me away at Shapley, and now they have followed me! I will act for myself, and take the risks."

Then he walked boldly on, crossed the road, and entered the big Hotel de Louvre et Paix. To appear unconcerned he had a drink at the bar, and ascending in the lift, called the floor-waiter, asked for his bill, and packed his bag.

"Ah!" he said to himself. "If I could only get to know where The Sparrow is and ask him the truth! He may be at that address in Paris which he gave me."

After a little delay the bill was brought and he paid it. Then in a taxi he drove to the station where he deposited his bag in the cloak-room.

Close by the *consigne* a woman was standing. He glanced at her, when, to his surprise, he saw that she was the same woman who had been sitting in the cafe with a male companion.

Was she, he wondered, in league with his so-called friend? And if so, what was intended.

Sight of that woman lounging there, however, decided him. She was, no doubt, awaiting his coming.

He walked out of the great railway terminus, and, inquiring the way to the Rue Beauvau, soon found the garage where a powerful open car was awaiting him in the roadway outside.

A smart driver in a dark overcoat came forward, and apparently recognizing Hugh from a description that had been given to him, touched his cap, and asked in French:

"Where does m'sieur wish to go?"

"To the station to fetch my coat and bag," replied the young Englishman, peering into the driver's face. He was a clean-shaven man of about forty, broad-shouldered and stalwart. Was it possible that the car had been hired by the police, and the driver was himself a police agent?

"Very well, m'sieur," the man answered politely. And Hugh having entered, he drove up the Boulevard de la Liberte to the Gare St. Charles.

As he approached the *consigne*, he looked along the platform, and there, sure enough, was the same woman on the watch, though she pretended to be without the slightest interest in his movements.

Hugh put on his coat, and, carrying his bag, placed it in the car.

"You have your orders?" asked Hugh.

"Yes, m'sieur. We are to go to Cette with all speed. Is not that so?"

"Yes," was Hugh's reply. "I will come up beside you. I prefer it. We shall have a long, dark ride to-night."

"Ah! but the roads are good," was the man's reply. "I came from Cette yesterday," he added, as he mounted to his seat and the passenger got up beside him.

Hugh sat there very thoughtful as the car sped out of the city of noise and bustle. The man's remark that he had come from Cette on the previous day gave colour to the idea that no net had been spread, but that the stranger was acting at the orders of the ubiquitous Sparrow. Indeed, were it not for the strange glance the undersized little man had given to the passer-by, he would have been convinced that he was actually once again under the protection of the all-powerful ruler of the criminal underworld.

As it was, he remained suspicious. He did not like that woman who had watched so patiently his coming and going at the station.

With strong headlights glaring—for the night was extremely dark and a strong wind was blowing—they were soon out on the broad highway which leads first across the plain and then beside the sea, and again across the lowlands to old-world Arles.

It was midnight before they got to the village of Lancon, an obscure little place in total darkness.

But on the way the driver, who had told Hugh that his name was

Henri Aramon, and who insinuated that he was one of The Sparrow's associates, became most affable and talkative. Over those miles of dark roads, unfamiliar to Hugh, they travelled at high speed, for Henri had from the first showed himself to be an expert driver, not only in the unceasing traffic of the main streets of Marseilles, but also on the dark, much-worn roads leading out of the city. The roads around Marseilles have never been outstanding for their excellence, and after the war they were indeed execrable.

"This is Lancon," the driver remarked, as they sped through the dark little town. "We now go on to Salon, where we have a direct road across the plain they call the Crau into Arles. From there the road to Cette is quite good and straight. The road we are now on is the worst," he added.

Hugh was undecided. Was the man who was driving him so rapidly out of the danger zone his friend—or his enemy?

He sat there for over an hour unable to decide.

"This is an outlandish part of France," he remarked to the driver presently.

"Yes. But after Salon it is more desolate."

"And is there no railway near?"

"After Salon, yes. It runs parallel with the road about two miles to the north—the railway between Arles and Aix-en-Provence."

"So if we get a breakdown, which I hope we shall not, we are not far from a railway?" Hugh remarked, as through the night the heavy car tore along that open desolate road.

As he sat there he thought of Dorise, wondering what had happened—and of Louise. If he had obeyed his father's wishes and married the latter all the trouble would have been avoided, he thought. Yet he loved Dorise—loved her with his whole soul.

And she doubted him.

Poor fellow! Hustled from pillar to post, and compelled to resort to every ruse in order to avoid arrest for a crime which he did not commit, yet about which he could not establish his innocence, he very often despaired. At that moment he felt somehow—how he could not explain—that he was in a very tight corner. He felt confident after two hours of reflection that he was being driven over these roads that night in order that the police should gain time to execute some legal formality for his arrest.

Why had not the police of Marseilles arrested him? There was some subtle motive for sending him to Cette.

He had not had time to send a telegram to Mr. Peters in London, or to Monsieur Gautier, the name by which The Sparrow told him he was known at his flat in the Rue des Petits Champs, in the centre of Paris. He longed to be able to communicate with his all-powerful friend, but there had been no opportunity.

Suddenly the car began to pass through banks of mist, which are usual at night over the low marshes around the mouths of the Rhone. It was about half-past two in the morning. They had passed through the long dark streets of Salon, and were already five or six miles on the broad straight road which runs across the marshes through St. Martin-de-Crau into Arles.

Of a sudden Hugh declared that he must have a cigarette, and producing his case handed one to the driver and took one himself. Then he lit the man's, and afterwards his own.

"It is cold here on the marshes, monsieur," remarked the driver, his cigarette between his lips. "This mist, too, is puzzling. But it is nearly always like this at night. That is why nobody lives about here."

"Is it quite deserted?"

"Yes, except for a few shepherds, and they live up north at the foot of the hills."

For some ten minutes or so they kept on, but Hugh had suddenly become very watchful of the driver.

Presently the man exclaimed in French:

"I do not feel very well!"

"What is the matter?" asked Hugh in alarm. "You must not be taken ill here—so far from anywhere!"

But the man was evidently unwell, for he pulled up the car.

"Oh! my head!" he cried, putting both hands to his brow as the cigarette dropped from his lips. "My head! It seems as if it will burst! And—and I can't see! Everything is going round—round! Where—where am I?"

"You are all right, my friend. Get into the back of the car and rest. You will be yourself very quickly."

And he half dragged the man from his seat and placed him in the back of the car, where he fell inert and unconscious.

The cigarette which The Sparrow had given to Hugh only to be used in case of urgent necessity had certainly done its work. The man, whether friend or enemy, would now remain unconscious for many hours.

Hugh, having settled him in the bottom of the car, placed a rug over him. Then, mounting to the driver's place, he turned the car and drove as rapidly as he dared back over the roads to Salon.

Time after time, he wondered whether he had been misled; whether, after all, the man who had driven him was actually acting under The Sparrow's orders. If so, then he had committed a fatal error!

However, the die was cast. He had acted upon his own initiative, and if a net had actually been spread to catch him he had successfully broken through it. He laughed as he thought of the police at Cette awaiting his arrival, and their consternation when hour after hour passed without news of the car from Marseilles.

At Salon he passed half way through the town to cross roads where he had noticed in passing a sign-board which indicated the road to Avignon—the broad high road from Marseilles to Paris.

Already he had made up his mind how to act. He would get to Avignon, and thence by express to Paris. The *rapides* from Marseilles and the Riviera all stopped at the ancient city of the Popes.

Therefore, being a good motor driver, Hugh started away down the long road which led through the valley to Orgon, and thence direct to Avignon, which came into sight about seven o'clock in the morning.

Before entering the old city of walls and castles Hugh turned into a side road about two miles distant, drove the car to the end, and opening a gate succeeded in getting it some little distance into a wood, where it was well concealed from anyone passing along the road.

Then, descending and ascertaining that the driver was sleeping comfortably from the effects of the strong narcotic, he took his bag and walked into the town.

At the railway station he found the through express from Ventimiglia—the Italian frontier—to Paris would be due in twenty minutes, therefore he purchased a first-class ticket for Paris, and in a short time was taking his morning coffee in the *wagon-restaurant* on his way to the French capital.

XXV

The Man Cataldi

On the day that Hugh was travelling in hot haste to Paris, Charles Benton arrived in Nice early in the afternoon.

Leaving the station it was apparent he knew his way about the town, for passing down the Avenue de la Gare, with its row of high eucalyptus trees, to the Place Massena, he plunged into the narrow, rather evil-smelling streets of the old quarter.

Before a house in the Rue Rossette he paused, and ascending to a flat on the third floor, rang the bell. The door was slowly opened by an elderly, rather shabbily-attired Italian.

It was Yvonne's late servant at the Villa Amette, Giulio Cataldi.

The old man drew back on recognizing his visitor.

"Well, Cataldi!" exclaimed the well-dressed adventurer cheerily. "I'm quite a stranger—am I not? I was in Nice, and I could not leave without calling to see you."

The old man, with ill-grace scarcely concealed, invited him into his shabby room, saying:

"Well, Signor Benton, I never thought to see you again."

"Perhaps you didn't want to—eh? After that little affair in Brussels. But I assure you it was not my fault. Mademoiselle Yvonne made the blunder."

"And nearly let us all into the hands of the police—including The Sparrow himself!" growled the old fellow.

"Ah! But all that has long blown over. Now," he went on, after he had offered the old man a cigar. "Now the real reason I've called is to ask you about this nasty affair concerning Mademoiselle Yvonne. You were there that night. What do you know about it?"

"Nothing," the old fellow declared promptly. "Since that night I've earned an honest living. I'm a waiter in a cafe in the Avenue de la Gare."

"A most excellent decision," laughed the well-dressed man. "It is not everyone who can afford to be honest in these hard times. I wish I could be, but I find it impossible. Now, tell me, Giulio, what do you know about the affair at the Villa Amette? The boy, Henfrey, went there to demand of Mademoiselle how his father died. She refused to tell him, angry words arose—and he shot her. Now, isn't that your theory—the same as that held by the police?"

The old man looked straight into his visitor's face for a few moments. Then he replied quite calmly:

"I know nothing, Signor Benton—and I don't want to know anything. I've told the police all I know. Indeed, when they began to inquire into my antecedents I was not very reassured, I can tell you."

"I should think not," laughed Benton. "Still, they never suspected you to be the man wanted for the Morel affair—an unfortunate matter that was."

"Yes," sighed the old fellow. "Please do not mention it," and he turned away to the window as though to conceal his guilty countenance.

"You mean that you *know* something—but you won't tell it!" Benton said.

"I know nothing," was the old fellow's stubborn reply.

"But you know that the young fellow, Henfrey, is guilty!" exclaimed Benton. "Come! you were there at the time! You heard high words between them—didn't you?"

"I have already made my statement to the police," declared the old Italian. "What else I know I shall keep to myself."

"But I'm interested in ascertaining whether Henfrey is innocent or guilty. Only two persons can tell us that—Mademoiselle, who is, alas! in a hopeless mental state, and yourself. You know—but you refuse to incriminate the guilty person. Why don't you tell the truth? You know that Henfrey shot her!"

"I tell you I know nothing," retorted the old man. "Why do you come here and disturb me?" he added peevishly.

"Because I want to know the truth," Benton answered. "And I mean to!"

"Go away!" snapped the wilful old fellow. "I've done with you all—all the crowd of you!"

"Ah!" laughed Benton. "Then you forget the little matter of the man Morel—eh? That is not forgotten by the police, remember!"

"And if you said a word to them, Signor Benton, then you would implicate yourself," the old man growled. Seeing hostility in the Englishman's attitude he instantly resented it.

"Probably. But as I have no intention of giving you away, my dear Giulio, I do not think we need discuss it. What I am anxious to do is to establish the guilt—or the innocence—of Hugh Henfrey," he went on.

"No doubt. You have reason for establishing his guilt—eh?"

"No. Reasons for establishing his innocence."

"For your own ends, Signor Benton," was the shrewd old man's reply.

"At one time there was a suspicion that you yourself had fired at Mademoiselle."

"What!" gasped the old man, his countenance changing instantly. "Who says that?" he asked angrily.

"The police were suspicious, I believe. And as far as I can gather they are not yet altogether satisfied."

"Ah!" growled the old Italian in a changed voice. "They will have to prove it!"

"Well, they declare that the shot was fired by either one or the other of you," Benton said, much surprised at the curious effect the allegation had upon the old fellow.

"So they think that if the Signorino Henfrey is innocent I am guilty of the murderous attack—eh?"

Benton nodded.

"But they are seeking to arrest the signorino!" remarked the Italian.

"Yes. That is why I am here—to establish his innocence."

"And if I were to tell you that he was innocent I should condemn myself!" laughed the crafty old man.

"Look here, Giulio," said Benton. "I confess that I have long ago regretted the shabby manner in which I treated you when we were all in Brussels, and I hope you will allow me to make some little amend." Then, taking from his pocket-book several hundred-franc notes, he doubled them up and placed them on the table.

"Ah!" said the old man. "I see! You want to *buy* my secret! No, take your money!" he cried, pushing it back towards him contemptuously. "I want none of it."

"Because you are now earning an honest living," Benton sneered.

"Yes—and Il Passero knows it!" was Cataldi's bold reply.

"Then you refuse to tell me anything you know concerning the events of that night at the Villa Amette?"

"Yes," he snapped. "Take your money, and leave me in peace!"

"And I have come all the way from England to see you," remarked the disappointed man.

"Be extremely careful. You have enemies, so have I. They are the same as those who denounced the signorino to the police—as they will no doubt, before long, denounce you!" said the old man.

"Bah! You always were a pessimist, Giulio," Benton laughed. "I do not fear any enemies—I assure you. The Sparrow takes good care that we are prevented from falling into any traps the police may set," he added after a moment's pause.

The old waiter shook his head dubiously.

"One day there may be a slip—and it will cost you all very dearly," he said.

"You are in a bad mood, Giulio—like all those who exist by being honest," Benton laughed, though he was extremely annoyed at his failure to learn anything from the old fellow.

Was it possible that the suspicions which both Molly and he had entertained were true—namely, that the old man had attempted to kill his mistress? After all, the hue-and-cry had been raised by the police merely because Hugh Henfrey had fled and successfully escaped.

Benton, after grumbling because the old man would make no statement, and again hinting at the fact that he might be the culprit, left with very ill grace, his long journey from London having been in vain.

If Henfrey was to be free to marry Louise, then his innocence must first be proved. Charles Benton had for many weeks realized that his chance of securing old Mr. Henfrey's great fortune was slowly slipping from him. Once Hugh had married Louise and settled the money upon her, then the rest would be easy. He had many times discussed it with Molly, and they were both agreed upon a vile, despicable plot which would result in the young man's sudden end and the diversion of his father's fortune.

The whole plot against old Mr. Henfrey was truly one of the most elaborate and amazing ones ever conceived by criminal minds.

Charles Benton was a little too well known in Nice, hence he took care to leave the place by an early train, and went on to Cannes, where he was a little less known. As an international crook he had spent several seasons at Nice and Monte Carlo, but had seldom gone to Cannes, as it was too aristocratic and too slow for an *escroc* like himself.

Arrived at Cannes he put up at the Hotel Beau Site, and that night ate an expensive dinner in the restaurant at the Casino. Then, next day, he took the *train-de-luxe* direct for Calais, and went on to London, all unconscious of the sensational events which were then happening.

On arrival in London he found a telegram lying upon his table among some letters. It was signed "Shaw," and urged him to meet him "at the usual place" at seven o'clock in the evening. "I know you are away, but I'll look in each night at seven," it concluded.

It was just six o'clock, therefore Benton washed and changed, and just before seven o'clock entered a little cafe off Wardour Street, patronized mostly by foreigners. At one of the tables, sitting alone, was a wiry-looking, middle-aged man—Mr. Howell, The Sparrow's friend.

"Well?" asked Howell, when a few minutes later they were walking along Wardour Street together. "How did you get on in Nice?"

"Had my journey for nothing."

"Wouldn't the old man tell anything?" asked Howell eagerly.

"Not a word," Benton replied. "But my firm opinion is that he himself tried to kill Yvonne—that he shot her."

"Do you really agree with me?" gasped Howell excitedly. "Of course, there has, all along, been a certain amount of suspicion against him. The police were once on the point of arresting him. I happen to know that."

"Well, my belief is that young Henfrey is innocent. I never thought so until now."

"Then we must prove Cataldi guilty, and Henfrey can marry Louise," Howell said. "But the reason I wanted to get in touch with you is that the police went to Shapley."

"To Shapley!" gasped Benton.

"Yes. They went there the night you left London. Evidently somebody has given you away!"

"Given me away! Who in the devil's name can it be? If I get to know who the traitor is I—I'll—by gad, I'll kill him. I swear I will!"

"Who knows? Some secret enemy of yours—no doubt. Molly has been arrested and has been up at Bow Street. They also arrested Louise, but there being no charge against her, she has been released. I've sent her up to Cambridge—to old Mrs. Curtis. I thought she'd be quite quiet and safe there for a time."

"But Molly arrested! What's the charge?"

"Theft. An extradition warrant from Paris. That jeweller's affair in the Rue St. Honore, eighteen months ago."

"Well, I hope they won't bring forward other charges, or it will go infernally bad with her. What has The Sparrow done?"

"He's abroad somewhere—but I've had five hundred pounds from an unknown source to pay for her defence. I saw the solicitors. Brigthorne, the well-known barrister, appeared for her."

"But all this is very serious, my dear Howell," Benton declared, much alarmed.

"Of course it is. You can't marry the girl to young Henfrey until he is proved innocent, and that cannot be until the guilt is fixed upon the crafty old Giulio."

"Exactly. That's what we must do. But with Molly arrested we shall be compelled to be very careful," said Benton, as they turned toward Piccadilly Circus. "I don't see how we dare move until Molly is either free or convicted. If she knew our game she might give us away. Remember that if we bring off the Henfrey affair Molly has to have a share in the spoils. But if she happens to be in a French prison she won't get much chance—eh?"

"If she goes it will be ten years, without a doubt," Howell remarked.

"Yes. And in the meantime much can happen—eh?" laughed Benton.

"Lots. But one reassuring fact is that, as far as old Henfrey's fate is concerned, Mademoiselle's lips are closed. Whoever shot her did us a very good turn."

"Of course. But I agree we must fix the guilt upon old Cataldi. He almost as good as admitted it by his face when I taxed him with it. Why not give him away to the Nice police?"

"No, not yet. Certainly not," exclaimed Howell.

"It's a pity The Sparrow does not know about the Henfrey business. He might help us. Dare we tell him? What do you think?"

"Tell him! Good Heavens! No! Surely you are fully aware how he always sets his face against any attempt upon human life, and no one who has taken life has ever had his forgiveness," said Howell. "The Sparrow is our master—a fine and marvellous mind which has no equal in Europe. If he had gone into politics he could have been the greatest statesman of the age. But he is Il Passero, the man who directs affairs of every kind, and the man at the helm of every great enterprise. Yet his one fixed motto is that life shall not be taken."

"But in old Henfrey's case we acted upon our own initiative," remarked Benton.

"Yes. Yours was a wonderfully well-conceived idea. And all worked without a hitch until young Henfrey's visit to Monte Carlo, and his affection for that girl Ranscomb."

"We are weaning him away from her," Benton said. "At last the girl's suspicions are excited, and there is just that little disagreement which, broadening, leads to the open breach. Oh! my dear Howell, how could you and I live if it were not for that silly infection called love? In our profession love is all-conquering. Without it we could make no progress, no smart coups, no conquests of women who afterwards shed out to us money which at the assizes they would designate by the ugly word 'blackmail.'"

"Ah! Charles. You were always a philosopher," laughed his companion—the man who was a bosom friend of The Sparrow. "But it carries us no nearer. We must, at all costs, fix the hand that shot Yvonne."

"Giulio shot her—without a doubt!" was Benton's quick reply.

They were standing together on the kerb outside the Tube station at Piccadilly Circus as Benton uttered the words.

"Well, my dear fellow, then let us prove it," said Howell. "But not yet, remember. We must first see how it goes with Molly. She must be watched carefully. Of course, I agree that Giulio Cataldi shot Yvonne. Later we will prove that fact, but the worst of it is that the French police are hot on the track of young Henfrey."

"How do you know that?" asked his companion quickly.

"Well," he answered, after a second's hesitation, "I heard so two days ago."

Then Howell, pleading an urgent meeting with a mutual friend, also a crook like themselves, grasped the other's hand, and they parted.

XXVI

LISETTE'S DISCLOSURES

At ten o'clock on the morning that Hugh Henfrey left Avignon for Paris, The Sparrow stood at the window of his cozy little flat in the Rue des Petits Champs, where he was known to his elderly housekeeper—a worthy old soul from Yvetot, in the north—as Guillaume Gautier.

The house was one of those great old ones built in the days of the First Empire, with a narrow entrance and square courtyard into which the stage coaches with postilions rumbled before the days of the P.L.M. and aircraft. In the Napoleonic days it had been the residence of the Dukes de Vizelle, but in modern times it had been converted into a series of very commodious flats.

The Sparrow, sprightly and alert, stood, after taking his *cafe au lait*, looking down into the courtyard. He had been reading through several letters and telegrams which had caused him some perturbation.

"They are playing me false!" he muttered, as he gazed out of the window. "I'm certain of it—quite certain! But, Gad! If they do I'll be even with them! Who could have given Henfrey away in London—*and why?*"

He paced the length of the room, his teeth hard set and his hands clenched.

"I thought they were all loyal after what I have done for them—after the fortunes I have put into their pockets. Fancy! One of them a well-known member of Parliament—another a director of one of the soundest insurance companies! Nobody suspects the really great crooks. It is only the little clumsy muddlers whom the police catch and the judge makes examples of!"

Then crossing back to the window, he said aloud:

"Lisette ought to be here! She was due in from Toulouse at nine o'clock. I hope nothing further has happened. One thing is satisfactory—young Henfrey is safe."

As a matter of fact, the girl had spoken to The Sparrow from her hotel in Toulouse late on the previous night, and told him that her "friend Hugh" was in Marseilles.

Even to the master criminal the whole problem was increasingly complicated. He could not prove the innocence of young Henfrey, because of the mysterious, sinister influence being brought to bear against him. He had interested himself in aiding the young fellow to evade arrest, because he had no desire that there should be a trial in which he and his associates might be implicated.

The Sparrow hated trials of any sort. With him silence was golden, and very wisely he would pay any sum rather than court publicity.

Half an hour went past, but the girl he expected did not put in an appearance.

Monsieur Gautier—the man with the gloved hand—was believed by his old housekeeper to be a rich and somewhat eccentric bachelor, who was interested in old clocks and antique silver, and who travelled extensively in order to purchase fine specimens. Indeed it was by that description he was registered in the archives of the Surete, with the observation that notwithstanding his foreign name he was an Englishman of highest standing.

It was never dreamed that the bristly-haired alert little man, who was so often seen in the salerooms of Paris when antique silver was being sold, was the notorious Sparrow.

Lisette's failure to arrive considerably disturbed him. He hoped that nothing had happened to her. Time after time, he walked to the window and looked out eagerly for her to cross the courtyard. In those rooms he sometimes lived for weeks in safe obscurity, his neighbours regarding him as a man of the greatest integrity, though a trifle eccentric in his habits.

At last, just before eleven, he saw Lisette's smart figure in a heavy travelling coat crossing the courtyard, and a few moments later she was shown into his room.

"You're late!" the old man said, as soon as the door was closed. "I feared that something had gone wrong! Why did you leave Madrid? What has happened?" he asked eagerly.

"Happened!" she echoed in French. "Why, very nearly a disaster! Someone has given us away—at least, Monsieur Henfrey was given away to the police!"

"Not arrested?" he asked breathlessly.

"No. We all three managed to get away—but only just in time! I had a wire to-night from Monsieur Tresham, telling me guardedly that within an hour or so after we left Madrid the police called at my hotel—and at Henfrey's."

"Who can have done that?" asked The Sparrow, his eyes narrowing in anger, his gloved hand clenched.

"Your enemy—and mine!" was the girl's reply. "Franklyn is in Switzerland. Monsieur Henfrey is in Marseilles—at the Louvre et Paix—and I am here."

"Then we have a secret enemy—eh?"

"Yes—and he is not very far to seek. Monsieur Howell has done this!"

"Howell! He would never do such a thing, my dear mademoiselle," replied the gloved man, smiling.

"Oh! wouldn't he? I would not trust either Benton or Howell!"

"I think you are mistaken, mademoiselle. They have never shown much friendship towards each other."

"They are close friends as far as concerns the Henfrey affair," declared mademoiselle. "I happen to know that it was Howell who prepared the old man's will. It is in his handwriting, and his manservant, Cooke, is one of the witnesses."

"What? *You know about that will, Lisette?* Tell me everything."

"Howell himself let it out to me. They were careful that you should not know. At the time I was in London with Franklyn and Benton over the jewels of that ship-owner's wife, I forget her name—the affair in Carlton House Terrace."

"Yes. I recollect. A very neat piece of business."

"Well—Howell told me how he had prepared the will, and how Benton, who was staying with old Mr. Henfrey away in the country, got him to put his signature to it by pretending it to be for the purchase of a house at Eltham, in Kent. The house was, indeed, purchased at Benton's suggestion, but the signature was to a will which Howell's man, Cooke, and a friend of his, named Saunders, afterwards witnessed, and which has now been proved—the will by which the young man is compelled to marry Benton's adopted daughter before he inherits his father's estates."

"You actually know this?"

"Howell told me so with his own lips."

"Then why is young Henfrey being made the victim?" asked The Sparrow shrewdly. "Why, indeed, have you not revealed this to me before?"

"Because I had no proof before that Howell is *our* enemy. He has now given us away. He has some motive. What is it?"

The bristly-haired little man of twenty names and as many individualities pondered for a moment. It was evident that he was both apprehensive and amazed at the suggestion the pretty young French girl had placed before him.

When one finds a betrayer, then in order to fix his guilt it becomes necessary to discover the motive.

The Sparrow was in a quandary. Seldom was he in such a perturbed state of mind. He and his accomplices could always defy the police. It was not the first time in his career, however, that he had found a traitor in his camp. If Howell was really a traitor, then he would pay dearly for it. Three times within the last ten years there had been traitors in the great criminal organization. One was a Dutchman; the second was a Greek; and the third a Swiss. Each died—for dead men tell no tales.

The Sparrow ordered some *cafe noir* from his housekeeper and produced a particularly seductive brand of liqueur, which mademoiselle took—together with a cigarette.

Then she left, he giving her the parting injunction:

"It is probable that you will go to Marseilles and meet young Henfrey. I will think it all over. You will have a note from me at the Grand Hotel before noon to-morrow."

XXVII

The Inquisitive Mr. Shrimpton

An hour later Hugh stood in The Sparrow's room, and related his exciting adventure in Marseilles and on the high road.

"H'm!" remarked the man with the gloved hand. "A very pretty piece of business. The police endeavoured to mislead you, and you, by a very fortunate circumstance, suspected. That cigarette, my dear young friend, stood you in very good stead. It was fortunate that I gave it to you."

"By this time the driver of the car has, of course, recovered and told his story," Hugh remarked.

"And by this time the police probably know that you have come to Paris," remarked The Sparrow. "Now, Mr. Henfrey, only an hour ago I learnt something which has altered my plans entirely. There is a traitor somewhere—somebody has given you away."

"Who?"

"At present I have not decided. But we must all be wary and watchful," was The Sparrow's reply. "In any case, it is a happy circumstance that you saw through the ruse of the police to get you to Cette. First the Madrid police were put upon your track, and then, as you eluded them, the Marseilles police were given timely information—a clever trap," he laughed. "I admire it. But at Marseilles they are even more shrewd than in Paris. Maillot, the *chef de la Sureté* at Marseilles, is a really capable official. I know him well. A year ago he dined with me at the Palais de la Bouillabaisse. I pretended that I had been the victim of a great theft, and he accepted my invitation. He little dreamed that I was Il Passero, for whom he had been spreading the net for years!"

"You are really marvellous, Mr. Peters," remarked Hugh. "And I have to thank you for the way in which you have protected me time after time. Your organization is simply wonderful."

The man with the black glove laughed.

"Nothing really wonderful," he said. "Those who are innocent I protect, those who are traitors I condemn. And they never escape me. We have traitors at work now. It is for me to fix the identity. And in this you, Mr. Henfrey, must help me. Have you heard from Miss Ranscomb?"

"No. Not a word," replied the young man. "I dare not write to her."

"No, don't. A man from Scotland Yard went to see her. So it is best to remain apart—my dear boy—even though that unfortunate misunderstanding concerning Louise Lambert has arisen between you."

"But I am anxious to put it right," the young fellow said. "Dorise misjudges me."

"Ah! I know. But at present you must allow her to think ill of you. You must not court arrest. We now know that you have enemies who intend you to be the victim, while they reap the profit," said The Sparrow kindly. "Leave matters to me and act at my suggestion."

"That I certainly will," Hugh replied. "You have never yet advised me wrongly."

"Ah! I am not infallible," laughed the master criminal.

Then he rose, and crossing to the telephone, he inquired for the Grand Hotel. After a few minutes he spoke to Mademoiselle Lisette, telling her that she need not go to Marseilles, and asking her to call upon him again at nine o'clock that night.

"Monsieur Hugh has returned from the south," he added. "He is anxious to see you again."

"*Tres bien, m'sieur*," answered the smart Parisienne. "I will be there. But will you not dine with me—eh? At Vian's at seven. You know the place."

"Mademoiselle Lisette asks us to dine with her at Vian's," The Sparrow said, turning to Hugh.

"Yes, I shall be delighted," replied the young man.

So The Sparrow accepted the girl's invitation.

On that same morning, Dorise Ranscomb had, after breakfast, settled herself to write some letters. Her mother had gone to Warwickshire for the week-end, and she was alone with the maids.

The whole matter concerning Hugh puzzled her. She could not bring herself to a decision as to his innocence or his guilt.

As she sat writing in the morning-room, the maid announced that Mr. Shrimpton wished to see her.

She started at the name. It was the detective inspector from Scotland Yard who had called upon her on a previous occasion.

A few moments afterwards he was shown in, a tall figure in a rough tweed suit.

"I really must apologize, Miss Ranscomb, for disturbing you, but I have heard news of Mr. Henfrey. He has been in Marseilles. Have you heard from him?"

"Not a word," the girl replied. "And, Mr. Shrimpton, I am growing very concerned. I really can't think that he tried to kill the young Frenchwoman. Why should he?"

"Well, because she had connived at his father's death. That seems to be proved."

"Then your theory is that it was an act of vengeance?"

"Exactly, Miss Ranscomb. That is our opinion, and a warrant being out for his arrest both in France and in England, we are doing all we can to get him."

"But are you certain?" asked the girl, much distressed. "After all, though on the face of things it seems that there is a distinct motive, I do not think that Hugh would be guilty of such a thing."

"Naturally. Forgive me for saying so, miss, but I quite appreciate your point of view. If I were in your place I should regard the matter in just the same light. I, however, wondered whether you had heard news of him during the last day or two."

"No. I have heard nothing."

"And," he said, "I suppose if you did hear, you would not tell me?"

"That is my own affair, Mr. Shrimpton," she replied resentfully. "If you desire to arrest Mr. Henfrey it is your own affair. Why do you ask me to assist you?"

"In the interests of justice," was the inspector's reply.

"Well," said the girl, very promptly, "I tell you at once that I refuse to assist you in your endeavour to arrest Mr. Henfrey. Whether he is guilty or not guilty I have not yet decided."

"But he must be guilty. There was the motive. He shot the woman who had enticed his father to his death."

"And how have you ascertained that?"

"By logical deduction."

"Then you are trying to convict Mr. Henfrey upon circumstantial evidence alone?"

"Others have gone to the gallows on circumstantial evidence— Crippen, for instance. There was no actual witness of his crime."

"I fear I must allow you to continue your investigations, Mr. Shrimpton," she said coldly.

"But your lover has deceived you. He was staying down in Surrey with the girl, Miss Lambert, as his fellow-guest."

"I know that," was Dorise's reply. "But I have since come to the conclusion that my surmise—my jealousy if you like to call it so—is unfounded."

"Ah! then you refuse to assist justice?"

"No, I do not. But knowing nothing of the circumstances I do not see how I can assist you."

"But no doubt you know that Mr. Henfrey evaded us and went away—that he was assisted by a man whom we know as The Sparrow."

"I do not know where he is," replied the girl with truth.

"But you know The Sparrow," said the detective. "You admitted that you had met him when I last called here."

"I have met him," she replied.

"Where does he live?"

She smiled, recollecting that even though she had quarrelled with Hugh, the strange old fellow had been his best friend. She remembered how the White Cavalier had been sent by him with messages to reassure her.

"I refuse to give away the secrets of my friends," she responded a trifle haughtily.

"Then you prefer to shield the master criminal of Europe?"

"I have no knowledge that The Sparrow is a criminal."

"Ask the police of any city in Europe. They will tell you that they have for years been endeavouring to capture Il Passero. Yet so cleverly is his gang organized that never once has he been betrayed. All his friends are so loyal to him."

"Yet you want me to betray him!"

"You are not a member of the gang of criminals, Miss Ranscomb," replied Shrimpton.

"Whether I am or not, I refuse to say a word concerning anyone who has been of service to me," was her stubborn reply. And with that the man from the Criminal Investigation Department had to be content.

Even then, Dorise was not quite certain whether she had misjudged the man who loved her so well, but who was beneath a cloud. She had acted hastily in writing that letter, she felt. Yet she had successfully warned him of his peril, and he had been able to extricate himself from the net spread for him.

It was evident that The Sparrow, who was her friend and Hugh's, was a most elusive person.

She recollected the White Cavalier at the ball at Nice, and how she had never suspected him to be the deputy of the King of the Underworld—the man whose one hand was gloved.

Within half an hour of the departure of her visitor from Scotland Yard, the maid announced Mr. Sherrard.

Dorise, with a frown, arose from her chair, and a few seconds later faced the man who was her mother's intimate friend, and who daily forced his unwelcome attentions upon her.

"Your mother told me you would be alone, Dorise," he said in his forced manner of affected elegance. "So I just dropped in. I hope I'm not worrying you."

"Oh! not at all," replied the girl, sealing a letter which she had just written. "Mother has gone to Warwickshire, and I'm going out to lunch with May Petheridge, an old schoolfellow of mine."

"Oh! Then I won't keep you," said the smug lover of Lady Ranscomb's choice. He was one of those over-dressed fops who haunted the lounges of the Ritz and the Carlton, and who scraped acquaintance with anybody with a title. At tea parties he would refer to Lord This and Lady That as intimate friends, whereas he had only been introduced to them by some fat wife of a fatter profiteer.

Sherrard saw that Dorise's attitude was one of hostility, but with his superior overbearing manner he pretended not to notice it.

"You were not at Lady Oundle's the night before last," he remarked, for want of something better to say. "I went there specially to meet you, Dorise."

"I hate Lady Oundle's dances," was the girl's reply. "Such a lot of fearful old fogies go there."

"True, but a lot of your mother's friends are in her set."

"I know. But mother always avoids going to her dances if she possibly can. We had a good excuse to be away, as mother was packing."

"Elise was there," he remarked.

"And you danced with her, of course. She's such a ripping dancer."

"Twice. When I found you were not there I went on to the club," he replied, with his usual air of boredom. "When do you expect your mother back?"

"Next Tuesday. I'm going down to Huntingdon to-morrow to stay with the Fishers."

"Oh! by the way," he remarked suddenly. "Tubby Hall, who is just back from Madrid, told me in the club last night that he'd seen your friend Henfrey in a restaurant there with a pretty French girl."

"In Madrid!" echoed Dorise, for she had no idea of her lover's whereabouts. "He must have been mistaken surely."

"No. Tubby is an old friend of Henfrey's. He says that he and the girl seemed to be particularly good friends."

Dorise hesitated.

"You tell me this in order to cause me annoyance!" she exclaimed.

"Not at all. I've only told you what Tubby said."

"Did your friend speak to Mr. Henfrey?"

"I think not. But I really didn't inquire," Sherrard replied, not failing, however, to note how puzzled she was.

Lady Ranscomb was already assuring him that the girl's affection for the absconding Henfrey would, sooner or later, fade out. More than once he and she had held consultation concerning the proposed marriage, and more than once Sherrard had been on the point of withdrawing from the contest for the young girl's heart. But her mother was never tired of bidding him be patient, and saying that in the end he would obtain his desire.

Sherrard, however, little dreamed how great was Dorise's love for Hugh, and how deeply she regretted having written that hasty letter to Shapley.

Yet one of Hugh's friends had met him in Madrid in company with what was described as a pretty young French girl!

What was the secret of it all? Was Hugh really guilty of the attempt upon the notorious Mademoiselle? If not, why did he not face the charge like a man?

Such were her thoughts when, an hour later, her mother's car took her out to Kensington to lunch with her old school friend who was on the point of being married to a man who had won great distinction in the Air Force, and whose portrait was almost daily in the papers.

Would she ever marry Hugh, she wondered, as she sat gazing blankly out upon the London traffic. She would write to him, but, alas! she knew neither the name under which he was going, nor his address.

And a telephone message to Mr. Peters's house had been answered to the effect that the man whose hand was gloved was abroad, and the date of his return uncertain.

XXVIII

The Sparrow's Nest

Mademoiselle Lisette met her two guests at Vian's small but exclusive restaurant in the Rue Daunou, and all three had a merry meal together. Afterwards The Sparrow smoked a good cigar and became amused at the young girl's chatter.

She was a sprightly little person, and had effectively brought off several highly successful coups. Before leaving his cosy flat in the Rue des Petits Champs, The Sparrow had sat for an hour calmly reviewing the situation in the light of what Lisette had told him and of Hugh's exciting adventure on the Arles road.

That he had successfully escaped from a very clever trap was plain, but who was the traitor? Who, indeed, had fired that shot which, failing to kill Yvonne, had unbalanced her brain so that no attention could be paid to her wandering remarks?

He had that morning been on the point of trying to get into touch with his friend Howell, but after Lisette's disclosures, he was very glad that he had not done so. His master-mind worked quickly. He could sum up a situation and act almost instantly where other men would be inclined to waver. But when The Sparrow arrived at a decision it was unalterable. All his associates knew that too well. Some of them called him stubborn, but they had to agree that he was invariably right in his suspicions and conclusions.

He had debated whether he should tell Hugh what Lisette had alleged concerning the forgery of his father's will, but had decided to keep the matter to himself and see what further proof he could obtain. Therefore he had forbidden the girl to tell Henfrey anything, for, after all, it was quite likely that her statements could not be substantiated.

After their coffee all three returned to the Rue des Petits Champs where Lisette, merry and full of vivacity, joined them in a cigarette.

The Sparrow had been preoccupied and thoughtful the whole evening. But at last, as they sat together, he said:

"We shall all three go south to-morrow—to Nice direct."

"To Nice!" exclaimed Lisette. "It is hardly safe—is it?"

"Yes. You will leave by the midday train from the Gare de Lyon—and go to Madame Odette's in the boulevard Gambetta. I may want you. We shall follow by the *train-de-luxe*. It is best that Mr. Henfrey is out of Paris. The Surete will certainly be searching for him."

Then, turning to Hugh, he told him that he had better remain his guest that night, and in the morning he would buy him another suit, hat and coat.

"There will not be so much risk in Nice as here in Paris," he added. "After all, we ought not to have ventured out to Vian's."

Later he sat down, and after referring to a pocket-book containing certain entries, he scribbled four cryptic telegrams which were, apparently, Bourse quotations, but when read by their addressees were of quite a different character.

He went out and himself dispatched these from the office of the Grand Hotel. He never entrusted his telegrams of instructions to others.

When he returned ten minutes later he took up *Le Soir*, and searching it eagerly, suddenly exclaimed:

"Ah! Here it is! Manfield has been successful and got away all right with the German countess's trinkets!"

And with a laugh he handed the paper to Lisette, who read aloud an account of a daring robbery in one of the best hotels in Cologne—jewels valued at a hundred thousand marks having mysteriously disappeared. International thieves were suspected, but the Cologne police had no clue.

"M'sieur Manfield is always extremely shrewd. He is such a real ladies' man," laughed Lisette, using some of the *argot* of the Montmartre.

"Yes. Do you recollect that American, Lindsay—with whom you had something to do?"

"Oh, yes, I remember. I was in London and we went out to dinner together quite a lot. Manfield was with me and we got from his dispatch-box the papers concerning that oil well at Baku. The company was started later on in Chicago, and only two months ago I received my dividend."

"Teddy Manfield is a very good friend," declared the man with the gloved hand. "Birth and education always count, even in these days. To any ex-service man I hold out my hand as the unit who saved us from becoming a German colony. But do others? I make war upon those who have profited by war. I have never attacked those who have remained honest during the great struggle. In the case of dog-eat-dog

I place myself on the side of the worker and the misled patriot—not only in Britain, but in all the countries of the Allies. If members of the Allied Governments are profiteers what can the man-in-the-street expect of the poor little scraping-up tradesman oppressed by taxation and bewildered by waste? But there!" he added, "I am no politician! My only object is to solve the mystery of who shot poor Mademoiselle Yvonne."

The pretty decoy of the great association of *escrocs* smoked another cigarette, and gazed into the young man's face. Sometimes she shuddered when she reflected upon all she knew concerning his father's unfortunate end, and of the cleverly concocted will by which he was to marry Louise Lambert, and afterwards enjoy but a short career.

Fate had made Lisette what she was—a child of fortune. Her own life would, if written, form a strange and sensational narrative. For she had been implicated in a number of great robberies which had startled the world.

She knew much of the truth of the Henfrey affair, and she had now decided to assist Hugh to vanquish those whose intentions were distinctly evil.

At last she rose and wished them *bon soir*.

"I shall leave the Gare de Lyon at eleven fifty-eight to-morrow, and go direct to Madame Odette's in Nice," she said.

"Yes. Remain there. If I want you I will let you know," answered The Sparrow.

And then she descended the stairs and walked to her hotel.

Next evening Hugh and The Sparrow, both dressed quite differently, left by the Riviera *train-de-luxe*. As The Sparrow lay that night in the *wagon-lit* he tried to sleep, but the roar and rattle of the train prevented it. Therefore he calmly thought out a complete and deliberate plan.

From one of his friends in London he had had secret warning that the police, on the day he left Charing Cross, had descended upon Shapley Manor and had arrested Mrs. Bond under a warrant applied for by the French police, and he also knew that her extradition for trial in Paris had been granted.

That there was a traitor in the camp was proved, but happily Hugh Henfrey had escaped just in time.

For himself The Sparrow cared little. He seemed to be immune from arrest, so cleverly did he disguise his true identity; yet now that some person had revealed his secrets, what more likely than the person, whoever it was, would also give him away for the sake of the big reward which he knew was offered for his apprehension.

Before leaving Paris that evening he had dispatched a telegram, a reply to which was handed him in the train when it stopped at Lyons early next morning.

This decided him. He sent another telegram and then returned to where Hugh was lying half awake. When they stopped at Marseilles, both men were careful not to leave the train, but continued in it, arriving at the great station of Nice in the early afternoon.

They left their bags at a small hotel just outside the station, and taking a cab, they drove away into the old town. Afterwards they proceeded on foot to the Rue Rossetti, where they climbed to the flat occupied by old Giulio Cataldi.

The old fellow was out, but the elderly Italian woman who kept house for him said she expected him back at any moment. He was due to come off duty at the cafe where he was employed.

So Hugh and his companion waited, examining the poorly-furnished little room.

Now The Sparrow entertained a strong suspicion that Cataldi knew more of the tragedy at the Villa Amette than anyone else. Indeed, of late, it had more than once crossed his mind that he might be the actual culprit.

At last the door opened and the old man entered, surprised to find himself in the presence of the master criminal, The Sparrow, whom he had only met once before.

He greeted his visitors rather timidly.

After a short chat The Sparrow, who had offered the old man a cigarette from a cheap plated case much worn, began to make certain inquiries.

"This is a very serious and confidential affair, Cataldi," he said. "I want to know the absolute truth—and I must have it."

"I know it is serious, signore," replied the old man, much perturbed by the unexpected visit of the king of the underworld, the elusive Sparrow of whom everyone spoke in awe. "But I only know one or two facts. I recognize Signor Henfrey."

"Ah! Then you know me!" exclaimed Hugh. "You recognized me on that night at the Villa Amette, when you opened the door to me."

"I do, signore. I recollect everything. It is all photographed upon my memory. Poor Mademoiselle! You questioned her—as a gentleman would—and you demanded to know about your father's death. She prevaricated—and—"

"Then you overheard it?" said Hugh.

"Yes, I listened. Was I not Mademoiselle's servant? On that night she had won quite a large sum at the Rooms, and she had given me—ah! she was always most generous—five hundred francs—twenty pounds in your English money. And they were acceptable in these days of high prices. I heard much. I was interested. Mademoiselle was my mistress whom I had served faithfully."

"You wondered why this young Englishman should call upon her at that hour?" said The Sparrow.

"I did. She never received visitors after her five o'clock tea. It was the habit at the Villa Amette to lunch at one o'clock, English tea at five o'clock, and dinner at eight—when the Rooms were slack save for the tourists from seven till ten. Strange! The tourists always think they can win while the gambling world has gone to its meals! They get seats, it is true, but they always lose."

"Yes," replied The Sparrow. "It is a strange fact that the greatest losses are sustained by the players when the Rooms are most empty. Nobody has yet ever been able to account for it."

"And yet it is so," declared old Cataldi. "I have watched it day by day. But poor Mademoiselle! What can we do to solve the mystery?"

"Were you not with Mademoiselle and Mr. Benton when you both brought off that great coup in the Avenue Louise, in Brussels?" asked The Sparrow.

"Yes, signore," said the old man. "But I do not wish to speak of it now."

"Quite naturally. I quite appreciate it. Since Mademoiselle's—er—accident you have, I suppose, been leading an honest life?"

"Yes. I have tried to do so. At present I am a cafe waiter."

"And you can tell me nothing further regarding the affair at the Villa Amette?" asked The Sparrow, eyeing him narrowly.

"I regret, signore, I can tell you nothing further," replied the staid, rather sad-looking old man; "nothing." And he sighed.

"Why?" asked the man whose tentacles were, like an octopus, upon a hundred schemes, and as many criminal coups in Europe. He sought a solution of the problem, but nothing appeared forthcoming.

He had strained every effort, but he could ascertain nothing.

That Cataldi knew the key to the whole problem The Sparrow felt assured. Yet why did not the old fellow tell the truth?

At last The Sparrow rose and left, and Hugh followed him. Both were bitterly disappointed. The old man refused to say more than that he was ignorant of the whole affair.

Cataldi's attitude annoyed the master criminal.

For three days he remained in Nice with Hugh, at great risk of recognition and arrest.

On the fourth day they went together in a hired car along the winding road across the Var to Cannes.

At a big white villa a little distance outside the pretty winter town of flowers and palms, they halted. The house, which was on the Frejus road, was once the residence of a Russian prince.

With The Sparrow Hugh was ushered into a big, sunny room overlooking the beautiful garden where climbing geraniums ran riot with carnations and violets, and for some minutes they waited. From the windows spread a wide view of the calm sapphire sea.

Then suddenly the door opened.

XXIX

The Story of Mademoiselle

Both men turned and before them they saw the plainly dressed figure of a beautiful woman, and behind her an elderly, grey-faced man.

For a few seconds the woman stared at The Sparrow blankly. Then she turned her gaze upon Hugh.

Her lips parted. Suddenly she gave vent to a loud cry, almost of pain, and placing both hands to her head, gasped:

"*Dieu!*"

It was Yvonne Ferad. And the cry was one of recognition.

Hugh dashed forward with the doctor, for she was on the point of collapse at recognizing them. But in a few seconds she recovered herself, though she was deathly pale and much agitated.

"Yvonne!" exclaimed The Sparrow in a low, kindly voice. "Then you know who we really are? Your reason has returned?"

"Yes," she answered in French. "I remember who you are. Ah! But—but it is all so strange!" she cried wildly. "I—I—I can't think! At last! Yes. I know. I recollect! You!" And she stared at Hugh. "You—you are *Monsieur Henfrey!*"

"That is so, mademoiselle."

"Ah, messieurs," remarked the elderly doctor, who was standing behind his patient. "She recognized you both—after all! The sudden shock at seeing you has accomplished what we have failed all these months to accomplish. It is efficacious only in some few cases. In this it is successful. But be careful. I beg of you not to overtax poor mademoiselle's brain with many questions. I will leave you."

And he withdrew, closing the door softly after him.

For a few minutes The Sparrow spoke to Mademoiselle of Monte Carlo about general things.

"I have been very ill," she said in a low, tremulous voice. "I could think of nothing since my accident, until now—and now"—and she gazed around her with a new interest upon her handsome countenance—"and now I remember!—but it all seems too hazy and indistinct."

"You recollect things—eh?" asked The Sparrow in a kindly voice, placing his hand upon her shoulder and looking into her tired eyes.

"Yes. I remember. All the past is slowly returning to me. It seems ages and ages since I last met you, Mr.—Mr. Peters," and she laughed lightly. "Peters—that is the name?"

"It is, mademoiselle," he laughed. "And it is a happy event that, by seeing us unexpectedly, your memory has returned. But the reason Mr. Henfrey is here is to resume that conversation which was so suddenly interrupted at the Villa Amette."

Mademoiselle was silent for some moments. Her face was averted, for she was gazing out of the window to the distant sea.

"Do you wish me to reveal to Monsieur Henfrey the—the secret of his father's death?" she asked of The Sparrow.

"Certainly. You were about to do so when—when the accident happened."

"Yes. But—but, oh!—how can I tell him the actual truth when—when, alas! I am so guilty?" cried the woman, much distressed.

"No, no, mademoiselle," said Hugh, placing his hand tenderly upon her shoulder. "Calm yourself. You did not kill my father. Of that I am quite convinced. Do not distress yourself, but tell me all that you know."

"Mr. Peters knows something of the affair, I believe," she said slowly. "But he never planned it. The whole plot was concocted by Benton." Then, turning to Hugh, Mademoiselle said almost in her natural tone, though slightly high-pitched and nervous:

"Benton, the blackguard, was your father's friend at Woodthorpe. With a man named Howell, known also as Shaw, he prepared a will which your father signed unconsciously, and which provided that in the event of his death you should be cut off from almost every benefit if you did not marry Louise Lambert, Benton's adopted daughter."

"But who is Louise actually?" asked Hugh interrupting.

"The real daughter of Benton, who has made pretence of adopting her. Of course Louise is unaware of that fact," Yvonne replied.

Hugh was much surprised at this. But he now saw the reason why Mrs. Bond was so solicitous of the poor girl's welfare.

"Now I happened to be in London, and on one of your father's visits to town, Benton, his friend, introduced us. Naturally I had no knowledge of the plot which Benton and Howell had formed, and finding your father a very agreeable gentleman, I invited him to the furnished flat I had taken at Queen's Gate. I went to the theatre with him on two occasions, Benton accompanying us, and then your father returned to the country. One day, about two months later Howell happened to be in London, and presumably they decided that the plot was ripe for execution, for they asked me to write to Mr. Henfrey at Woodthorpe, and suggest that he should come to London, have an early supper with us, and go to a big charity ball at the Albert Hall. In due course I received a wire from Mr. Henfrey, who came to London, had supper with me, Benton and Howell being also present, while Howell's small closed car, which he always drove himself, was waiting outside to take us to the ball."

Then she paused and drew a long breath, as though the recollection of that night horrified her—as indeed it did.

"After supper I rose and left the room to speak to my servant for a moment, when, just as I re-entered, I saw Howell, who was standing behind Mr. Henfrey's chair, suddenly bend, place his left arm around your father's neck, and with his right hand press on the nape of the neck just above his collar. 'Here!' your father cried out, thinking it was a joke, 'what's the game?' But the last word was scarcely audible, for he collapsed across the table. I stood there aghast. Howell, suddenly noticing me, told me roughly to clear out, as I was not wanted. I demanded to know what had happened, but I was told that it did not concern me. My idea was that Mr. Henfrey had been drugged, for he was still alive and apparently dazed. I afterwards heard, however, that Howell had pressed the needle of a hypodermic syringe containing a newly discovered and untraceable poison which he had obtained in secret from a certain chemist in Frankfort, who makes a speciality of such things."

"And what happened then?" asked Hugh, aghast and astounded at the story.

"Benton and Howell sent me out of the room. They waited for over an hour. Then Howell went down to the car. Afterwards, when all was clear, they half carried poor Mr. Henfrey downstairs, placed him in the car, and drove away. Next day I heard that my guest had been found by a constable in a doorway in Albemarle Street. The officer, who first thought he was intoxicated, later took him to St. George's Hospital, where he died. Afterwards a scratch was found on the palm of his hand, and the doctors believed it had been caused by a pin infected with some poison. The truth was, however, that his hand was scratched in opening a bottle of champagne at supper. The doctors never suspected the tiny puncture in the hair at the nape of the neck, and they never discovered it."

"I knew nothing of the affair," declared The Sparrow, his face clouded by anger. "Then Howell was the actual murderer?"

"He was," Yvonne replied. "I saw him press the needle into Mr. Henfrey's neck, while Benton stood by, ready to seize the victim if he resisted. Benton and Howell had agreed to kill Mr. Henfrey, compel his son to marry Louise, and then get Hugh out of the world by one or other of their devilish schemes. Ah!" she sighed, looking sadly before her. "I see it all now—everything."

"Then it was arranged that after I had married Louise I should also meet with an unexpected end?"

"Yes. One that should discredit you in the eyes of your wife and your own friends—an end probably like your father's. A secret visit to London, and a mysterious death," Mademoiselle replied.

She spoke quite calmly and rationally. The shock of suddenly encountering the two persons who had been uppermost in her thoughts before those terrible injuries to her brain had balanced it again. Though the pains in her head were excruciating, as she explained, yet she could now think, and she remembered all the bitterness of the past.

"You, M'sieur Henfrey, are the son of my dead friend. You have been the victim of a great and dastardly conspiracy," she said. "But I ask your forgiveness, for I assure you that when I invited your father up from Woodthorpe I had no idea whatever of what those assassins intended."

"Benton is already under arrest for another affair," broke in The Sparrow quietly. "I heard so from London yesterday."

"Ah! And I hope that Howell will also be punished for his crime," the handsome woman cried. "Though I have been a thief, a swindler, and a decoy—ah! yes, I admit it all—I have never committed the crime of murder. I know, messieurs," she went on—"I know that I am a social outcast, the mysterious Mademoiselle of Monte Carlo, they call me! But I have suffered. I have indeed in these past months paid my debt to Society, and of you, Mr. Henfrey, I beg forgiveness."

"I forgive you, Mademoiselle," Hugh replied, grasping her slim, white hand.

"Mademoiselle will, I hope, meet Miss Ranscomb, Mr. Henfrey's fiancee, and tell her the whole truth," said The Sparrow.

"That I certainly will," Yvonne replied. "Now that I can think I shall be allowed to leave this place—eh?"

"Of course. I will see after that," said the man known as Mr. Peters. "You must return to the Villa Amette—for you are still Mademoiselle of Monte Carlo, remember! Leave it all to me." And he laughed happily.

"But we are no nearer the solution of the mystery as to who attempted to kill you, Mademoiselle," Hugh remarked.

"There can be but one person. Old Cataldi knows who it is," she answered.

"Cataldi? Then why has he not told me? I questioned him closely only the other day," said The Sparrow.

"For certain reasons," Mademoiselle replied. "He *dare* not tell the truth!"

"Why?" asked Hugh.

"Because—well—" and she turned to The Sparrow. "You will recollect the affair we brought off in Brussels at that house of the Belgian baroness close to the Bois de la Cambre. A servant was shot dead. Giulio Cataldi shot him in self-defence. But Howell knows of it."

"Well?" asked The Sparrow.

"Howell was in Monte Carlo on the night of the attempt upon me. I met him in the Casino half an hour before I left to walk home. He no doubt recognized Mr. Henfrey, who was also there, as the son of the man whom he had murdered, watched him, and followed him up to my villa. He suspected that Mr. Henfrey's object was to face me and demand an explanation."

"Do you really think so?" gasped Hugh.

"Of that I feel positive. Only Cataldi can prove it."

"Why Cataldi?" inquired Hugh.

"See him again and tell him what I have revealed to you," answered Mademoiselle of Monte Carlo.

"Who was it who warned me against you by that letter posted in Tours?"

"It was part of Howell's scheme, no doubt. I have no idea of the identity of the writer of any anonymous letter. But Howell, no doubt, saw that if he rid himself of me it would be to his great advantage."

"Then Cataldi will not speak the truth because he fears Howell?" remarked the notorious chief of Europe's underworld.

"Exactly. Now that I can think, I can piece the whole puzzle together. It is all quite plain. Do you not recollect Howell's curious rifle fashioned in the form of a walking-stick? When I halted to speak to Madame Beranger on the steps of the Casino as I came out that night, he passed me carrying that stick. Indeed, he is seldom without it. By means of that disguised rifle I was shot!"

"But you speak of Cataldi. How can he know?"

"When I entered the house I told him quickly that I believed Howell was following me. I ordered him to watch. This no doubt he did. He has ever been faithful to me."

"Buy why should Howell have attempted to fix his guilt upon Mr. Henfrey?" asked The Sparrow. "In doing so he was defeating his own aims. If Mr. Henfrey were sent to prison he could not marry Louise Lambert, and if he had married Louise he would have benefited Howell! Therefore the whole plot was nullified."

"Exactly, m'sieur. Howell attempted to kill me in order to preserve his secret, fearing that if I told Mr. Henfrey the truth he would inform the police of the circumstances of his father's assassination. In making the attempt he defeated his own ends—a fact which he only realized when too late!"

CONCLUSION

The foregoing is perhaps one of the most remarkable stories of the underworld of Europe.

Its details are set down in full in three big portfolios in the archives of the Surete in Paris—where the present writer has had access to them.

In that bald official narrative which is docketed under the heading "No. 23489/263—Henfrey" there is no mention of the love affair between Dorise Ranscomb and Hugh Henfrey of Woodthorpe.

But the true facts are that within three days of Mademoiselle's recovery of her mental balance, old Giulio Cataldi made a sworn statement to the police at Nice, and in consequence two gendarmes of the Department of Seine et Oise went one night to a small hotel at Provins, where they arrested the Englishman, Shaw, alias Howell, who had gone there in what he thought was safe hiding.

The arrest took place at midnight, but Howell, on being cornered in his bedroom, showed fight, and raising an automatic pistol, which he had under his pillow, shot and wounded one of the gendarmes. Whereupon his companion drew his revolver in self-defence and shot the Englishman dead.

Benton, a few months later, was sentenced to forced labour for fifteen years, while his accomplice, Molly Bond, received a sentence of ten years. Only one case—that of jewel robbery—was, however, proved against her.

Dorise, about six weeks after Mademoiselle Yvonne's explanation, met her in London, and there she and Hugh became reconciled. Her jealousy of Louise Lambert disappeared when she knew the actual truth, and she admired her lover all the more for his generosity in promising, when the Probate Court had set aside the false will, that he would settle a comfortable income upon the poor innocent girl.

This, indeed, he did.

The Sparrow has never since been traced, though Scotland Yard and the Surete have searched everywhere for him. But he is far too clever. The writer believes he is now living in obscurity, but perfectly happy, in a little village outside Barcelona. He loves the sunshine.

As for Hugh, he is now happily married to Dorise, and as the Probate Court has decided that Woodthorpe and the substantial income are his, he is enjoying all his father's wealth.

Yvonne Ferad is still Mademoiselle of Monte Carlo. She still lives on the hill in the picturesque Villa Amette, and is still known to the habitues of the Rooms as—Mademoiselle of Monte Carlo.

On most nights in spring she can be seen at the Rooms, and those who know the truth tell the queer story which I have in the foregoing pages attempted to relate.

A Note About the Author

William Le Queux (1864–1927) was an Anglo-French journalist, novelist, and radio broadcaster. Born in London to a French father and English mother, Le Queux studied art in Paris and embarked on a walking tour of Europe before finding work as a reporter for various French newspapers. Towards the end of the 1880s, he returned to London where he edited *Gossip* and *Piccadilly* before being hired as a reporter for *The Globe* in 1891. After several unhappy years, he left journalism to pursue his creative interests. Le Queux made a name for himself as a leading writer of popular fiction with such espionage thrillers as *The Great War in England in 1897* (1894) and *The Invasion of 1910* (1906). In addition to his writing, Le Queux was a notable pioneer of early aviation and radio communication, interests he maintained while publishing around 150 novels over his decades long career.

A Note from the Publisher

Spanning many genres, from non-fiction essays to literature classics to children's books and lyric poetry, Mint Edition books showcase the master works of our time in a modern new package. The text is freshly typeset, is clean and easy to read, and features a new note about the author in each volume. Many books also include exclusive new introductory material. Every book boasts a striking new cover, which makes it as appropriate for collecting as it is for gift giving. Mint Edition books are only printed when a reader orders them, so natural resources are not wasted. We're proud that our books are never manufactured in excess and exist only in the exact quantity they need to be read and enjoyed.

bookfinity™

Discover more of your favorite classics with Bookfinity™.

- Track your reading with custom book lists.
- Get great book recommendations for your personalized Reader Type.
- Add reviews for your favorite books.
- AND MUCH MORE!

Visit **bookfinity.com** and take the fun Reader Type quiz to get started.

Enjoy our classic and modern companion pairings!

Classic & Modern

Printed in the USA
CPSIA information can be obtained
at www.ICGtesting.com
JSHW022327140824
68134JS00019B/1350